Wicked Favor

(The Wicked Horse Vegas Series)

By
Sawyer Bennett

Find Sawyer on the web!
sawyerbennett.com
twitter.com/bennettbooks
facebook.com/bennettbooks

Table of Contents

CHAPTER 1

Jerico

THERE'S A LOT of moaning coming from The Orgy Room, which is par for the course. I step in to take a peek, and there's not an ounce of shame when I say the view of all those people fucking and writhing and orgasming never fails to arouse me. Perhaps I'll end up here tonight.

It is my favorite room here at The Wicked Horse Vegas. It's not where you see the kinkiest shit—that would be The Silo Room—but it is where the lust permeates the air so thickly there's a wildness that sort of inhabits you when you join in.

It overtakes you.

Possesses you.

Then frees you.

Yeah… I'll be back here tonight.

I make my way back to the foyer and push open the heavy double doors to The Social Room. The sound of the sexy music, moaning, and flesh slapping against flesh is totally muted here, and it looks like nothing more than an upscale bar. It is a long and rectangular room with a bar running along one wall in Brazilian rosewood trimmed in chrome. There are no stools at the bar—standing-room only—but there are several velour seats and couches done in muted colors of taupe, cream, gray, and brown. This room is sedate, elegant, and designed to encourage conversations over a cocktail or two.

To keep in line with the elegance of our decor, there is a dress code. It's not overly stifling, but it is enforced. Most people dress up because they want to be noticed and can afford the best clothes. A one-day membership is five hundred dollars… so that pretty much weeds out the tourists who can't afford to look like they belong in a place like this.

After being passed my preferred drink of vodka on the rocks from one of the bartenders, I move down to the end of the bar. As owner of this club, I watch everything. Because of my background in military special ops, I observe details others wouldn't, even if they were sitting right in front of them.

It's still early—just past nine PM—but there's already a hefty crowd here for a Wednesday.

Movement at the entrance catches my attention, and I see Helena exiting the elevator. The Wicked Horse sits on the 46th floor of the Onyx Casino. To get into the club, the patrons have to make it past security on the first floor to gain entrance to the elevator that comes right to

The Wicked Horse.

Helena is absolutely stunning. She's wearing a simple, yet no doubt expensive, red dress that's molded to her body. It is so expertly tailored that it is in no way sleazy. Black heels, bare legs, and chocolate hair that flows down her back. Her skin is golden, her eyes an expressive light brown, and she's probably the most beautiful woman in the club right now. Not going to lie—it makes my dick stir when she locks eyes on me before moving my way with a sexy swing to her hips and a knowing smirk on her mouth.

We are going to have fun tonight.

"Jerico," she murmurs as she reaches me, leans in, and accepts a light kiss to her cheek.

When she pulls back, I tell her, "You look gorgeous. Haven't seen you around in a while."

"Steven has not been traveling as much and when he's home, he gets all my attention as you know," she says before turning to the bartender to order a glass of wine.

"How is Steven?" I ask, because Helena's husband is also a member here. They are big-time swingers and like to switch partners, which is pretty much what constitutes our regular members. Most people in here are in committed relationships, but they like a little debauchery in their sex lives. Steven doesn't mind Helena coming here on her own, nor does she mind if he does. Their relationship is very odd, but it totally works for them.

"He's tired," she says as she turns back to me with clear worry in her voice. "I wish he'd cut back on his travel, but you know he'll never slow down."

I nod in understanding. When you love what you do, it's not like a job. Steven is a diamond broker, and Helena is an attorney. Both are locals here in Vegas. They've been members since the doors opened, but they aren't in here often because they work their asses off.

The bartender sets Helena's wine on the bar.

"Put that on my tab," I tell him.

The bartender nods, and Helena smiles at me as she takes her glass in a perfectly manicured hand. I know from firsthand experience those nails like to scratch backs while lost in desire. "Thanks, love. That's sweet."

Taking a slight step in so I can lean closer to her, I murmur. "Will you join me tonight?"

"I thought you'd never ask," she says with a grin above her wineglass as she looks at me with hot eyes.

Chuckling, I lean back and pick up my vodka to take a sip. "You've been here all of thirty seconds."

She laughs, too, and we make idle chatter as we have our drinks. Helena likes at least two glasses of wine before she goes to one of the rooms, so she's loosened up. A few regulars come up to us to say hello, and we mingle with them a bit. But eventually, Helena takes her last sip of wine and sets the glass on the bar. I'd stopped after one vodka because I don't like anything dulling my senses.

Placing a hand on my chest, Helena closes it around my necktie, just below the knot. She gives it a playful tug. "Want to tie me up with this thing?"

"I was thinking of locking you up instead." My voice is husky as I start to imagine what I want to do to her.

"Lock me up?" she asks with genuine interest.

"We installed some stocks over in The Silo," I tell her, watching her eyes flame with even more interest. It's become my new favorite toy. We used reclaimed wood and cast iron to have it made so it looks positively medieval. I had read once that stocks were originally used as a form of physical punishment involving public humiliation, and well… having sex in public while being locked up tight by your head and wrists can be totally humiliating to some. "Thought I'd lock you in it and let you suck my cock for a bit. After that, I think I'm going to fuck your pussy, then your ass. Going to own every piece of you tonight while you're unable to move."

"God," Helena says on a breathy moan. "You are so damned dirty."

"It's why you like me so much," I tell her with a smile as I take her by the elbow.

"It's why I adore you," she clarifies. "I wish you'd teach Steven some of that dirty talk. He's amazing in the sack, but he's way too quiet."

"Yeah, I am not going to be teaching your husband how to talk dirty to you," I tell her dryly as I turn her from the bar. "But if he wants to do a threesome with you and me, he can listen in on how I do it."

"Now that's a fabulous idea," Helena says with a laugh as we turn to walk toward the doors that lead to a foyer beyond The Social Room. From there, we can access one of four rooms in which we can have every dirty desire fulfilled, but it's The Orgy Room I want tonight.

Before we can even make it three steps, we're stopped by a woman standing in our path looking at me expectantly.

She's very pretty in a natural sort of way. Not a lush, exotic beauty like Helena, but more of a free spirit. I drink that in immediately, knowing it only from the look in her eyes. They're a champagne color with thick lashes, but the message inside is that she's slightly uncomfortable but ready to accept a challenge. Zooming out, I take in more. Tall but with the right amounts of curves, she wears a simple black dress that's not overly sexy, but with her body, it doesn't need to be. Caramel-colored hair sets off the whole package. Next to her eyes, it's her best feature. Long and wild looking, like she just walked across a breezy beach, yet I know it's how she actually styled it. It's parted on the side, a very long set of bangs coming down over her right eye. It's a very Veronica Lake sort of look.

"Mr. Jameson," she says as she lifts her chin confidently even though I can tell she's worried. Those eyes... so expressive. "I was wondering if I could have a word with you."

Too bad she hadn't shown up before Helena, because there's no doubt I'd love to take this woman out for a spin. She's a damn knockout with legs that go on for miles, an ass made to be slapped, and a husky, raspy voice that sounds like she's been screaming in rapture for days.

Sadly though, I have committed to someone else right now.

"I'm sorry... but I've just made plans with this lovely lady," I reply as I nod my head to Helena. "But perhaps after?"

The woman wrings her hands with worry, glances at the elevator and then back to me. Before she can respond, Helena adds, "Or... you could join us. Jerico loves some girl-on-girl action."

The beauty's eyes widen in shock.

"Um... no thank you," she stammers to Helena before turning to me. "I apologize for interrupting you. I know this is incredibly rude, but this is important. I need a favor."

"I don't do favors," I tell her truthfully, tightening my grip on Helena's elbow. I'm immediately disappointed this woman isn't going to end up in my bed. She'll probably end up booted out the doors if she's here to scam someone. "Now if you'll excuse us—"

"My name is Trista Barnes," she blurts out as we start to brush past her. "My brother is Jayce Barnes."

I freeze in mid-step, the shock of hearing that name temporarily paralyzing me before it fills me with rage. Slowly, I look over my shoulder at her and I can't withhold the menace in my voice when I say, "Why are you here?"

She's takes a slight step back, indicating her wariness and yet I can't do anything but glower at her simply because of who she's related to.

Trista takes a deep breath and it comes out shaky, showing me her confidence level has dropped severely. "I'm in a bit of trouble, and Jayce said you could help me. He says you owe him a favor. That he wants to collect on it in the form of helping me. Please... I just spent five hundred dollars I didn't have to spend to get in here to see you. I just need five minutes of your time."

"Christ," I mutter as I release Helena's arm and scrub my fingers through my dark hair. I glare hard at the woman, hoping to perhaps frighten her into just leaving. I'll even gladly refund her entrance fee. While I have no fucking desire to have anything to do with Jayce Barnes' sister, I'm slightly impressed and maybe a little turned on when she lifts her chin up and holds my eyes. I love to watch a woman reach out for an inner confidence she's not sure she has just yet.

Beyond pissed at myself because I'm actually a little intrigued, I turn my gaze to Helena and try to lighten my voice. "Rain check, okay?"

"Of course," she says, laying a hand lightly on my

forearm. I bend over and brush my lips against her cheek.

Helena is a classy woman. She even gives a small smile of encouragement to Trista before she turns back to the bar.

"Follow me," I say to Trista tersely as I walk through The Social Room. I don't even look behind me to see if she's keeping up with my long strides, but she slips through the double wooden doors right behind me. We end up in a semicircle foyer that has the same paneled walls and Italian marble as the room we just came from. From here, there are five hallways branching off like spokes on a wheel, each closed off by an ornately carved wooden door. There are signs above each—The Waterfall Room, The Deck, The Orgy Room, The Silo—which is a nod to the original Wicked Horse in Wyoming. One is marked Private.

I veer to the right, taking the private hall that leads to my office. It's the last door on the right, sitting adjacent to my apartment door. In fact, my office connects to my apartment by an interior door that leads right into the kitchen, so my home-to-work commute couldn't be any shorter.

There's a security pad on the wall. I punch in my five-digit code after angling my body so Trista can't see, then I push the door open and step back to let her go in first.

I gave the designer free license to decorate my office

and apartment however she saw fit as long as she didn't use the colors pink or green. She did a superb job, going with an industrial design I really liked. The ceilings are exposed steel beams with air conditioning ductwork painted in black to match. The floors are done in light maple, and my simple desk has a roughly finished wooden top with iron legs. There's a light blue rug with a wavy pattern in cream as well as two chairs done in gray leather. One wall houses a set of built-in cabinets that hold my records on The Wicked Horse, which aren't all that interesting or secretive since this business is about as legit as they come. Only in Vegas, right?

As such, I don't have any locks on the cabinets and I don't use the safe built into my wall. The security pad outside the door is plenty for what's in here.

Now my other business, The Jameson Group, is a different matter since I do contract work for the government, and by government, I mean CIA. That's next-level top secret and remains secured at my other offices in the business district across town. But since I'll soon be retiring from there at the ripe old age of thirty-five, I prefer to focus my attention on this new endeavor. Who would have thought Jerico Jameson, one of the most sought-after private security contractors, would end up leaving that business to open a sex club?

I know my parents—God rest their souls—would have never seen this coming.

"Take a seat," I order Trista, pointing to one of the

chairs. I round my desk to do the same. Placing my elbows on the tabletop and steepling my fingers in front of my mouth, I take a harder look at the woman who just turned what was promising to be a very good night into a really shitty one.

I don't see any of Jayce in her. His hair and eyes were dark brown. Trista's hair is lighter... almost a bronze color. She's got high cheekbones and a slender nose. Jayce's face was round with a wide nose. Trista's eyebrows are perfectly arched while Jayce's sat rather flat. I remember everything about that douche.

"You don't look like your brother," I observe as I lean back in my chair and place my hands on the armrests.

"Different mothers," is all she says. "But we grew up together."

"Why did he send you to me?" I ask the question again, expecting a better answer than a favor.

"I'm desperately in need of money," she explains quickly. "I don't know what favor he owes you, but he said you had money and you'd help me in exchange for wiping the slate clean between you two."

I have to struggle not to snort my disbelief. The slate would never be clean between us. I hate that mother-fucker so much he could be standing in front of me dying, with a drink of water the only thing to save him, and I'd pour it out on the ground beside him.

"He said he saved your life once," she says quietly, as

if she needs to remind me why she's sitting here.

It's true… and I hate the reminder.

That bastard saved my life from certain death, and I owe him big time. While pinned down in a firefight with insurgents from the Nazwad district of the Helmund Province, I took a bullet through my leg that nicked an artery. Jayce had thrown me over his shoulder, ran through a hail of bullets, and got me to a Humvee that held our field medic. The medic was able to hold the bleed and give me a unit of blood until the chopper came in to pick me up and take me to a field hospital. I was dangerously close to dying, but three more units of blood and stitching up my artery brought me back from the brink of death. Had Jayce not gotten me out of there, I wouldn't have made it to the hospital. I was weak, disoriented, but completely grateful when I told him as he sat beside my bed, "Jayce… buddy… I'm not sure how I can ever repay you, but if you need anything at all, you come to me and it's yours."

It's been almost ten years since then and he's never asked for that favor, so I just assumed he knew to keep his distance from me. I'm sure he knew I'd probably attack him on sight, not to kill him, but to beat the shit out of him. I'd hurt him badly if he were standing in this office right now. He knows it because I've already done it once before, but it wasn't enough to dull my fury at him.

Given the circumstances, it would probably be totally acceptable if I were to even consider the debt paid already and kick his sister out of my office. It's true he saved my life, but when I caught him fucking my fiancée about four years later, I didn't kill him. That fucker was invited by me to join The Jameson Group because I trusted him and he'd saved my life. But whenever I was on a mission and Jayce was off duty, he was apparently banging Michelle stateside. I didn't kill him, but I should have. I stopped after I broke a few of his ribs and knocked some teeth out. By my reasoning, not killing him means I saved his life. So we should be even, right?

In fact, I should tell her that right now. Inform her to tell her brother to suck my dick—that I wouldn't help him or her if their lives depended on it.

But I don't.

Because two things strike me at once.

The first being an attack of conscience. I might be a mean son of a bitch and a ruthless leader when warranted, but I don't ever renege on a promise. I owe him a favor, so he'll get it.

Second, it occurs to me I could indeed help Jayce's sister. She says she needs money and with a loan of funds, a repayment plan is in the cards. Add in the fact she's fucking gorgeous as hell, and well…

I have an excellent idea on how she could repay me.

A way that would not make Jayce happy at all.

Let's just call it a little bit of sweet revenge.

CHAPTER 2

Trista

I ALTERNATE BETWEEN tugging the hem of my stretchy skirt down my legs and making sure my face stays angled in such a way that my fall of long bangs keeps my eye covered.

The bruise I'm hiding is hideous looking. I'm very self-conscious about it, and not because Jerico Jameson has to be the best-looking man I've ever seen in my life. The pictures I saw when I Googled him do not do him justice. There's no way I could have imagined his hair was actually so dark it was indeed black, or that his green eyes are so light I'd call them the color of bleached jade, but they're streaked with slivers of rust, which makes them beyond beautiful. And that face... so perfectly put together that he doesn't seem real.

But I'm not here for his looks.

I'm here for his money, and Jayce assured me Jerico has what I need.

"What kind of money are we talking about?" Jerico

asks as he critically studies me.

"Twenty-five thousand," I say nervously.

"That's a lot of cash to ask of someone," he says pensively. "But I do owe Jayce a favor, and I happen to be wealthy."

"So you'll help me?" I ask, hope welling up in my chest. For the first time in days, I'm not burdened down with overwhelming fear.

"Maybe," he says as he leans forward in his chair, crossing his forearms on the desk. "Why do you need it?"

"Family emergency," I say quickly… maybe a little too quickly because it sounds like a lie.

Jerico's eyebrows draw inward as his gaze pierces straight through me. "You owe someone the money."

My eyes go wide with surprise, and I totally give myself away by stammering, "How could you possibly know that?"

He smiles at me like the cat that just ate the canary, because I just admitted it to him. I didn't want him to know because the details aren't his business. I just need the money and an agreement by a decent guy to let me pay it back when I'm able to sell my house. Jayce assured me Jerico was the man.

"That bruise beside your right eye that goes down into your cheekbone…" Jerico says, nodding at me. "You're not hiding it very well. When a woman is beaten and needs money, my first guess is someone's trying to let her know time is up and it's going to hurt if she doesn't pay. The other choice would have been an abused woman needing money to skip town on whatever douche is beating her, but you carry yourself with a little too much confidence for that."

Okay, so he has me sort of pegged, but he has no clue how weird this "loan shark" thing really is. He'd never believe the deep hole I've dug myself into, nor would he respect the circumstances that brought me here to beg for help.

"What was the original loan amount?" Jerico asks.

"Thirteen thousand dollars," I tell him.

I was loaned thirteen. Now, I owe twenty-five as payment plus interest. But I don't begrudge any of this because I needed that money and was willing to do anything to get it. The fact that the sale of my house fell through and I couldn't get the equity out to pay off the loan didn't really touch my lender's heart. He came after me and roughed me up good, imposing a final deadline I had better make or I would be hurt a lot worse.

I had four weeks to come up with the funds or my dead, bullet-riddled body would be put out in the Nevada desert for coyotes to tear apart. Okay, that's an exaggeration, but I don't want to incur his wrath any further. I just want him out of my life.

I'm pinning my hopes on Jerico Jameson to bail me out, hoping he'll work out some type of reasonable payment plan. I'm assuming he's an honorable guy as Jayce seemed positive he'd give me the money with easy repayment terms and a much lower interest.

"What was the money for?" Jerico asks again. "And when do you need it by?"

"Like I said… family emergency." This was very much true, but he didn't need to know the details.

My six-year-old niece, who I help my mom care for, needed a heart-valve replacement. Since she's uninsured, the hospital wanted a deposit before they'd do the surgery. I was able to cash out twenty-seven thousand from my 401K plan, but I had to borrow the other thirteen. It came at a huge risk, but I figured I'd just sell my house, take the equity out of it—which wasn't much but would at least cover the loan payoff—and all would be fine. Except the people who were going to buy it backed out at the last second, so now I was up shit creek without a paddle.

Since Jerico has asked me twice what the money was for, I expect him to push the issue. Instead, he asks, "What are you offering in terms of repayment?"

I blink at him in surprise. He wants me to suggest something? "Um… well, I need twenty-five to pay off the loan within thirty days. I could maybe pay it back over five years with some interest, of course, for your trouble."

Jerico gives a bark of laughter, but his expression is not amused. "Miss Barnes, I'm not a bank. I don't make long-term loans. I'll give you the money… but at a twenty-two percent rate that would be due thirty days after I give you the money."

"Impossible," I whisper. My house was not going to sell, so I couldn't pay it back that fast. The reason the buyers had backed out was that the home inspection revealed there was major termite damage. It was going to cost thousands to fix it. The house was a no-go. "That puts me in the same exact situation I'm in now."

"That's my offer," he says softly. And the implication is "take it or leave it."

"Mr. Jameson," I say as I lean forward in my chair and try to push the tears back. "I really, really need your help. My brother saved your life. The favor I'm asking is not for the actual money, but a reasonable way I can repay it. I can't get that much money together in thirty days. Can't you please work something out with me that I can actually succeed at?"

He appraises me critically again. This time, he lets his gaze roam over my entire body as I sit in the chair opposite of him. When his eyes come back to mine, he says, "Are you willing to work off the debt?"

"Work off the debt?" I repeat skeptically. He owns a sex club after all.

"Yes. Here at The Wicked Horse," he explains.

This perks my interest because I happen to need a job, and I'm insanely curious about what happens inside of this place. I've always been adventurous that way. When Corinne was in the hospital for her heart-valve replacement, I had to miss work. My employers were not forgiving, and they gave my job away to the temp who had replaced me. I'd been there six years and had hardly missed work, but I asked for a week off and they fired me.

Assholes.

So I'm unemployed right now and could use a job. While my mom's paycheck helps cover half the expenses, it doesn't pay for everything and my meager savings are about exhausted.

Leaning forward in my chair, I ask, "What does that mean... work here?"

"You know what this club is?" he counters.

I nod. "A sex club."

"What would my job duties be?" I ask.

"They'd be whatever I tell you they were," he says.

A little taken aback, I wonder if I am mistaking that look in his eyes.

Sinister?

Lustful?

But I must be mistaken because he says, "For example, I might have you work the hostess stand in The Social Room, or tend the bar. This may seem shocking to you, but I might use you as a waitress who sells condoms and lube and such. Or it could be something as mundane as cleaning my apartment. Let's say you'd be my personal employee for whatever was needed."

This has potential. It is all stuff I can do, and none of what he listed bothers me in the slightest.

"There are a variety of other jobs that mainly involve cleaning and making the club look beautiful at all times," he adds on. "It's physical work."

"But I wouldn't be expected to have sex with anyone?" I ask cautiously, because while I like sex a whole hell of a lot, I'm not whoring myself out.

"I don't run a brothel, Miss Barnes," he drawls, and I can tell I've offended him.

"I'm sorry—"

He talks right over me to clarify. "I do not expect you to have sex with any of the members as part of your repayment of the loan."

"How much time is needed to pay you back the loan?" This sounds too easy.

"Four weeks. That's when your deadline is, right?"

"All you want is four weeks of work for twenty-five thousand dollars?" I ask incredulously. "Because I'm sorry… nothing in life is that easy."

Jerico cocks an eyebrow at me. "While I have no clue about your work ethic or any particular talents you may have, Miss Barnes, I'm requiring four weeks of work so that—for all intents and purposes—we have a legitimate deal. My granting you the favor I owe your brother isn't the money I'm giving you. As you said, it's the easy repayment plan that will wipe my debt clean with him."

Well, there you go. Now we're on the same page.

"One last thing," I say quickly. "I lost my job a few weeks ago, so I'm hunting for a new one. Would my hours here be evenings or day shifts? I just need to know how to narrow my search. Still have to pay my bills, you know?"

"Tell you what," Jerico says as he stands up and walks over to a cabinet on the adjacent wall to his desk. "I'll give you extra shifts at time and a half to add onto the front or back of your regular shifts. If you're working the condiment trays, you can make pretty good money in tips. More than enough to cover your bills, I'm sure."

My mind races through everything to make sure I haven't missed anything. I get twenty-five thousand for working at The Wicked Horse for a month. I don't have to have sex with the members. He'll give me extra work at overtime rate so I can pay my share of the living expenses. I can then walk away debt free and start my life over again, leaving these hellish weeks behind.

Sucking in a big breath, I let it out as I stand from my chair to face him. "Then I gratefully accept, Mr. Jameson."

His back is to me as he pulls a painting away from the wall to reveal a safe behind it. He looks over his shoulder at me briefly. "Let's just make it Jerico."

"Okay… Jerico," I agree.

Oddly, he opens the safe with a pull to the handle, indicating it's not locked. This surprises the hell out of me because he steps back holding a wad of cash in his hand. Jerico walks to me and without a word, he takes my wrist and turns my hand over so the palm is facing up.

My skin tingles from his touch, which is so disconcerting I stammer out, "You don't lock your safe?"

Jerico's eyebrow arches. "Who would dare steal from me?"

Good point. I know from Jayce that he was special ops military, which is where they met, then he created a company that did the same type of work on the civilian side. Jayce worked there with him for a few years, and Jayce isn't a man I'd mess with, so I'm assuming Jerico is the same or probably worse.

Without needing an answer from me, he starts counting out hundred dollar bills into my hand. I silently count out ten thousand. Surprisingly, it's not as large a stack as I thought it would be. The bills are brand new, crisp, and lay cleanly flat. The resulting stack is no thicker than an inch.

"What's this for?" I ask dumbfounded as I look up at him.

His thick-lashed fern-colored eyes are so brilliant this close that I'm almost mesmerized. He gives me a smile, the first one he's bestowed upon me since we met. "Take that to the loan shark and give it to him. Tell him he'll have the rest by the due date."

I open my mouth to question this, but he cuts me off by putting five more hundred dollar bills in my hand and saying, "That's your entrance fee back since you're not using the club tonight."

Caught completely off guard by his generosity, especially because this meeting started out so rocky, I overcompensate with my gratitude. "Thank you so much, Mr. Jameson… I mean, Jerico. I really didn't have five hundred to spare, but this was an emergency. I'm really grateful you're giving it back because I need it for bills, and—"

He holds his hand up to cut me off and nods down to the money. "Take that tonight. Don't wait."

"But why?"

"Because many sharks like to send their goons out again before the due date to impress upon people the importance of meeting the deadline. And I can't have you unable to work, now can I?"

I'm touched he thought enough to do that for me, but I'm in no way thinking that makes him a good guy. He just wants to keep me healthy so I can work off my debt to him.

I nod in understanding and finally close my hand around the stack of money in my hand. Raising my gaze, I ask Jerico, "When do you want me to start working?"

♦

TURNS OUT, JERICO wanted me to start working that night, although he said it would not count toward the thirty days I owed him. To be clearer, he really wanted to show me around the place because he told me it would be shocking to my system if I'd never been in a sex club before, and he didn't want me to look like a scared rabbit tomorrow when I had my first full shift.

I understood his logic, and I was even grateful for the head's-up.

I was not, however, prepared for the things I saw, even though I'm pretty openminded and liberal when it comes to sex.

I am by no means a prude, but as Jerico walked me through the various rooms, I was torn between watching with avid fascination and turning my face away with disgust. Some of the stuff was beautifully erotic. Some of the stuff turned my stomach.

Regardless, Jerico kept me there for two hours, taking the time to explain what people were doing and how the entire system of a sex club worked. From the tour, I was most surprised to learn that most people who came were couples who either liked the public nature of the club or wanted to swap partners. It was eye opening, but it was humiliating too, because there was a part of me that was greatly turned on. When I left, my panties were wet. For some reason, I felt Jerico knew that because his parting words were, "I hope you enjoyed the tour." I wasn't sure how in the hell I was supposed to work and be professional with that going on around me. In fact, I sneaked a peek at Jerico's crotch from time to time and he was totally without a hard-on, so there must be some way to make yourself immune to all this stuff.

Now it's just after midnight, and I'm exhausted. Yet

before I can make my way to my house, where my mom and Corinne will already be sound asleep, I decide to go ahead and drop the ten thousand off to the asshole I made the mistake of doing business with.

I pull my car up to the aluminum-sided trailer that sits off the highway on a barren and dusty lot. I note with relief that the lights are on.

Trudging wearily up the steps, I take deep breaths so I remain calm. Two sharp raps on the door, and then it's opened.

And there before me stands my brother, Jayce.

The loan shark.

He doesn't invite me in, which is fine because I don't want to go in. Instead, I reach into my purse and hand him the stack of money—less the five hundred Jerico refunded me. "Here's ten of the twenty-five I owe you."

Jayce's hand shoots out to snatch the money from me, and he counts it out quickly. When he looks back to me, I wonder how this man fell so far. His eyes are perpetually bloodshot and there are busted capillaries around his nose and cheeks, which tells me his dependence on alcohol has probably destroyed his liver as well. He's now a con artist and a drug dealer as well as a small-time grifter. After Jayce got out of the military and went to work for Jerico, he made some pretty big money. Still, you'd never know it by the way he lives now.

As such, Jayce was the last person I turned to for help because I honestly didn't think he had it. I was elated when he said he could give me the money, so I just assumed he'd saved it up and wasn't spending it.

Of course, the real shock was when he made it clear it was a loan with steep interest. God forbid the man would do something to help his niece out of the goodness of his heart.

I look past him into his dingy abode, sure the carpet and furniture are from the seventies. It's really old, and it smells that way too.

"Why only ten thousand?" he snaps at me.

"It's a good faith effort to show you I'll have the rest by your deadline."

"So Jerico is going to give you the money?" he asks with an amused smile.

"Yes," I tell him. "I've got to work at his club for thirty days, but then we're square."

Jayce looks at me like he doesn't believe me for a moment, but then ultimately shrugs his shoulders in acceptance. He didn't care how I got the money, just as long as he got repaid. Frankly, I'm surprised he gave up such a large favor to bail my ass out of hot water, but really… it benefits him. He got his money back, plus a hefty profit. I still can't believe the asshole made me borrow it as Corinne is his niece too. You'd think he'd want to help save her life, but he's sank so low in his assholish ways that he doesn't care about anyone, including himself.

"How did he act when you told him who you were?"

Jayce asks.

"What do you mean?"

"What was his reaction? Surprised?"

"I guess," I say, trying to think back. I was so damn nervous I'm not sure. "He led me to his office to talk in private once I told him who I was."

"Did he say anything about me?"

"No."

"Did he hesitate to pay the favor he owes me?"

"Not at all," I assure him.

"Interesting," Jayce mumbles. He starts to back up so he can close the door, and he does this without looking back at me again.

Asshole.

My brother is a certifiable, living, breathing asshole.

In fact, most of my family are assholes. The man who sired Jayce and me ran off with another woman. My mom kept Jayce and raised him with me and my older sister, Danielle, but she's an asshole too. She left Corinne with me and Mom about six months ago, saying she was going on a short vacation, but she never came back. I suspect she knew Corinne was very sick with her heart condition, but didn't know what to do about it. Luckily, Mom and I got her right into a doctor who referred us to a cardiologist.

When we were told she needed the surgery, we had no clue what to do. We didn't even have formal guardianship papers on Corinne, much less insurance.

According to the doctor, time was of the essence in fixing her valve, so I scraped the money together.

Cashed in the 401K and went to my brother, Corinne's own uncle, and asked for help with the down payment. Of course, all I got from him was a "loan" with the agreement to let me wait until I could get the equity out of my house to pay him back. When that fell through, he gave me an additional ten days, which was impossible.

When I couldn't produce the twenty-five thousand, he got rough with me, landing a solid left hook to my temple. I don't think he was doing this per se to "act" like the stereotypical loan shark. I think he did it because he was drunk, possibly high and pissed I didn't have his money. Jayce wasn't a nice man on most days, but cross him and he could get vicious.

With a sigh, I turn around and trot down his porch steps and head back to my car. I want to get a good night's sleep because I have a feeling that working in a sex club starting tomorrow is not going to be conducive to restful nights over the next few weeks.

CHAPTER 3

Jerico

THERE'S A SHARP rap before my office door opens. Kynan walks in without waiting for permission, and he's the only one who's allowed to do that.

"Just get back?" I ask as I briefly glance up at him and then back down to the quarterly tax report on my desk.

"Few hours ago," he says as he drops down into one of the chairs opposite my desk and sighs with satisfaction.

"Let me guess," I say dryly without even looking up at him. "You stopped off in one of the rooms before you came in here."

"Orgy Room," he says, and I can hear the grin in his voice without even looking up. "Some dude in there whacked off while I banged his wife from behind."

Chuckling, I push the tax report away and lean back in my chair to look at my closest friend and my only confidant. I met Kynan McGrath while I was a young

2nd lieutenant with the Marine Corps. I was fresh out of college, fresher out of officer candidate school, and on my first deployment to Afghanistan. My unit was paired up with a unit from the Royal Marine Commandos, which was led by Kynan. We bonded as we spent months flushing Taliban from small villages, a tedious and dangerous job that was mentally stressful. I was impressed with Kynan, and he with me, and he was the first person I asked to join up with me as a civilian contractor. I knew I wanted out of the military after I'd gotten shot, not because I was afraid but because I was an entrepreneur. I figured if I was going to do dangerous shit in service to my country and its allies, I wanted to be paid well for it. So when my enlistment was up, I didn't look back. That was ten long, lucrative years ago, but we've worked together seamlessly ever since. I'm going to sell The Jameson Group to him when I fully retire. As it stands now, I'm pretty far removed from it. Kynan's been running everything for the past year and a half as I've devoted my attention to The Wicked Horse.

"So getting your rocks off was more important than reporting the final details of your operation to me?" I ask him with a straight face.

Kynan knows me well. His grin gets bigger. "I think you've gone soft, dude. You've been living in fancy suits and sitting in a comfortable chair for too long. Meanwhile, I've been freezing my ass off in the Pakistan mountains gathering intelligence for our country, eating freeze-dried food, and whacking off in my sleeping bag. So yeah… it was more important I visit The Orgy Room before coming here."

I smirk at Kynan because I agree with him. When I came off missions, first thing I always wanted to do was fuck. In my single days, that would be nameless, one-night stands. Then it was only Michelle, who I met three years after I started The Jameson Group, I wanted to fuck. I was twenty-eight and ready to settle down. We'd dated for only six months before I proposed, but I didn't have any doubts. She accepted, and I thought things were perfect. Less than ten months after that—and only two weeks before our wedding—I came off a mission a few days early to surprise her, and it was a surprise indeed when I caught her in our bed with Jayce.

The betrayal hurt. I could go into a million different ways in which that betrayal has changed me. But when it boils down to it, it was so much more than the fact she cheated on me. She and Jayce took away the one thing I wanted most in the world, and it's the reason why I hate them so much.

Nowadays, I fuck one-night stands and frankly, I don't find it to be unsatisfying at all. No annoying fiancée to please, no expensive wedding to hold, and the knowledge my heart would remain securely untouched.

"Everything go according to plan?" I ask Kynan, pushing my thoughts away from the bitter taste that floods my mouth when I think of Michelle and Jayce.

"Absolutely no problems," he responds to me.

There was a time when I felt compelled to have him give me a play by play of the mission, but these days, I find I don't care. It's a combination of inherently trusting Kynan and getting burned out with The Jameson group. Now that I've been running The Wicked Horse Vegas, I find myself completely fulfilled. I have more money than I know what to do with, and I get to have off-the-hook sex whenever I want. Tell me how I could have a better job?

I'll forever be grateful for the opportunity my former marine buddy, Cain Bonham, presented to me when he introduced me to his boss, Bridger Payne. Cain knew I was looking to back away from The Jameson group and that I had quite a bit of money to invest in a new business opportunity. Cain also knew Bridger was looking to franchise The Wicked Horse in Wyoming. He put us in touch and after several meetings as well as checking each other out, we formed a partnership to open The Wicked Horse Vegas. While the clubs are very different in setup and services offered, they are still clubs that allow people to indulge in their sexual fantasies. It's just that here in Vegas... we do it with a bit more showmanship and pizazz.

"We've been asked to bid on a contract by the French government for an operation they would like us to assist the French Foreign Legion with," I tell Kynan. "I sent the information to you through our encrypted server. Take a look at it and rough me up a proposal."

"Sure thing, boss," he replies confidently as he settles deeper in his chair, propping an ankle on top of the opposite knee. "Anything else before I head home and do about five loads of laundry?"

I hesitate for only a moment about whether to bring this up, but I decide it's good if someone else knows about it. "Jayce Barnes reared his ugly face again."

Kynan doesn't say anything, but his eyebrows rise with curiosity and surprise. He waits for me to continue.

"Actually, his sister showed up at the club yesterday. She asked to collect on the favor I owe Jayce for saving my life."

"What was the favor?" Kynan asks.

"She needed money. Got in trouble with a loan shark to the tune of twenty-five thousand, and he roughed her up a little bit. Jayce sent her to collect the favor."

"The favor is for you to give her twenty-five?" he asks for clarification.

Shaking my head, I lean back in my seat. I distract-edly pick at the leather armrests before admitting to him, "It was a loan she wanted with special repayment options. She's broke and doesn't have the ability to repay it, at least not in a timely manner."

"And…?" Kynan drawls out.

"So I made a deal with her. Told her I'd give her the money in exchange for working at The Wicked Horse for thirty days."

Kynan lets out a bark of laughter and then throws his head back to continue laughing even harder. When he finally looks back at me, he says, "Oh man, let me guess… she's a fucking knockout?"

I give him a grin and nod. "She's gorgeous. Doesn't look anything like her brother, thank fuck."

"What are you going to do—just have her do the nasty to you for the next thirty days? Because, dude, you don't need that as a repayment option. You got all the pussy you need here in this club."

My smile morphs, and I know there's a sparkle of malice in my eyes as I say, "I have something a little more involved for Miss Barnes."

Now I really have Kynan's attention as he leans forward in his chair, head tilted with curiosity. "What are you going to do?"

Kynan is well aware of my bad history with Jayce. While Kynan didn't have the personal hurt I did, he was just as offended because being on a team together and the nature of missions that we do, trust and loyalty are everything. While Kynan felt for me as any close friend would, he was more pissed about the breach of loyalty. He had no qualms with me beating the shit out of Jayce before expelling him from The Jameson Group. Kynan is also well aware I owe a debt to Jayce for saving my life and the fact I've been dreading the day I'd have to repay it. He can't really be surprised I'm not going to pay my debt in an aboveboard manner.

"While I do intend to have my fun with her over the next thirty days as part of the favor he owes me, I'm going to provide a little humiliation to Jayce by showing him the dirty things I'm going to do to his sister."

Kynan stares at me speculatively, and I can see the wheels in his brain turning. He's a guy with a bigger heart than me, so I know this is causing him concern. He won't hold his peace with me, though. He never has.

"She's an innocent pawn in this, brother," Kynan said softly. "You sure your conscience can handle that?"

"I'm not going to do anything to her that she doesn't want," I assure Kynan. "I'm just going to share the details of how my favor was repaid to Jayce. I'm thinking some photos and video would do nicely."

Kynan gives a shake of his head, and I can tell by the look on his face he doesn't like this idea. It's a good thing I don't need his permission to do this. It's a better thing that my conscience isn't as steadfast as his, because I always knew if there was a way to hurt Jayce more than the ass-kicking I gave him, I'd take it. After everything he destroyed, I'm not going to let this opportunity pass.

"Listen, Jerico," Kynan says, eyes intent. "This is not a good idea. You beat the shit out of Jayce, you kicked your cheating fiancée to the curb, and you went on to build a multimillion dollar empire. You have a good life now, dude. You need to let it go."

"You know this has nothing to do with Michelle and Jayce fucking around behind my back." My voice is hard as steel. "I was satisfied with the beating he got, and I'm thinking Michelle wasn't my true soul mate because I don't miss her a bit. You, more than anyone, know why I want further revenge on Jayce."

Kynan's face slackens and his eyes go soft with remorse. He knows I'm right. In fact, he's the only one who knows what is really driving me, and I can tell by the way he's looking at me that he's not going to support me, but he's also done trying to prevent me from doing it.

"What are you going to do with her?" Kynan asks curiously.

My lips tip upward into a wicked smile. "She works exclusively for me the next thirty days, so I'm going to do with her whatever I want. If I want her to scrub my bathroom floor, she'll do it. If I want her to suck my dick each night when she comes on duty, she'll do it. For thirty days, she's mine to do with what I want."

"Never seen you focus on one woman for that amount of time," Kynan observes.

I shrug. "Didn't say I was going to focus on her exclusively during the thirty days. Maybe I'll just insist she watch me with another woman."

Kynan rolls his eyes, but he knows I'll have not one ounce of hesitancy in doing something like that. The wonderful thing about owning this club is I can indulge in my wildest and kinkiest fantasies.

"You said she's gorgeous?" Kynan asks with pure

curiosity and no censure. "What's she look like?"

A soft knock on my door sends a jolt of adrenaline through me. Glancing at my watch, I see it's seven PM.

With a nod of my head toward the door, I tell him "You're fixing to find out."

"Come in," I call out in a deep voice.

Kynan turns around in his seat and watches as the door swings open slowly and Trista stands there, looking a bit wild-eyed. She licks her lips nervously, her eyes going back and forth between Kynan and me.

"I'm sorry if I'm interrupting," she says quickly. "I can come back later."

She starts to turn away from the door, but with just one word, I assert my command over her.

"Stop."

Her body goes rigid and after a few moments, she turns slowly to face me. I wave her into my office as Kynan stands up from his chair.

"Trista," I say as a means of introduction. "This is my closest friend, Kynan McGrath. He helps run my other business, The Jameson Group."

Kynan reaches a hand out to her and she shakes it tentatively, mumbling something under her breath. Looking over his shoulder at me, Kynan gives me a small shake of his head that I should so not be messing with this woman.

I ignore him. "Are you ready to get started?"

Trista swallows hard, and there is no mistaking the

uncertainty in her eyes. Still, she holds her back straight and keeps her chin lifted when she says with an unconvincing smile, "Sure am."

I'm glad her voice sounds strong because I don't feel like dealing with a meek little lamb.

"I'm going to head out," Kynan says. "I might come back later but if not, I'll catch you tomorrow."

I give a lift of my chin in acknowledgment before turning my attention back to Trista, hearing the door close behind Kynan.

I take a good look at Trista. She's wearing nothing but a faded pair of jeans and a red shirt that is flowy across the top but cinched tighter around her waist. Her hair is a wild mass of waves of various lengths pouring down her back, with streaks of different color in her hair. Various shades of brown to golden blonde, which gives it that dark honeyed color. Her makeup tonight is very light. In fact, I'm not sure she's wearing much of anything other than mascara. I'm smart enough to know that means she does not want to draw attention to herself. I had told her she would be provided with a uniform when she arrived. When she asked me last night what uniform she'd be wearing, I merely told her it depended on what job I had her doing.

If she's bartending, she'll wear a black miniskirt and black camisole. If working the condiment tray, she'll have on nothing but a thong to cover her pussy and the straps from the tray to cover her breasts. And if I have her on her knees before me, she'll be naked. I haven't decided quite yet what to do with her, but I know I'll have to ease her into it. I won't take her unwillingly. My preference would be to have her begging for it.

"Have a seat, Trista," I tell her as I point to one of the chairs. "I've had an employment contract drafted up, along with documentation of the money I'm going to give you in exchange."

"Okay," she says softly. When she takes her seat, I reach into a lateral file drawer to pull out the paper.

Handing it across to her, I say, "It's very simple. But then again, our deal is quite simple."

Trista takes the single page from me and starts to read it. I wasn't lying… it is very simple. I know this because I drafted it. It won't stand up in court, but all I need it to do is stand up within Trista's mind.

She takes her time, eyes moving over the words. It essentially says I have agreed to give her twenty-five thousand, and ten thousand of that has already been paid. In exchange, she agrees to work for me in The Wicked Horse for thirty days. It could be any of the jobs that are available, which she has already seen and been made aware. That was the reason I gave her the tour last night, because I wanted to make sure she knew everything she was getting into. And because Trista specifically mentioned sex with members as a no-go, I made sure to put that in there as well. I personally don't care if she has sex with other members when she is off duty, but she's going to be in for a surprise when she learns I'm not a member of this club and this agreement does not apply to me. It's not like I'm going to force her into anything because I don't need to. I can be very persuasive and Trista will end up wanting what I offer. It was obvious last night during the tour. I'd seen the subtle way she shifted on her feet and the change in her breathing patterns. She was turned on by what she saw, and I intend to introduce her to my world very soon. This contract is nothing more than a way to ensure she doesn't use the "no sex with members rule" as an excuse if she's nervous.

When she's done reading the contract, she places it on my desk and moves forward in her chair. Without a word, I hand a pen to her. She signs it, not asking a single question or showing a moment's hesitation. I'm wondering if that's because she believes I'm merely giving her a legitimate job in exchange for the loan or if she's so relieved to have the loan shark off her back, she truly doesn't care what she needs to do over the next thirty days.

I have to say, I'm hoping it's the latter. Having Trista Barnes at my beck and call without having any hesitancy from her would make this a very pleasant experience indeed.

CHAPTER 4

Trista

J ERICO PUTS HIS signature on the document and tucks it back into his desk drawer without asking me if I want a copy. I don't... but it would have been a nice offer.

I slowly wipe my palms across my denim-covered thighs, hoping it's a casual enough move that Jerico doesn't know they're sweating. Even though I'm relieved to know Jayce will consider the loan paid at the end of thirty days, I am quite nervous about working in a sex club. It's not for the reasons one would think, though. I have an adventurous sexual spirit, and I believe the few men I've had sexual relationships with have felt I was more than sufficient in the sack. There is no shame in working in a place that indulges in fantasy, kink, and fetish. Free world and all that stuff.

My concern is more personal.

I'm worried I'll want to experience this fully and I should be concerned because I liked what I saw last night. The grotesque displays of debauchery are going to affect me, but I'm not sure how. My fear is it will turn me on.

Draw me in.

Make me curious.

"You ready to get started?" Jerico asks as he stands up from his chair.

I take a moment… a brief one. One where I can check him out under the guise of merely holding conversation with him.

Standing slowly from my chair, I give him a confident smile that I'm not feeling and say "Sure."

As I'm doing that, I take the measure of the man before me while we're in the bright lights of his office. He's insanely tall. I bet he tops out around six-six. He's built and the tailoring of his dress shirt is so precise I can see the shape of his biceps under the silk material. So yeah, Jerico has the body. But what makes him so striking is his face. His eyes are the first thing I notice, and I have a tough time looking away from them.

Crystal-jade green.

Amazing.

Pair that with his midnight-black hair, which includes perfectly slashed eyebrows of almost the same color and thick lashes, his eyes become hypnotizing. That hair is something to behold. It looks like he walked straight out of a fashion magazine as it is cut in various layers. It's not too short, but not too long, and it looks like he did nothing more than run his fingers through it to style it. Finally, he wears a five o'clock shadow well. It's dark and gives him a rough-and-tumble look, which is very contrary to the stylish way he dresses.

He gives me a curt smile as he walks out from behind his desk, and my inspection is over. I watch as he opens a closet door and pulls out three hangers, each holding a different outfit.

He holds one up to me. I immediately recognize it as the bartending outfit. For the females, it's a black miniskirt that's not too obscenely short—I've worn shorter—and a camisole that's sexy but not too revealing.

"Here's your bartending uniform," he says as he hands it to me. "You brought black heels as I instructed, right?"

I nod, because it is the only thing he said I needed, so I'd grabbed one of only two pair I had. These had a modest heel of only three inches, with a pointed toe and a thin silver chain around the ankle.

Jerico holds up the second hanger, which also holds black clothing. "This is the uniform of a cleaner. I still want you in heels, though. You're not meant to be seen but if you are, at least the heels add some sex appeal."

The uniform looks very concealing, but very tight. Black stretchy pants with a slight shimmer and a small, extremely tight-looking black turtleneck with long sleeves. I suppose covering most of the skin in black is to camouflage the cleaners so they could be discreet when they swooped in to clean up the vinyl.

My eyes slide to the last hanger in his hand and there is a tiny scrap of flimsy silk folded over the bar. He hands it to me and says, "This is your uniform for the condiment tray. It's brand new."

My hand shakes as it takes the hanger from him. I swallow hard and ask, "And which job will I be performing tonight?"

Please don't be the thong. Please don't be the thong.

My breath comes out in a massive rush when he says, "We're going to start you easy tonight with cleaning duty. I'm going to be the one to train you."

My jaw drops open and my stomach flips at the thought of spending the evening with him in the midst of people having wild monkey sex. Talk about awkward and scintillating at the same time. My voice is raspy when I ask, "Why would you even bother training me?"

Jerico laughs, and there's no mistaking the taunt in it. "Relax, Trista… It's not because I think you're special or anything. It's just that you're a temporary employee and you're specifically working for me since I'm personally loaning you the money. I'm not going to waste any of my other staff's time to train you when it won't benefit the club in the long term."

It made sense. I guess.

Jerico turns toward his office door and issues a curt, "Come. Follow me."

"Please," I mumble softly under my breath so he

can't hear my backhanded rebuke for not being polite. I turn around and jog to keep up with him, clutching the three hangers to my chest. From his office, we turn left. Stopping, he points to a door that says *Locker Room*.

"It's unisex, but I have dressing rooms in there that are private," Jerico says. "Go get dressed. You can put your stuff in a locker. They have programmable digital locks. I'll wait here for you. We'll get started after that."

Jerico leans back casually against the wall and doesn't give me a second glance. I watch for only a moment as he pulls his smartphone out of his breast pocket and starts working it.

Not eager in the slightest to get started, I still make myself turn and walk into the locker room, my nerves humming with nervousness and some other emotion I can't quite put my finger on, but it's making me feel like I'm walking on a razor's edge.

♦

I HAD THOUGHT cleaning semen and other fluids off the furniture would be a completely humiliating task. What I found out, however, is that no one watches the people who do the cleaning. It's ingenious how the rooms are set up to accommodate that. For example, here in The Orgy Room, there are a multitude of beds and lounges covered in black vinyl and set into black acrylic and chrome frames. They sit low to the floor and are spread around the room in what appears to be a haphazard design. The floor is made up of large, square, frosted panels set into steel supports and run at a diagonal across the room. The colors change from a dusky rose to a cream color, which can enhance the mood of the music playing. From the ceiling, massive silk lampshades colored ice blue and formed into quirky shapes hang down. There are dozens of them, some wider and some longer, giving a very multidimensional look. The lampshades are fitted with muted lightbulbs to keep the atmosphere intimate but not completely dark. People definitely want to see what's happening in this room.

What isn't visible among the multitude of the lampshades hanging from the ceiling are very small but very bright lights that are aimed in a critical fashion on the beds and chaise lounges to provide a spotlight on any action that might occur there. When a couple or group is done with that piece of furniture, the light goes out. It indicates to the staff that the furniture needs cleaned. My job is to sweep in like a ghost to sanitize and dry the furniture. When it's clean, the spotlight is turned back on and it's opened for more fucking.

I'd asked Jerico about this last night as my curiosity was going to kill me. I was surprised about the semen. I mean… it's a public sex club and I assumed people would wear condoms. To his credit, Jerico didn't laugh at me. He explained that many of the couples here don't swing. Their pleasure is either having sex with others present or doing fetish stuff and as such, they didn't use condoms because they were monogamous. But he assured me the bulk of people suited up for protection, which meant I was mostly cleaning up sweat and perhaps lipstick if a woman was pushed facedown or something.

At least, that's how my imagination works.

But more importantly, no one watches the people who are cleaning the vinyl because they're busy ogling each other or other couples having sex. It becomes quickly apparent to me I am virtually unnoticeable in this job position, and I am freaking so grateful for it. Grateful to Jerico that he gave me an easy, inconspicuous job on my first night.

On the flip side, it's not a job that keeps me busy at all times. When there's nothing to clean, I have to stand at the perimeter of the room in the shadows and just watch the action. Looking away isn't an option because I have to be ready when a spotlight goes out. I make a mental note to myself to bring extra panties tomorrow.

Jerico has not left my side all evening, even though I've pretty much got the job down pat. Let's face it… it's not that hard to squirt the cleaner to get the nasty stuff up, and then wipe it away. I carry two towels. One to wipe the cleaning solution up and the other to dry the vinyl. When these towels reach their maximum usage, I go to the supply room and I restock. And thank God latex gloves are provided because otherwise, I would've had to politely decline this position.

I'm cleaning up other people's spunk and sweat and

while it is not the most humiliating job in the world, it's certainly not something I would ever aspire to do for the long term. It makes me wonder why the other cleaners in here are doing this job, and I can only figure they are in desperate times or something.

Jerico and I enter The Orgy Room. We'd spent a fair amount of time in The Waterfall Room—with its circular pool and platform in the center where people can have sex while a waterfall pours from the ceiling down onto them—as well as The Deck—with its acrylic see-through floor that gives the illusion of walking on air—before coming here.

So far tonight, I've been able to keep my wits about me. I try to concentrate on the fact that this is just a job. I've been pretty much able to tune out the noises, and I try not to keep my gaze focused anywhere for any length of time. Not only would it feel weird to stare at some of the things going on, but I don't want to inadvertently get drawn into it.

Let's face it… this club is filled with scenes that most people never see in their lifetime. I honestly can't imagine a more provocatively interesting place to people watch. While I'm currently single, I do wonder what it would be like to come with a serious partner. I would never consider coming as a single woman, but the thought of being with somebody I trusted in this environment has me curious. It's simply fascinating to me that many of the members here are in committed relationships with each other and this is a normal part of their sex lives.

I follow Jerico over to a far wall in The Orgy Room. We stand against it, taking an initial assessment of the activities. Jerico casually leans back against the wall, clasping his hands in front of him. Throughout the night, he has been approached by no less than a dozen different women trying to get him to join in their fun. It didn't surprise me. Jerico is one of the best-looking men I've ever seen, and I would imagine he partakes of the benefits of his club quite frequently. But he merely shook his head and politely declined, saying he was training the new employee. Of course, eyes would then turn to me in appraisal. Once they saw I was nothing more than a lowly cleaner, I was forgotten.

While Jerico remains casually posed, I stand ramrod straight, almost at military attention. Armed with a spray bottle of bleach in one hand and a towel in another with my drying cloth hooked into my belt, I'm locked and loaded.

My eyes scan the room and I estimate there are at least thirty pieces of furniture scattered about for people to use. On closer inspection, I see some padded benches and something that looks like a pommel horse in addition to the beds and lounges. There are also areas that are nothing more than an array of large stuffed pillows covered in a special type of vinyl that seems to be very lightweight and silky. Jerico assured me it could be cleaned with my solution.

It's starting to get busy. Probably half the furniture is in use. As I learned in The Waterfall Room, when a couple—or threesome or foursome or however many people can fit on a piece of furniture—take residence upon it, the spotlight shining down leaves nothing to the imagination.

I nearly jump out of my skin when I hear Jerico's voice near my ear. He's leaned over and although he's not actually touching me, I swear I can feel his lips move as he murmurs, "Tell me the difference between this room and The Waterfall Room."

I turn my head slightly to look at him and every time I connect with his eyes, I feel a sizzling warmth go through me. "What do you mean?"

"I mean," Jerico drawls as if I can't understand the English language. "What is the difference between the two rooms?"

"Um…" I stammer as I shrug my shoulders. "One has water and the other doesn't?"

"That's a naïve answer, Trista," Jerico says softly. "This is a sex club. Tell me the difference you have observed between the two rooms."

For the first time tonight, I allow myself a very slow perusal of the room. I had spent almost an hour in The Waterfall Room and while I didn't think I was paying that close attention to what was going on, I apparently absorbed more than I realized. Because as I look around

The Orgy Room, an immediate difference is clear.

Within The Waterfall Room, there is a much more apparent social aspect to the activities that go on in there. I'm not sure if it's because there is a pool where many of the patrons just lounge while sipping cocktails and talking, or the fact there are U-shaped seating areas that invite social intimacy. I realize there was less sex going on in there than in The Orgy Room.

From where I stand now as I look around the expanse and take in the activities, I am hit with the blatant realization that this room is for people who just want to fuck. No one is engaged in conversation, and the only sounds are of moaning, screaming, groaning, and flesh slapping.

Turning my head to face Jerico, I can feel my skin flush when I see how intently he is looking at me, waiting for my answer. My voice quavers when I tell him, "This room is only for sex. There's no socialization."

I want to look away, but his gaze has me absolutely locked in place. He stares at me a moment before giving a slight nod. Then he pulls back and leans against the wall. I turn around and keep my eyes rotating around the room for the next spotlight to go out and call me to my duties.

But Jerico isn't finished with the conversation. He's not leaning toward me, but he doesn't speak any louder when he says, "That's a very good observation, Trista.

It's why it's my favorite room."

I'm embarrassed that a full spinal shiver occurs from his words because if I had any doubts as to whether Jerico participated at The Wicked Horse, that has been dispelled. However, the shiver is more than likely because I can now picture Jerico on one of those pieces of furniture doing all kinds of amazing, kinky, and orgasmic things to women.

Over the next thirty days, I wonder if I'll observe him doing that… and if I'll ever be able to get those images out of my head afterward.

CHAPTER 5

Jerico

I STROLL INTO The Silo Room, my gaze sweeping the patrons. It's early, so it's only about half full, which lets me easily lock eyes onto Steven and Helena. They came tonight at my request because after three days of Trista working as a cleaner, it's time to start pushing her boundaries a little. She's not only getting promoted up to the condiment tray, but she's also going to understand her boss a little bit better tonight. Because what I have planned for her can't come as a great surprise, so I'm going to start exposing her to the dirty side of Jerico Jameson.

Joining Steven and Helena at the circular bar in the middle of the room, I quickly give him a handshake and press a soft kiss to Helena's cheek.

Next to The Orgy Room, this would be my favorite spot to fuck. I don't do any of the BDSM or fetish shit, but I admit it's interesting and arousing to watch sometimes. Admittedly, I'm not down with some of it, but most of it is erotic, so I like the vibe here.

This room is a smaller replica of Bridger's club in Wyoming. It's circular with little rooms on the perimeter done all in glass. Some rooms cater to fetishes, BDSM, or various other kink. Others are for members who just want to star in their own personal porn show. The main difference between this Silo and the one in Wyoming is that two of the rooms here offer privacy by long curtains that can be closed along the glass. This is usually done by a couple who comes in together and want to perhaps have a threesome. Their kink is the threesome and not in being watched, so I thought it was a nice touch to add.

"Want a drink?" Steven asks before he lets the last of his bourbon slide down his throat. I shake my head in the negative as he sits his glass back down. Helena's wineglass is empty, but I bet it's her second as I told her I only had limited time at seven, so I know she's ready to go.

It just so happens that seven is when Trista will come on duty. My cryptic text to her should have her showing up in this room in the next five minutes or so. All I texted her was, *New duties tonight. Find me when you get here.*

I've not seen her much the last two nights as she was able to work on her own and any more "training" by me would probably be considered stalking. So she worked, and I ignored her for the most part.

But not tonight.

"So what's your pleasure?" Helena asks in a husky voice as she steps into the front of my body. Steven comes up behind his wife and presses in tight, grinding his dick against her ass. I think it's a subtle suggestion I fuck her pussy while her husband gets her ass.

I smile at her, but then lift my eyes to Steven to get his permission. "I'd just love Helena's beautiful mouth on my cock tonight. I don't have a lot of time to play."

"I still think I'll take your ass, love," Steven whispers in Helena's ear. She shudders because that woman loves ass play.

"Then let's get to it," she murmurs as she takes my hand to lead me over to a low, black bench covered in buttoned vinyl. It sits directly in front of the glass room that houses the stocks, which are currently in use by two men. One has his neck and arms firmly enclosed in the hinged, swinging board while he's sucking his partner's cock. I've learned over the last year that Helena loves watching two men together, so it's no surprise she decided to set up shop in front of this room. I know she'd love for Steven and me to get physical with each other during our threesomes, but that's not my thing. Nothing against it, just not my cup of tea.

Because time is of the essence, Steven takes control of getting his wife ready. While feathering kisses along her neck, he removes her dress, bra, and panties while leaving on her high-heeled shoes. My dick doesn't start to get hard until Helena crawls onto the bench. With a sultry look, she crooks her finger at me to step closer. I do as requested. Coming to her knees, she starts to work at my belt and zipper. While I don't pay close attention to him, I can see Steven moving behind her with a bottle of lube in his palm.

Helena makes short work of pulling my cock free and with a few hard strokes of her hand, I'm ready to go. My eyes stay glued on her mouth as she takes me inside it, and I can't help the groan that rumbles out of me when the head of my cock slips into her throat. She hums in appreciation, and I feel that sensation straight through to my balls.

Helena bobs up and down on me for a few moments, but then her entire body jerks forward and my gaze rises to see Steven behind her with his dick against her ass. He rotates his hips and gently works himself into her before he sets up a leisurely pace as he is never in any hurry to get off. Because he always wants his wife to get off first, his fingers go between her legs and she makes more moaning and groaning sounds that feel amazing on my cock as she sucks me slowly but very deeply. She is a fucking master at blowing a guy.

My hands come up to cradle Helena's face so I can hold her in place. Because she has no problems with taking me deep, I take over and start to thrust, going faster than the pace she set. Helena breathes in through her nose to ensure she has adequate oxygen, but I know this isn't completely comfortable for her as her eyes start leaking tears. Had this been the first time I've been down her throat, I would be worried, but this is normal for her.

I can feel my orgasm starting to tingle as Helena brings a hand up to roll my balls. My head falls back with a deep groan and when I let it fall forward again, my gaze catches Trista standing in the doorway. She doesn't see me looking at her as her own gaze is riveted to where Steven is plowing his wife's ass. But then Trista's gaze slides slowly along Helena's body to where she's enthusiastically sucking my dick.

My orgasm starts to burn hotter and as I dig my fingers into the side of Helena's head, I fuck her mouth faster. I keep my eyes locked on Trista, and she finally dares to look at me.

My breath is coming out harshly, but I still manage to give Trista a wicked smile. She gives me nothing in return except wide eyes and a slightly parted mouth. She never does drop her gaze from mine and I'm guessing it's because she's too embarrassed to do so now that I caught her staring.

But I know she wants to.

I can also tell she wants to look more.

I know this because I can see her chest rising and falling, and her cheeks are flushed. She runs her tongue over her lower lip a few times and her hands are clasped together so tightly her knuckles are white. Add onto that, she's fidgeting by stepping from foot to foot and pressing her legs together slightly. I'd bet my life if I were to stick my hand down the front of her jeans, I would find her soaking wet.

And just the thought of my hand between her legs causes my climax to slam into me. I shove deeper into Helena's mouth and shoot my load straight down her throat with a long groan I know Trista can hear from across the room.

Fuck... that felt good.

Actually, I think that was the best orgasm I've ever had with Helena and I'm honest enough with myself to acknowledge it was because Trista was watching me do it.

Helena sucks every bit of me down, then gently licks around the base of my cock while her husband continues to fuck her ass. I pull away from her, gently stroking a thumb across her cheek. Leaning down, I press my lips to her forehead and whisper, "Thank you, Helena. You are amazing."

My head turns toward Trista as I tuck myself back into my pants and refasten my zipper and belt. Trista has stepped fully into the room, but she is no longer looking my way. Instead, her gaze is roaming around, but I can tell she's not taking anything in. As I've observed over the past few days, she tries her damnedest not to focus on the sex going on around her. It's not because she's not interested... because there is not one person who can step foot in this club and not have curiosity overtake them. My best guess is that Trista wants to look too badly and is perhaps afraid of the way it will affect her, so she tries very hard to remain aloof from it all.

I clasp Steven on the shoulder for a brief squeeze as he continues to fuck his wife before making my way across the interior of The Silo toward Trista.

Her gaze finally comes to me when I'm but a few feet from her. I glance at my watch, and then back to her. "You're right on time."

Trista merely shrugs. "Well, I take my job seriously."

"Good to know," I tell her as I take her by the elbow and lead her out of The Silo. "I'd hate to have to fire you before you fulfilled your end of the deal to get the rest of the money."

Trista stiffens minutely, but she doesn't say a word. She walks along with me willingly but silently as I take her to my office.

After punching in my security code, I open the door and motion her to walk in before me. I follow her in and shut the door.

"You said I was going to be working a different job tonight?" Trista asks, her nervousness clear in her tone.

I don't answer her right away. Walking to the closet, I open the door, reach in, and pull out a condiment tray. Turning to her, I say, "Lindsay normally works the Waterfall Room, but she's sick tonight. You're going to need to fill in for her."

I wait patiently to see what Trista will do. If I was a betting man, I would think she would balk at the idea.

Even though she knows this is an expected job duty, I can tell she's not the type of woman who is going to be comfortable wearing nothing but a thong and a couple of straps over her breasts.

Instead, she catches me off guard when she asks, "Do you do that often?"

I know exactly what she's asking, but I play stupid. "What do you mean?"

"Have sex with the club members," she says almost belligerently. I have to control myself not to laugh over her tone.

"Of course I do," I admit to her. "Why wouldn't I?"

Trista doesn't seem to have an answer for that, and her gaze drops to the floor.

I provide her a little bit of clarification about the type of man Jerico Jameson is. "Trista… I like sex. I like it kinky. I also like it in public sometimes. I own a sex club. It's only natural I would take advantage of what is presented to me since I like those things. Do you think I shouldn't?"

Trista's eyes come back to mine, and she shakes her head. "It's none of my business what you do. I was just curious. And… I've um… noticed that some of the other employees also have sex while they're on duty."

I walk over to my desk and set the condiment tray down on it. Leaning back, I sit on the edge and cross my arms over my chest. "I guess I failed to mention to you that any employee here also has an automatic membership."

"That doesn't surprise me," Trista says quickly. "I guess I was just surprised that employees would take advantage of the membership while they are working."

Understanding dawns, and I nod my head at her. "If things are super busy, my employees should be doing their duties. But if things are slow and there is an opportunity one of the employees wants to take, I encourage it."

"You do?"

"Most people who come in here don't have a lot of confidence in their sexual nature. They come for an experience, perhaps one that will only occur once in their lifetime. Sometimes, they are so nervous they won't take advantage of what the club has to offer them. In those cases, I encourage my employees to help make those patrons comfortable. I also ask any of my employees who come in while off duty to help facilitate those guests along."

Trista's face turns red, and she practically squeaks, "But you said that would not be required of me."

I give her a reassuring smile. "It is not a requirement to work here, Trista. Should you feel the desire to do so, and your duties would not suffer, then you are more than welcome to fuck someone."

Utter relief fills Trista's eyes. At the same time, I have a burning fire in my gut at the thought of Trista bending over a couch to take some stranger's dick into her.

Which makes me wonder… is she that type of girl?

"Does any of this offend you?" I ask as I push off the desk and come to stand before her.

She tilts her head back to look up at me. Worrying at her lower lip with her teeth for just a moment, she shakes her head. "Not in the slightest. I'm openminded and I don't begrudge anyone in this club."

Hmm. That doesn't exactly tell me what I want to know.

"Are you interested in that particular employee benefit?" I ask pointedly.

I can't believe the strength of the disappointment that flows through me when she vehemently shakes her head. "Oh no, I could never do something like that. Not in front of others."

Yes, that is very discouraging indeed.

I push off my desk and turn to the condiment tray so she cannot see the disappointment on my face. There's a polite smile there when I turn back to her. "Here you go. Take this in the locker room and get dressed. I'll wait for you outside so I can explain to you how this works and where you can get the supplies to fill it."

Trista doesn't take the tray from me, only stares at it as if it's a snake ready to strike at her. I know this is a huge leap to go from wearing clothing that covers from neck to toe to an outfit that's not going to leave much to the imagination.

I'd like to provide her some reassurance, but I've got

none to offer. If she is in any way shy, unsure, or has major inhibitions, nothing I say is going to put her at ease.

I will, however, spend the evening walking her through the job, and not for any altruistic reasoning. It's the first step in getting those pretty legs to open for me. My instinct is that Trista is turned on by this, and I want to watch that blossom even further.

CHAPTER 6

Trista

I SIT IN the dressing room on the padded bench with
one leg crossed over the other and my arms folded
over my bare breasts. I've been sitting here for five
minutes trying to work up the courage to put on the
condiment tray and step out of the locker room.

So far, all I've managed to do is to take my clothes
off and put the slinky black thong on. I looked at myself
in the mirror for all of three seconds before my butt
slammed down onto the bench, and I covered myself.

I cannot do this.

I cannot go out and look Jerico in the eye while I
have silk running up the crack of my ass and my boobs
squished by the straps of the tray. It is completely odd
and a little humiliating that I'm more worried about
Jerico seeing me in this getup than I am the hundreds of
other people in this club.

But there is no way Jerico is going to let me hang out
in here all night, so I take a deep breath and resolve to

get this over with. I stand up on the exhale and jolt when I hear Jerico call out, "Trista… are you okay in there?"

My ass slams back down to the bench as my arms cover my chest protectively. My mouth opens, but no words come out.

"Trista?" Jerico says, his voice practically on the other side of the dressing room door.

I'm still not able to answer him, and frankly, I'm barely able to breathe. I just saw this man get a blow job… watched his face morph into pleasure so intense I wondered what it would be like to be that woman, and…

I have no words for him.

There's a gentle tapping on the louvered door that separates me from Jerico, and he asks again, "Trista… is there a problem?"

I swallow hard, and my voice practically squeaks, "No, I'm okay."

"You don't sound okay," Jerico says, and it pisses me off that I hear humor in his voice.

Pisses me off so much I can't help but snap at him, "I'm a little embarrassed to be wearing this."

Jerico doesn't say anything for a moment, but then he cautiously points out, "You had no objections to this when I told you about it a few days ago."

"I know," I snap at him again. "Just give me a minute."

"Sure," he says congenially, as if he has all the time in

the world to wait for me.

I hear him take a few steps back and then what sounds like his body leaning against the wall opposite the dressing room door. I can imagine him looking all sinfully sophisticated, replete with male satisfaction, while he waits for the scared little girl to get over herself.

"Surely you know you have a beautiful body," Jerico says, and the shock of his words cause me to jolt even as I tighten my arms over my breasts.

I don't even know what to say. In a million years, I would never think a man as gorgeous as Jerico Jameson would consider me to be beautiful.

Apparently, Jerico doesn't expect a response from me because he continues. "You truly have nothing to be embarrassed about, Trista. No one in this club will think twice about you wearing that uniform. Besides that, I'll stick with you tonight to ensure that everything goes okay."

I still don't know what to say.

The silence continues, but then it becomes awkward.

Finally, Jerico commands in a low, firm voice. "Trista… open the door and step out here."

I hesitate only a second. This is my job, and I need the money Jerico is going to give me. I've got to suck this up, put on my big-girl panties—or thong—and get this over with. It's only twenty-seven more days of my life, and then I can move on.

Standing up from the bench, I pick up the condiment tray and set the hooked harness over my shoulders, pull my hair out from under it, and situate the straps to come down over the middle of each breast. When I look in the mirror, my face flushes red as I take myself in. My boobs, which are a hefty C cup, are smashed in a way that doesn't hurt but causes them to round outward. Even though the underside of the strap has a soft, velvety feel, it chafes a little against my nipples. This, of course, makes my nipples hard, and I grit my teeth over the realization that I'm not sure if it's the sensation of the straps rubbing against them or the knowledge Jerico will be seeing me like this in a matter of seconds.

Just below my breast, the strap on each side splits in two and the four ends anchor to the corners of the tray so I don't have to support its weight. In addition to being able to see almost all my boobs except my areolas and nipples, my entire abdomen is exposed as the edge of the tray sits right below my navel. I give a slight turn in the same strappy black heels I've been wearing the last three nights, and then look at my ass in the mirror. The thong is a dark black satin that is thankfully not see-through—not that it matters when my entire ass is exposed. At least I've always thought I had a good butt. It's not too flat but not too bubbly. I also have good legs, which are long and tanned, and I have to admit there is a small part of me—way deep down inside—that admits I look sexy.

"Trista?" Jerico calls out to me.

I give a slight cough to clear the nervousness from my throat and say, "I'm coming."

I take a deep breath, turn, and open the door to the dressing room, coming face to face with Jerico.

If I thought there might be some measure of a gentleman within him, I would be wrong because his gaze slowly runs down my body in an appreciative, slightly leering manner. He takes his time, letting his eyes wander back up, but they make it no higher than my breasts.

"I'm going to show you a trick that will make this more comfortable," he says softly before raising his eyes to meet mine. He steps closer to me and slips his fingers under the strap covering my right breast, but about three inches below it so he's not touching my skin. The breath I suck in involuntarily is embarrassing, and my body locks solid.

Jerico gives me a wicked smile, and then he murmurs, "I'm just going to make a slight adjustment on you."

Before I can think to object to him touching me, he pulls the strap away from my breast and with his other hand, he places his palm on the underswell. He lifts it up, and his fingers feel like fire upon my skin. My heart thumps so hard I'm sure it might burst out of my chest. He then lays the strap back over my breast, and I have to admit it feels more comfortable as his hands fall away. My breast doesn't feel as smashed, but the nipple is harder. Damn it.

My head lifts, and Jerico grins at me. There is no doubt there is wicked intent there. "Want me to adjust the other one?"

My voice is entirely raspy as I shake my head before turning away from him. "I can manage on my own."

Jerico chuckles as I repeat the same maneuver to my other boob and almost sigh over the feeling of relief it produces. When I turn back around, Jerico doesn't spare me at all, roaming his eyes over me again. This causes me to fidget in place, much the way I did when I found him in The Silo Room getting his dick sucked while the woman who was pleasuring him was getting her ass fucked. I want to deny to myself that said fidgeting is anything more than just nervousness. However, I can't lie to myself, although I'd deny it to anyone else, but I was insanely turned on by watching Jerico. I'm not stupid. I know he planned it, because he knew what time I would be showing up and he specifically told me to find him.

I have no clue what his reasoning for it was, but it's probably something as simple as the fact he truly didn't care if I saw him doing that. Let's face it, I know nothing about this man other than he is insanely attractive. Much to my shame, I'm greatly intrigued by the wickedness of him and his club.

♦

THE JOB OF selling things from my condiment tray is not very hard. I worked in retail before, so it's merely a matter of a customer picking out what he wants to buy and me taking the money. I learn quickly enough that the toys on my tray—such as butt plugs and tiny vibrators—are not big sellers. It's mostly condoms and the occasional tube of KY jelly that sell. Ensuring I learn my job, Jerico explained to me that the regulars who come here bring their own paraphernalia. It's usually only the people who are here for a single night that will need condoms or lube, and they usually don't want to spend the extra money on a toy because let's face it… deviant and public sex in this place is better than any toy.

I'm only working The Waterfall Room tonight and as promised, Jerico is sticking by my side even though I've assured him I'm good on my own. Truth be told, he's absolutely freaking me out tonight. He has not even bothered to hide his appreciation of my body because he continued to admire it even after we left the locker room. My job is to walk around the room so I can be available to customers who may be in the heat of the moment and can wave me over to them. Jerico has made it a habit all evening to walk behind me at a discreet distance so it doesn't look as if he's training me, but any time I've looked back at him, his eyes have been pinned on my ass. I was horrified by a rush of pride knowing I'd caught the attention of a man who could have any woman in this club, and was even more horrified to realize during my bathroom break a few minutes ago that my thong is absolutely drenched in the crotch.

In addition, even though I've discreetly adjusted my breasts when I can, my nipples are still chafing. This is not really because of the straps, but because they are constantly hard. I'm going to go ahead and blame that on Jerico as well. Tonight I've had to pay better attention to my surroundings because the patrons who want to purchase from me are usually already involved in some heavy foreplay. As such, I've had to keep my attention on the action. But that came only after Jerico pointed out to me I couldn't do my job effectively unless I paid attention.

I walk the outer perimeter of the lounge chairs set around the pool and notice a man waving me over to him. He's naked with his legs sprawled out along the length of the couch and an equally naked woman kneels between them as she gives him a blow job.

I like The Waterfall Room a lot. The cascade of water that pours down from the ceiling onto the pool's center platform is spectacular. It runs through a sleek crystal ceiling light that is nothing more than long strings of lit crystals that hang down in various lengths above the pool. The water sparkles with a million refracting lights as it passes by the clear sparkling gems. While the waterfall is a beautiful centerpiece to the room, it's functional as well. The platform can hold up to four people who might want to fuck under the spray of warm water.

Around the edge of the pool, the flooring is black cement done in a super-fine texture with silver sparkles in it that prevents slipping but doesn't hurt the feet. Most people in the waterfall room wear bathing suits or nothing at all. No one ever wears shoes except the employees, and I'm thankful that the floor is non-slip as I walk in my heels.

The man who beckoned me is reclining on one length of U-shaped low-back couches covered in water-repellent vinyl of deep purple that shimmers. Vinyl is the name of the game as it's easily cleaned in between uses. There are silver pleated curtains draping the double glass doors that lead out to The Deck, and swags of fabric in the same silver hang in arcs from the center of the ceiling starting just outside the waterfall to the perimeter. It sort of reminds me of what the inside of a tent that belonged to a grand Sheik would look like. Or just a fancy circus tent, as the things that go on in here could be considered circus-like.

"What can I get for you?" I ask the man as I come to a stop just a few feet from where he's lying.

I have to admit the guy is very good looking. I've gotten used to the fact that there are all shapes, sizes, and ages in this club. Sometimes, it's not all that easy to watch an old, wrinkly man getting it on, but I try not to focus in on those sexcapades. It makes me appreciate, however, the men like this one when they need something from me. I'd estimate he's in his late thirties with sandy-blond hair and warm brown eyes. His haircut is precise and stylish, so I peg him for a lawyer or something like that.

While his partner's head bobs up and down on him, he does nothing more than consider the items on my tray. He casually peruses them and doesn't even seem to be affected by what the woman is doing to him. Finally, he looks back to me and asks, "What would you suggest?"

"Pardon me?"

His smile turns salacious as he nods down to the tray. "What would you suggest I use on my girl here? Should I plug her ass while I fuck her pussy?"

I'm completely caught off guard, and my answer is stammered out with a complete lack of finesse. "Um... I have... Um... Well, I'm really not sure—"

The man laughs. I can tell he's not charmed by me, but takes some pleasure in my embarrassment. His hand goes to the woman's head, his fingers grasping her hair tightly. He spares her a short glance and growls at her, "Faster," then uses the grip on her hair to push her roughly up and down on his stick.

Again, it's extremely weird that he doesn't seem turned on by any of this but rather seems more interested in embarrassing me because he says, "Why don't you join us? I'll let Lila here eat you out while I fuck you from behind."

I have to suppress the groan of embarrassment welling up inside of me. Not only am I highly offended, but I am also slightly turned on by the prospect of what was just offered. I don't know if it's from an abundance of hormones thickening the air or if I just suddenly became susceptible to the wickedness of this place, but for the first time, I wonder if I would ever take up Jerico's offer to get my rocks off during a slow shift.

"Leave her the fuck alone, Willis," Jerico growls from behind me. And I mean right behind me, so close I can feel his suit jacket brush against my bare ass.

The man—who is apparently named Willis—uses his grip on the woman's head to pull her off him, swinging his legs off the couch and placing his bare feet on the floor. He stands up. His dick is wet with lipstick marks and only standing at half mast, so I don't think the girl was doing a very good job. The man glares at Jerico. "What's your problem? You never mind your employees joining in the fun."

Jerico's voice is low and commanding as well as final. "That's true, but this one is off limits. Now if you'll excuse us, I hope you have a good evening."

And with that, Jerico's hand comes to the back of my neck. He uses it to turn me away from Willis and pushes me toward the opposite side of the room.

He guides me to the wall adjacent to the entrance door. There are no people congregated here, and it's fairly quiet away from the drone of lusty moans and slapping sex. With his hand still at the back of my neck, Jerico turns me around to face the pool and the sexual activity going on around it.

"Did you want to join that man and woman?" he asks me softly.

I shake my head immediately, and his fingers squeeze my neck in what I take to be approval.

"But the idea doesn't turn you off?"

Did he just ask me that?

I feel like my breath has been stomped out of my lungs by the personal question, mostly because I don't want to tell him the truth. Jerico, however, is not a man who will go unanswered.

"Trista," he says almost harshly to get my attention. "Tell me the truth… are you turned on right now?"

I shake my head vehemently, giving him a total and absolute nonverbal lie. I've been turned on since the moment I stepped out of the dressing room and Jerico looked at my body.

No, strike that. Since I saw him getting pleasured in The Silo room.

Jerico gives a dark laugh and whispers in my ear, "Little liar."

"I'm not," I deny, but it sounds weak.

I'm surprised when Jerico's hand falls from my neck, and he turns to stand right beside me as we look out over the interior of The Waterfall Room. He even casually tucks his hands in his pockets.

"I'll make you a deal, Trista," Jerico says.

My head turns in surprise to look at him, but he keeps his profile to me. "What's that?" I asked hesitantly.

He's not looking at me, but I can see from the side he's smirking when he says with utter confidence, "I think you are turned on. Confident, in fact. So if you let me stick my hand between your legs right now and you're dry, I'll hand you the other fifteen grand I owe you and you can walk out of here and never come back."

My heart starts to jackhammer at the thought of Jerico's hand between my legs, but there is no way I'm ever going to let myself get embroiled with a man like him. Still, you know how curiosity killed the cat and all that, so I ask him, "And what happens if I'm not dry?"

Jerico turns his head to look at me. He's no longer smirking and his eyes are dark and sinful looking as they bore into mine. "If you're wet, Trista, I'm probably going to bend you over one of these couches and take care of your problem."

My jaw drops so far I know I look utterly ridiculous. Blinking at him in astonishment, I take an involuntary step away.

"What do you say, Trista? Can I inch my fingers into your pussy for a little feel?"

Every cell in my body screams out, "Yes!"

Well, every cell except the ones in my brain who know this would be a very stupid mistake to make. I shake my head, taking a breath in to answer with what

I'm proud to note is a firm and steady voice. "I don't think that would be a good idea. I think I'll pass on your little bet."

Jerico doesn't say anything at first. He just continues to peer at me intently, perhaps wondering if I'll repeal that lie I just told. When I don't, he gives a shrug of his shoulders and says, "If you change your mind, all you have to do is ask."

"I won't change my mind," I say firmly.

Jerico gives a taunting nod and by the curl of his lips, I can tell he doesn't believe a word I'm saying. And to make matters worse, he offhandedly remarks, "If you do change your mind, I might be interested in working out something with you to lessen the amount of days you have to work at The Wicked Horse."

My eyebrows shoot straight into my hairline. "Are you saying if I have sex with you, I won't have to work here for another twenty-seven days and you'll still give me the money?"

Jerico gives me a wicked grin. "I don't know... are you interested in something like that if I am indeed offering?"

My eyes narrow at him. I know it's stupid to be offended seeing as how I am working in a sex club and I've been turned on ever since I watched Jerico get his dick sucked, but I snap at him, "I'm not a whore."

I didn't think this would strike a chord with Jerico, so I'm surprised when his head actually jerks back.

"That's not what I was thinking."

I can't hide the sarcasm in my voice. "Well, when you give a woman money for sex, it makes her a whore."

Jerico gives me an apologetic smile and an acknowledging nod of his head. "My apologies, Trista. Let's forget what I just said."

"Gladly," I say, still pissed off even though he's apologized. If I had to guess why I'm having this weird reaction, it's because part of me feels let down that I won't be having sex with Jerico Jameson.

Oh my God… I'm going crazy I think, and by the look on his face, he knows I'm struggling with this.

Jerico smiles at me and then bends his head so his mouth is within a hair's breadth of mine. I think he's going to kiss me but instead he just murmurs, "Putting money and our deal aside, if you ever want me to scratch that itch of yours, all you have to do is ask, Trista. I'll give it to you."

I actually go dizzy and my head spins from his words. He is basically offering to pleasure me if I ask, and only in consideration of my need and not our deal. I don't even know what to make of it but before I can even think about a coherent response, Jerico turns on his heel and walks out of the room.

CHAPTER 7

Jerico

FOR THREE NIGHTS, I've watched her.

By any definition, I'd totally be considered a stalker.

But from the comfort of my office, I can pull up the security feeds on my monitor and take note of the subtle changes in Trista as she works the condiment tray. Truth be told, I don't need her working that job and have a much greater need for her to go back to cleaning, but fuck if she doesn't look a hell of a lot sexier in a thong than a turtleneck and pants.

Part of my training in the military was gathering intelligence, so I can pick up on the slightest of details that could tell me a very important story, and there were a lot of changes I noticed over the last three days with Trista as she settled into her job routine.

The most important and pleasing thing was that Trista's stopped hiding her sexual curiosity. When I first started working here, she looked around a room in a vague way, not taking in too many details. I think she was afraid to watch.

Afraid of what it would do to her body.

But that has definitely changed.

Now, Trista watches what the patrons are doing. Sometimes, she stares for long moments and much to my delight, the kinkier the acts, the longer she stares. My trained eyes take in her chest rising and falling to keep up with what I'm sure was a racing pulse. She'd adjust the straps covering her breasts in a very minute way either because the pressure on her nipples was too much, or because she wanted to create some friction.

Naughty, naughty girl.

My favorite though was when she would cross one long leg over the other and squeeze her thighs together as she watched, and I had no doubt her clit was probably pulsing with desire.

Trista was getting braver too. She never once took any man up on an offer to join, and there had been some I'd seen. I had told her she could if business was slow, but I also made a spectacle in front of Willis that she was off limits. Perhaps Trista thinks she's off limits to everyone, and it's fine by me if she wants to think that.

But while Trista may not have had sex with anyone, she certainly had a frisky side that shocked the shit out of me. She was working The Orgy Room one evening as I sat in my office, enjoying a nice scotch while watching her on the video feed. She walked the room, and even her walk was different. Her shoulders were held back, chin up, and there was extra sway in her hips as she wound her way in and out of the various pieces of furniture.

She stopped at a long, low chaise that was currently occupied by a man and a woman. Both naked, engaged in some heated foreplay. The man asked Trista for something, and she pulled a bottle of lube from her tray. The man didn't take it at first, but merely flipped the woman over on her belly before hauling her to her hands and knees. He positioned himself behind her, one knee pressed into the vinyl cushioning and the other foot planted firmly on the floor for leverage.

He said something else to Trista, who laughed with delight but shook her head. My hand clenched, wondering if he invited her to join in and because I'd never seen Trista laugh like that, I thought perhaps she could be persuaded.

The man grinned at Trista and gripped the woman's ass before him, spreading her cheeks apart. The man nodded his head that way, and I could practically read his lips—come on—and the expression on his face was pleading.

The woman turned her head to Trista, and it appeared she was appealing to her as well.

To do what to the woman's ass was beyond me, but my lungs froze as I watched.

I swear I saw a mischievous glint start to sparkle in

Trista's eyes, and then she opened the lube. Stunned, I watched as she first turned it over the woman's ass, and then squirted some right over the exposed seam and without a moment of hesitation, she turned to the man. He took his cock in hand, leaned his hips forward a bit, and let Trista squirt lube down his length.

He must have asked her to stroke him, but she just laughed again as she shook her head, putting the top back on the lube and placing it on the floor near the couple's discarded clothes. The man started stroking his dick, but he nodded toward his clothes and said something to Trista. She squatted down gracefully, knees to the side but balancing the tray, and grabbed the man's wallet. He directed her to open it, and she pulled out a bill. Trista made change and started to put the remainder back in the wallet, but the man said something else to her.

I assumed he was offering her a tip.

Trista shook her head again, but she pulled her bottom lip between her teeth as if she was perhaps reconsidering. The man nodded to the money in her hand, then to his cock, and my body went tight.

Trista nodded as she stood up and I also stood up from my chair—to do what I don't know. Would I intervene if she participated?

Luckily, it wasn't necessary because all Trista did was stand there and watch.

Watch as the guy gave her a huge grin before lining

the head of his cock up to the woman's anus and started to work his way in. Trista didn't display one telling sign of shyness about standing there watching a man fuck a woman's ass. She watched... crossed those legs... pressed her thighs together.

It was sexy as fuck to watch her watch that couple, and I sat right back down in my chair and palmed my own swelling dick. I bet if I called her into my office right then and slid my fingers in that thong, she would have been drenched.

My cock got harder, then, so I jerked off as I watched Trista watch what turned out to be a pretty hot ass fucking.

Tonight though, I won't get to watch her. She came to me and made a good point about needing at least one night off a week. I wanted to argue with her, but I didn't, and tonight was that night.

Sad I wouldn't be able to watch her, wondering what would be running through her head. Wondering if she masturbated right in the locker room at the end of her shift because watching all that kinky fucking had made her horny.

Or maybe she waited until she got home. I could see her using the hand-held sprayer to pulse water over her clit, or maybe she waited until she was naked in bed. Legs spread wide with her slicked fingertips rubbing herself. Perhaps thinking of that couple she watched fuck up close, or maybe she even thought of Helena sucking me off.

She'd look fabulous in a bed made with black satin sheets, legs spread wide and begging me to fill her up. Fuck her slowly.

No wait... I don't want her in a bed. I won't make love to her. I want her on her knees before me or better yet... locked in the stocks while I fuck her. I want her in every dirty way I can imagine, and let's face it... I'd take her on black satin sheets and make love to her all right.

I wonder if I put the moves on her, would she submit to me? I either need to step up my game or forget about using Trista to get my revenge on Jayce.

Standing from my desk, I make my way out of my office and lock up behind me. I'll hang out in The Social Room for a bit and see if anyone interesting comes through. If not, I'll probably call it an early night and catch a late baseball game on TV. Granted, owning a sex club means that I have sex.

A lot.

But I don't have it every night, and there are times I'm not even interested. A beer, pizza, and ESPN preferable.

On the flip side, there are times I can get in a mood and want to do something totally whacked on the kink scale, and there's not much I haven't tried.

Tonight... I'm ambivalent, but I will give a quick peek inside to see if there are any regulars who interest me.

Just as I reach over to flip my monitor off, something catches my eye on the security feed. While I have a security team that monitors the activity in the rooms in person and from a security office down the private hall, I also occasionally watch the feeds. I'm not interested in the patrons or what they're doing, but the general flow of things and to make sure my business is being well run. That the bartenders are filling drinks quickly, and the cleaners are doing their job as efficiently as possible.

Yes, so I may have excessively watched Trista over the last few days, but it's my fucking club. She's also part of my fucking favor owed, and I will be using her to my satisfaction before her thirty days are up.

What catches my eye on the monitor is shocking, and I sit back down in my chair so I can be sure about what I'm seeing.

It's Trista.

Walking through The Social Room toward the bar.

She's wearing a short, black skirt and a white camisole-type top that's loose but is cut in a "V" practically down to her navel, with crisscross strings tying the sides somewhat together. The inside swells of her breasts are visible but not much else. The sexiest part is she's not wearing a bra and the material is very thin. Her nipples are clearly evident, and I wonder if it's taking all that bravery she's learned the last few days as she has opened up her acceptance to this club and turned it onto herself. Those long legs are made longer by a pair of obscenely high-heeled ankle boots. The spikes on those heels would look glorious pressed into my shoulders.

Everything about what I'm seeing now pleases me beyond understanding.

She walks through the foyer doors, and my eyes flip to the security feed. It shows her heading to The Orgy Room. If I had to guess, it's Trista's favorite just as she seems more interactive in there with patrons than the other rooms.

I sit down in my chair and watch. If I'd been asked what I thought the chances were that Trista Barnes would come to The Wicked Horse on her day off, the answer would have been "not a snowball's chance in hell."

But here she is… and I'm on edge to see what happens.

♦

Thirty minutes later, I'm pushing out of my chair with only one destination in mind.

The Silo to talk to Trista.

I watched as she drank a glass of wine and chatted with the bartender. She stayed no more than twenty minutes and left as soon as she finished her drink.

My pulse raced, thinking she might be leaving, but I was relieved when I saw her walk through the foyer and down the hall to The Silo, and that's when it hit me.

She's here to try the lifestyle out.

And dressed the way she is, feeling brave, adventurous, and loosened up with a few drinks, she was going to get well laid tonight.

I make it to The Silo only seconds after she does, and she's still walking toward the circular bar in the middle as I enter. My Silo here in Vegas is very similar to the one in Wyoming, except for one huge difference. The Silo in Wyoming is well lit, and there's no mystery to the fucking that goes on there. The glassed rooms are bright and so is the circular interior.

I had this room decorated in black and deep purples with incandescent lighting. There were spotlights to showcase the action in the glass rooms, but there were also the curtains for privacy. And in the interior away from the circular bar, there was plush seating—again in a washable vinyl—where patrons could make out, fondle, or fuck. It's not overly dark, but it is dim, maybe even a little romantic feeling but for all that highly kinky shit going on in those rooms, and still completely rocking a sinful vibe.

Trista walks up to the circular bar, which is outfitted with stools, unlike the other bars, to encourage people to move around. The Silo is a bit different as it has more of a show quality since most of the action goes on inside the glass rooms with the people on the exterior watching so they should be able to do so comfortably.

I come up behind her just as she orders a glass of white wine, then perches that phenomenal ass on a stool.

The one to her right is empty and I slide onto it, and the movement gets her attention. She turns to look at me, her eyebrows rising in surprise.

"Oh, come on now," I admonish her with a smirk, and then let my eyes slide to the bartender who walks up. I place a quick order as I feel like a good scotch tonight. "I'll have a Laphroaig, and put her wine on my tab."

The bartender bobs his head and I turn back to Trista. She still has that same stunned look.

"You can't be surprised to see me in here," I tell her casually. "I do own this place."

Her facial muscles relax and she gives me a hesitant smile. "Of course I'm not surprised. I'm just... well, I guess I'm a bit nervous to be in here and was hoping I could just observe unobtrusively."

"Ah," I hazard a guess. "You're a voyeur. You like to watch."

The bartender returns with the drinks, and Trista immediately picks hers up to take a sip before giving a shake of her head. Those honeyed lengths fall over her golden, bare shoulders. Her eyes peek up to mine, her smile sheepish. "I have no clue what the hell I'm doing here. Curiosity, I guess."

Fuck yes.

This was even better than I anticipated. The signs are all adding up.

Her increased comfortability the last three days. The way she watched more of the action and was clearly affected by it. And finally... having the actual guts to come in and watch some more. Watching Trista fidget in her seat, seemingly needing more wine to calm her nerves, I realize she wants something from this club, but she has no clue how to go about getting it.

Her sexual curiosity has not only been awakened... it's been poked and prodded. Now she wants to know more.

And I'm just the guy who's going to do it for her.

The only guy, I decide.

CHAPTER 8

Trista

MY ENTIRE BODY feels as tight as a rubber band, and I have the feeling that Jerico is intent on making it snap. I can see it in his eyes… The calculation, the challenge, and deep within those green irises, I clearly see lust.

What does he see when he looks at me?

Can he tell how nervous I am to be sitting here?

Over the last week working at The Wicked Horse, I have learned something incredibly important.

Sex is not what I thought it was.

I've had sex. Lots of it. Most of it has been very good, while some of it has been mediocre.

None of it, though, has been like what happens inside The Wicked Horse. As I've watched couples, triples, and hell, even groups of people with so many arms and legs sticking out I had no clue how many were participating, I realized my sex life has been utterly lacking. I've never screamed like some of the women I've seen here, and I've never had a man take hours with me just to see how many orgasms he could wring out. That's right… I've seen some men spend hours on just one woman, working her over until she was nothing but a pile of goo.

The question remains, however…do I really have the guts to give this a try?

I'm quite sure the answer to is "no" as long as Jerico is sitting beside me. While he may be the epitome of my fantasy man, he intimidates the shit out of me. I could never relax around him.

If I can get Jerico to leave, I resolve I will at least make an effort to meet someone who has potential for a hook up. That will be my promise to myself so this trip tonight will not have been in vain.

"So what do you want?" Jerico asks, and his words cause me to jump in my seat so that my wine sloshes over the edge.

I don't bother looking at him as I sit my glass down and use the bar napkin to wipe the wetness from my fingers. But I answer his question with all the vagueness I can muster, "I have no clue what you're talking about."

Jerico chuckles. He laughs in a way that pretty much says he thinks I'm full of shit.

He doesn't pull any punches and tells me just how it is. "Trista, you're here because you want to get fucked like you've never been fucked before. Don't be embarrassed about it. Accept the fact that there is not one person in this building who will judge you for participating in and fulfilling your desires."

I stare at him, contemplating what he just said. His words are the perfect thing I need to hear and yet they do nothing to alleviate my nervousness. "This is so far out of the box for me; I'm really not sure I can do this."

"Want my help?" Jerico asks casually as he picks up his glass of scotch and takes a sip.

His offer doesn't surprise me. Jerico is an extremely sexual creature. While I know there are women in here a million times more beautiful and sexy than I am, he's a guy and he's not going to pass up an easy fuck.

Still, there's no way I can accept. I shake my head and politely say, "No offense, but I don't think it's a good idea to bang my boss."

Jerico's head falls back, and he lets out a peel of rich, sensual laughter. When he looks at me, his eyes are filled with mirth and his teeth flash at me with amusement.

"God, you're fucking adorable," Jerico says with a grin. "You have no idea how much I would enjoy defiling you."

I know he's half kidding me, but I decide to play along with his joking demeanor.

I cock an eyebrow at him and with a skeptical voice, I ask, "Defile me? That sounds very criminal."

The amusement slides right off Jerico's face and instead his eyes burn with something I can't identify as he looks at me. "Oh, Trista, the things I want to do to you are very criminal, but there is no doubt in my mind you would enjoy them."

A full-body shudder runs through me, and I'm completely mortified Jerico witnesses it. I know he recognizes it as my body betraying me, essentially telling him I very much like the idea of him doing criminal things to me.

Reaching his hand out, Jerico takes the stem of my wineglass in between his thumb and forefinger and slides it toward me. "How about you sip at your wine and let me show you a few things as we sit here at the bar?"

I pick up my glass and take a gulp. After setting my glass down, I ask for clarification. "And just how would you show me?"

Jerico gives a nod of his head toward the glassed rooms. "I'll sit here with you, and we'll watch the various shows that are going to happen. As you know, there will be some kinky-ass shit. If you have any questions, you can ask me. If you have any interest in trying something, I volunteer. If I'm not your cup of tea, I'll find someone to take you in one of those rooms and give you your fantasy. But for now, we'll just sit here and watch."

I stare at Jerico, weighing my options. I know that this is a very dangerous game I could be entering. I've already seen enough inside The Wicked Horse to know my body is going to react. I know that I'm going to want things. Worse yet, I'm sitting next to a man who seems more like a God than a human being and who has offered to give me what I want.

I should leave.

I should get up, politely decline Jerico's offer, and leave.

Instead, I spin my barstool so my back is to the bar and I'm facing the glass rooms. Without even looking at Jerico, I mutter, "Okay. We'll watch for a while, and you can answer any questions I have."

That's the most I'm willing to commit to, although even that sounds hollow to me.

Jerico swivels his stool so he's also facing outward. The move causes his knee to brush against my bare thigh and goosebumps to break out.

My eyes scan across the four glassed-in rooms that are visible from where I sit. All have action going on inside. Before I can even focus on anyone in particular, Jerico leans toward me, draping his arm on the bar behind my back.

"The third room," he says quietly.

My gaze slides there, and my breath catches as I take in the beauty of what is happening inside.

It might be every woman's number-one fantasy, or at the very least in the top three.

The room itself is stark and bare. The walls are a cream color. There is a raised platform in the center upon which a mattress draped in lavender silk sheets rests. During the nights I've worked in The Silo, I've noticed this room is usually used by a couple or threesome who enjoy performing publicly.

The three bodies on the mattress are certainly putting

on a show. A woman with pale blonde hair is sandwiched between two men. They are both tall, well muscled, and equally well endowed. Their hands and mouths are everywhere, and even the two men share a deep kiss.

"What do you think of that?" Jerico asks, his voice sounding like pure sex.

I don't even think to lie. "What woman wouldn't love that?"

Jerico chuckles, but then his voice turns even silkier. "I expect the woman who doesn't love cock in her ass wouldn't. Do you like anal?"

My spine tingles with the prospect of what Jerico is asking me, but I have to answer him honestly. I turn my face so he can look in my eyes and know I'm hiding nothing. "I don't know if I like it or not."

Jerico nods in understanding before turning to look back at the room. I let my eyes follow as we watch the threesome for a few silent moments as they kiss, stroke, suck, and bite at each other.

One of the men rolls to his back, taking the woman with him until she's straddling right over his dick. She reaches her hand down and guides him inside. His hands go to her breasts as she starts undulating on top of him. I cross one of my legs over the other, which doesn't give me any relief from the throbbing between my legs. If anything, I can feel my clit pulsing in cadence with my heartbeat and my breathing starts to become shallow because I know what's coming next.

The other man crawls behind the woman, places a hand at the back of her neck, and pushes her forward until she has to balance herself with her hands on the other man's chest.

I don't know whether to be appalled or turned on by the crudity of it, but the man simply spits in his hand, wipes it on the end of his dick, and then drives it into the woman's ass. My own ass puckers at the thought of that invasion, which I know could not have felt good. The woman, however, immediately starts moaning as she lets both men do the work. Holding her body still, the man underneath her thrusts his hips upward while the other pounds her ass from behind.

"That's not how it would be your first time," Jerico says. I'm too mortified to look at him as we discuss the potential of me engaging in anal sex. He continues, "That woman has a lot of experience, and she likes it rough and painful. Not many can take a cock like that."

I watch the unbelievably dirty and erotic threesome, getting more turned on because it's clear they are enjoying themselves immensely. At the same time, while it could be my utmost fantasy to be with two men, the thought of taking a dick back there scares the living crap out of me.

I'm probably going to regret this, but I can't help but ask, "How did she work up to that?"

Jerico's hand comes to my jaw, which causes me to jerk in surprise. He turns my face so I have to look at him, and he chastises me. "Be honest, Trista. You're not asking how *she* worked up to it. You're wanting to know how *you* could work up to it."

I try to shake my head in denial, but his grip on my jaw is firm.

"Just ask me, Trista." His voice rumbles with command. "I'll tell you whatever you want to know. I'll *show* you whatever you want to know."

His hand falls away from my jaw, but I am powerless to look away from him. His jade eyes promise me so many things that my head spins. My entire body feels electrified, and I swear pure adrenaline is flowing through my veins.

I lick my lips. In a hoarse voice, I ask, "How would *I* work up to something like that?"

I swear flames leap in Jerico's eyes, and he gives me a wicked smile. He answers me by standing up from the stool so fast to position his body in front of me that I gasp in surprise.

His large hands go to my legs. When he puts pressure on them, they uncross and spread apart. He steps in closer, placing his hands on the bar behind me, effectively caging me in.

Jerico leans his face toward mine until his mouth is just inches away and I can feel his warm breath... smell the smoky peat of his scotch.

"I'd take my time with you," Jerico whispers with such seductive promise that my legs start to close involuntarily so I can squeeze against the ache between them. Instead, the insides of my thighs hit Jerico's legs and practically tremble when he continues, "I'd loosen you up first with a really good orgasm... Probably with my mouth between your legs. Then I'd fuck you slowly from behind, while using my fingers in your ass. Or, if I felt like you could take it, I'd use a plug. Regardless, I would work that tight little ring of muscle very gently so that by the time I slid my cock in your ass, you'd be begging for it."

I can't say anything. I can't even move because I'm afraid it would be to get down on my hands and knees and beg Jerico to do what he just said. Instead, I let my breath out in a slow gust and stare right back into his heated eyes.

He gives me a slow smile as he drops one hand from the bar to come to rest on my thigh. His hand slides up slowly, going right under my skirt until his thumb grazes the edge of my panties. He does this without ever taking his eyes from mine.

"But you're not ready for that yet," Jerico murmurs as his thumb does nothing but stroke me. "I'd start off with something a little bit different."

My heart is pounding so hard I feel like it's going to explode out of my chest. My fear should be ruling my actions as I would be best served to hightail it out of here. But I'm too far gone.

"How would you start off with me?" I'm slightly

embarrassed over how young, naïve, and even needy my voice sounds.

Jerico's hand goes still on my leg, his eyes boring into mine as he assesses the legitimacy of my request. "Do you want me to tell you or show you?"

This is bad.

Really, really bad.

I want him to show me. Absolutely I want it, and I want it so much it physically hurts. There's an ache between my legs that I know only action will satisfy. I am so freaking attracted to this man in a way I've never been attracted to anything. Not even chocolate. He makes me feel beautiful and desirable, and I know he will be the best sex of my life.

I just know it.

But he's also an ass, and he's my boss, and he's just a means to an end for me. He owns a freaking sex club, for God's sake, and the list of negatives could go on and on. This is a man unlike any other. I've never dealt with someone who has his magnetism, confidence, or command. I've never wanted to just roll over and submit to someone so much. I'm afraid if I do that, I'll lose myself forever.

This is so bad.

But I've made my decision.

With a hard swallow and without ever letting my eyes waver from his, I tell him, "I want you to show me."

I do not mistake it, and it amazes me, but Jerico's

expression is one of relief. It's fleeting, and his eyes immediately darken. With one hand still under my skirt and resting on my hip, the other comes up to wrap around the back of my neck. He gives me a squeeze—perhaps of warning, maybe of reassurance—and says, "Are you sure?"

No. I'm totally not sure.

"Yes," I whisper. "I'm sure."

Again, relief morphs into lust as he pulls his hands away from me. "Let's go to my office. We need to set a few ground rules first."

I'm not sure what I was expecting, but it most definitely wasn't a talk to discuss rules. I thought perhaps he'd just take me into one of the rooms. But I can't ponder that because Jerico has my hand in his and is pulling me off the stool to drag me out of The Silo.

CHAPTER 9

Jerico

I HOLD HER hand tightly, afraid she'll realize she probably just made a deal with the devil and try to run from me. But it's too late for that. She said she was sure. Looked right in my eyes and told me she wanted me to show her my world. I can feel her right below my belt as my mind starts to spin with the possibilities of what I will do to her. Have her do to me. Endless pleasure for us both if she's brave enough to push forward after we have our talk.

It hits me as we walk out of The Silo I'm getting what I wanted first and foremost… to have carnal knowledge of Trista. But I'm also getting more.

This is the beginning of my revenge on her brother.

I have a small flicker of conscience that makes me feel like shit for a moment. Will she get hurt in the process?

Not physically by me, of course. In fact, for the next few weeks, I'm going to make damned fucking sure she receives ultimate pleasure by my hands... tongue... dick... whatever.

Whatever happens between us, I have to remember Trista Barnes will not be my problem. How her brother reacts to what I'm going to do to his sister is also not going to be my problem, but rather my pleasure. I'll just have to reassure myself that Trista has enough backbone to withstand the humiliation she may have when facing her brother. In fact, I know she can handle it. I've watched her enough the last three days to know she's got fucking steel running up her spine.

That makes me feel marginally better about using her for my own vengeful gain, so I'll keep repeating that to myself.

Once inside my office, I release my hold on her. I shrug out of my suit jacket and throw it on my desk chair before pulling at my tie to loosen it just a bit. "Would you like another drink?"

Trista shakes her head. "I'm good."

I know virtually nothing about this woman, including whether she has a good tolerance for alcohol, but I'm glad she didn't accept. I certainly don't want her coming back to me tomorrow claiming she was drunk and didn't know what she was doing. As it stands now, she seems fairly sober and in control of herself, although her eyes are shimmering somewhat. Could be a slight buzz or could be desire, I'm not sure. I only know it makes her eyes practically glow like a bubbling glass of champagne held up to the light.

Trista lets her gaze wander around my office, and I use the opportunity to just look at her. She is truly a stunning woman, and she doesn't seem to have a clue about it. Maybe that's exactly what makes her stunning.

When her attention falls to my desk, she leans over and grabs a framed photo. After studying it briefly, she turns it to me and asks, "How long were you in the military?"

My eyes flick to the photo, but they rest there no more than a second as I know it well. It was taken a long time ago when I was deployed to Afghanistan and was nothing more than my unit at the time posing for a group picture. It was given to me shortly after we returned to the States by my men. It doesn't hold any special significance to me other than the fact I enjoyed my time in the military, and it was an honor for me to serve.

"That was taken about twelve years ago," I tell her as she sets the photo back down. "I was in the Marine Corps for four years."

"You mentioned the other day when you introduced me to your friend Kynan that he helps run The Jameson group. What is that?"

I'm not into small chitchat, and I let her know it. "Well, aren't you full of all kinds of questions? Wasn't our discussion about anal sex exciting enough for you?"

Trista's cheeks turn pink even as she glares at me.

"Excuse me for trying to get to know you."

In three long steps, I'm standing in front of her. One hand goes to the back of her head where I easily fist that glorious, thick hair. The other goes to her ass to pull her in close to me.

Trista doesn't make a sound as her body presses to mine, but that's rectified when I slide her skirt up and inch my fingers under the thin silk of her panties covering her ass. I spread my fingers and palm her butt cheek before giving it a rough squeeze.

She rewards me with a moan and a fluttering of her eyes before she opens them wide with expectation and a tiny hint of fear.

"This isn't a date, Trista," I tell her in a gruff voice. "It's sex. Hot, no-holds-barred, scream-until-your-throat-is-raw sex. If you're looking for anything other than that, you need to walk right out of this office and find someone else to scratch that itch."

Before she can answer me, however, I stack the deck in my favor by pushing my fingers down the crease of her ass until they can skim the back edge of her pussy. As expected, I find it slick. The knowledge she's wet and I've hardly done anything but make dirty promises has my dick turning as hard as stone. With the hand that's on her ass and teasing between her legs, I pull her into my groin so she can feel I'm as turned on as she is.

Trista's eyes glaze over with lust and her chest is practically heaving, so I think I know the answer to my question. "Are you leaving or are you staying?"

Her answer is immediate if not breathless. "Staying."

"Good choice," I praise her before pulling my hand out of her panties.

Trista makes a sound of regret and longing, but I ignore it.

"Ground rules," I say as I take a step back to break the intimacy because this is business. My dick actually hurts, but rules come first. "We've already covered the fact that this is just sex and nothing more."

Trista nods and murmurs, "Understood."

"This gets you no special consideration or privileges over the other employees," I continue.

Heat sparks in her eyes as she snaps at me, "I would never expect that."

I don't bother responding to her ire. "And this has absolutely nothing to do with the favor I'm doing for you or your work for me. This is just you and me wanting one another."

"Agreed," she says with a smirk I want to kiss off her face. Or fuck her mouth to get rid of it.

I finish by saying, "And there will be no jealousy. This is a sex club. I fuck who I want and when I want."

Trista studies me for a moment, and I think that may have been a deal breaker. I know women like Trista. She wants to explore her adventurous side but when it boils down to it, most women get proprietary. Unless she fully immerses herself in the swinging lifestyle, she'll never accept sharing.

"Agreed," she says firmly. The confidence in her voice says she's not giving me lip service. She's really going into this just looking to get her rocks off.

I expect to feel relief over her easy acceptance of my conditions, but something about the fact she doesn't have any qualms with me fucking other women puts me a bit on edge. It's just not normal, and I feel jittery about really knowing what her feelings are on the matter. That makes me even more uneasy because I never worry about women's emotional well-being. I'll give them unbelievable physical pleasure, but I never waste my time wondering how they feel inside.

And yet, I am now, and fuck... totally freaked about that.

But... the best way to take the edge off anything is to fuck it out of my system.

I grab Trista by the hand and start pulling her toward the office door. She immediately digs in her heels and yanks back against me.

Turning to face her, I impatiently ask, "What's the problem?"

"Well... I just sort of figured we'd maybe start in here. You know... just having some privacy..."

I laugh at her naïveté as I shake my head at her absurdity. "I'm sure there will come a time when I'll fuck you in my office more for convenience sake than anything else, but it's more important that we pop your cherry tonight."

Trista jerks her hand away from me and takes a wary step back. "You said I wasn't ready for anal sex."

Chuckling, I snag her hand back in mine and pull it up for a soft kiss over her knuckles—a move that's totally out of character for me, but I want to reassure her. "You are utterly fucking adorable. And you're right... you are not ready for anal sex. I'm talking about popping your exhibitionism cherry."

Trista's perfectly arched eyebrows pull inward with confusion. "Excuse me?"

I jerk my head toward my office door. "You're going to go into one of the rooms, and then we're going to fuck in front of other people."

Trista sucks in air through her nose and her eyes swim with turbulence. "I can't—"

"You can and you will," I tell her as I start to pull her toward the door. "It's what you came here for."

I expect her to argue with me, but she holds her silence. At least in her mind, she seems to admit that truth to herself. Part of the allure of this club is having people watch you, and it's exactly why she's following docilely behind me.

"Do you do this with your employees often?" she asks me.

"Not often." I don't elaborate further because it's none of her business.

I lead Trista to The Orgy Room because I know it's

her favorite. My three days of stalking her over the security feeds has given me good information, and besides… it's the easiest place for her to lose her inhibitions because of all the naked people lying around have sex in every way imaginable.

The room is busy, approximately three quarters full. Most of the people in here are actively engaged in some form of sexual activity, and the sounds of moans and grunts almost drowns out the seductive music playing in the background. My gaze sweeps the room, noting several available pieces of furniture, and I head straight for one that has the most people surrounding it. I want as many eyes on Trista as possible as I know her embarrassment will heighten her pleasure, and just the thought of this being her first time fucking in front of people makes my cock go even harder.

I stop beside a chaise lounge that's wide enough to easily accommodate a couple. It sits low to the ground and has a slanted, rolled back on one end that is good for bending a woman over or to lounge her back against while she rides cock.

I turn on Trista, giving her one last chance to have some control over her immediate fate. "Do you want this?"

She swallows hard and I wouldn't be surprised if she were to bolt out of here like a scared rabbit. Instead, she just nods her head and I'm practically slayed by the look of trust in her eyes.

Some of that trust is deserved. She's not going to regret what I'm getting ready to do to her. She's going to feel fucking fantastic when I'm done. But what happens after this is all over will never be in her best interest because she will first and foremost be my pawn to get back at her brother. I want her more than I've wanted a woman in a long damned time, but I can't lose sight of my original intention, which is revenge. My need for that trumps any attack of conscience that makes me question my plans.

"Take off your top," I murmur.

Her gaze upon me never wavers, her hesitation lasting no longer than a second before she reaches to the hem and pulls the top over her head. She's not wearing a bra, but I already knew that and my eyes immediately drop to her breasts.

They're fucking fantastic. Round, plump with light pink nipples that are already contracted tightly. I cannot wait to play with them. My gaze slides back up to find Trista staring at me intently.

I give her a knowing smile. Taking a moment to swivel my head left, then right, I take in our audience. The regulars in here know me, and a lot of people like to watch me fuck. Several pairs of eyes are watching.

I give my attention back to Trista, who is still staring at me almost as if her life depends on it. It's obvious it's because she is afraid to look around and acknowledge the fact that she is now a spectacle for other people's viewing pleasure.

I reach out and take her gently by the jaw, using pressure to turn her face away from me.

"Look around you, love," I lean into her to whisper. "You have a ton of people who can't wait to see what I'm going to do to you."

I almost groan as Trista's entire body shudders just from the raw promise. I bet if she wasn't wearing panties, she be dripping right now.

Releasing her jaw, I slowly take my tie off and throw it onto the chaise. My dress shirt and the white t-shirt underneath follow, dropping carelessly to the floor. I finally get a reaction from Trista as her eyes roam over my chest and torso, and I must say, I like her looking at me.

"Take your panties off," I tell her as I remove my belt. That falls on the chaise as well. I'm not sure if I'll use it or the tie.

Trista's hands go to the zipper at the back of her skirt, but I give a hard shake of my head. "Leave the skirt on."

I pop the button and release the zipper on my pants as Trista reaches under her skirt and shimmies out of her underwear. They land on the floor next to my clothing.

I make no further move to disrobe but instead hold my hand out to Trista. Without hesitation, she places her palm against mine and I wrap my fingers around hers. With a gentle tug, I pull her closer to the chaise lounge and order, "Straddle it."

She follows my command beautifully, lifting a gorgeous leg over until she's standing over the furniture with her legs spread. Her eyes are slightly glazed, and she's fallen into a sexual haze where you let your instincts and needs guide you. She's pliable right now, and I'm impressed. She seems to have given in completely to the experience.

"Pull your skirt up. Let me see what you have under there."

Her hands tremble as she does my bidding, baring her pussy to me and that gorgeous ass to the people standing behind the chaise watching.

I raise my head to meet Trista's eyes again, and I'm surprised to see they are swimming with uncertainty now and I almost feel sorry for her.

Almost.

I won't bother to alleviate her fears right now because it's the discomfort of this situation, she'll soon found out, that makes this so arousing. I'm going to push her hard because of that.

"Touch yourself," I tell her with a nod down toward her pelvis.

She lets out a quavering breath, her eyes fluttering closed. But when she opens them, they are filled with determination and that right there turns me on. She's a trooper. To my complete delight, ramping up my horniness by about a million degrees, she slides her hand over her pubic bone and through the trimmed hairs of her pussy before dipping one finger inside of herself. She drags it out slowly, right over her clit, which causes her to let out a small moan. My cock presses painfully against my zipper, but I ignore it. Instead, I take Trista by the shoulders and push her down to sit on the chaise lounge. This leaves her legs spread wide, which is a good start but I want more.

I bring one knee down to the cushion and run my hands along her bare thighs.

"Keep your skirt pulled up so I can see you," I tell her softly, my eyes pinned to her glistening cunt.

"Jerico," Trista says in a quavering voice, and my eyes snap up to hers.

Her bottom lip trembles, but no words come out. She's torn between seeking the ultimate pleasure or giving into her fears.

"You're beautiful," I tell her softly. I look up at the couples standing around and watching us before smiling at Trista. "Everyone here thinks you're beautiful. I need you to let go of your fears and trust in this."

Trista's pink tongue slides out. She gives a nervous swipe over that full bottom lip before giving me a hesitant smile. "Okay… let's do this. I'm good."

A wave of lust washes through me so forcefully I almost groan out loud. I reach out and caress her face in complete juxtaposition to the way I want to jump on her and fuck her hard. "Good thing… Because I'm not stopping again."

CHAPTER 10

Trista

OH, GOD. OH, GOD. Oh, God.
This is it.

My life is getting ready to change. Not in a catastrophic way, but in a way where I'm going to learn something that will make me look at the world differently from here on out.

I'm ready.

Words can't even describe the man kneeling between my legs. He's been seducing me all night with his words, promises, and gruff commands. Hell, even the fact he's not treating me delicately and is throwing me into the deep end of the pool is a complete turn on because it shows his confidence in me to take what he dishes out.

But damn.

Jerico Jameson, half naked and kneeling between my legs, has got to be without a doubt the most beautiful thing I have ever seen in my life. I can't seem to stop looking at his chest, which is muscled and tanned, and leads down to a rolling six-pack of lickable abs. His chest is lightly sprinkled with hair while his stomach is smooth. There's a trail as black as midnight just below his navel disappearing down into his pants, and I want to skim my fingers through it. His button has been undone and his zipper pulled halfway down, but all I can see is the black elastic waistband of his underwear and the outline of his erection beneath his dress pants. I want him to remove all his clothes so he will feel as vulnerable as I do, but then I merely laugh to myself because that man would never feel vulnerable in this situation.

Jerico's hands slide along the tops of my thighs with his thumbs skimming the inside. Well before he gets to the juncture of my legs, he slides them back down and then turns his wrists so he's gripping the back of my legs.

"Lean back," he orders and without a thought, I comply. My back comes to rest against the cushion of the chaise lounge.

I cry out in surprise when Jerico pulls me by my legs so I slide down until I'm flat on my back. He gives me a wicked grin, and I'm completely confused when he says, "Can I get a little help here?"

"What do you mean—" I start to say, but then I gasp as two sets of strange hands clasp onto my ankles.

My head frantically turns left, then right, and I see two men standing there holding my legs for Jerico. One of them is older, maybe in his early fifties, but he looks fit and quite handsome. I'm not sure if it relieves me or makes me uncomfortable, but he's fully dressed. The other man holding my ankle mortifies me. He's also completely dressed, but I immediately recognize him as Jerico's friend, Kynan, who he introduced me to the other day.

It hits me all at once that Jerico may intend to share me tonight, and I'm completely horrified with myself that my sex convulses at the thought as a brief image of me sandwiched between Jerico and Kynan flits through my brain.

What in the ever-loving hell?

I'm not that type of girl.

You are.

I shake my head to clear my thoughts, but there's nothing I can do about the pounding of my heart or the racing of the blood through my veins. I am so primed for something… anything… I can feel my pulse thumping within my clit.

"Spread her wide," Jerico orders the men, and I groan as my legs are raised and pulled apart further. Jerico stares hungrily at my pussy, but my eyes slide over his shoulder to see a few people have come to stand behind him who are also staring where he is.

I am flooded with shame and mortification. Yet at the same time, my nipples get harder and my clit screams out for some type of relief. A trickle of my own wetness slides down the crack of my ass.

"Trista," Jerico says softly and I focus back on him.

"I'm going to feed on you."

"What?" I practically squeak out, wondering if this is some weird vampire kink or something. Jerico grins at me, bringing his other knee to the chaise before flattening out on his stomach. His face hovers right above my sex, and he reiterates, "I'm going to feast on you. I'm going to eat this pussy. Devour it. Suck it down my throat not until *you're* satisfied, but until *I'm* satisfied."

"Oh, God," I mutter as my eyes rise to the ceiling and I hear Jerico softly laughing at me.

I'm oh-so-happy he's delighted by my ignorance.

But his mouth is on me, and my back arches off the chaise as my elbows dig into the cushion. A harsh pleasured cry tears free from my throat, and I raise my head to look down my body. Jerico's eyes... those beautiful, green, sinful, greedy eyes... are locked onto mine. His mouth is open wide, and he is indeed feeding on me. Because my legs are being held by others, Jerico uses his hands to pull me apart and expose the most sensitive part of me, but he keeps his focus on me. I feel hypnotized by the beauty of his face, which is awash with pleasure and satisfaction over what he's doing right now.

My blood quickens and even though his mouth has been pressed between my legs for less than thirty seconds, I can feel an orgasm brewing.

Jerico slips a thumb inside of me and presses downward at the same time his lips curve around my clit where he gently sucks at me.

"Fuck, that's hot," I vaguely hear someone say, but I don't bother trying to look. I totally agree... what he's doing to me is beyond hot.

It's magical.

Jerico's eyes flutter closed briefly, and he groans in appreciation before opening them back up to watch me. I can feel the vibration of it clear down to my toes. His teeth scrape along my flesh briefly before his tongue starts lapping at me. He starts out slowly but then builds momentum. His tongue lashes my clit back and forth before rolling around it in a circle. He repeats this faster and faster, and I realize I'm urging him on by saying, "Yes, yes, yes."

Jerico latches onto my clit, slides two fingers into me, and sucks hard. In the blink of an eye and with no warning at all, my entire world explodes. A shriek of pleasure bursts from deep within my chest before careening up my throat and tearing out of my mouth. My hips buck so hard the older man loses his grip on my ankle. That's okay as my leg comes down over Jerico's shoulder. I curl it around the back of his neck, squeezing his mouth tighter to me as he continues to lick and suck. Another orgasm rolls, punching pleasure so hard through me my hips fly off the chaise again.

Jerico finally lifts his head and although he looks only at me, his words are for Kynan, "You can let her go."

Kynan doesn't drop my leg, but gently lowers it until

it's also draped over Jerico's shoulder.

Jerico bestows a carnal smile at me and then proceeds to crawl his way up my body. With his elbows resting beside my ribs and his face hovering right over my face, he murmurs, "I want you to taste how delicious my meal was."

I don't need any further explanation. My hands slip into his hair as I pull his mouth down onto mine, feeling my wetness and then tasting it. Jerico's tongue mates with mine as he grinds his rock-hard shaft against my pussy.

I give a tug on his hair, and he lifts his head to stare down at me in question.

"I want to do that to you," I tell him softly and now with no shame I'm publicly displaying myself. "Let me do that to you."

His eyes bore into mine intently. I can't tell whether my offer pleases him or not, but he shakes his head and says, "That will be for another time. I've got something else planned."

A violent tremor runs through me at the pure sensuality in his voice, and I think it actually might be another mini-orgasm.

Next thing I know, Jerico is pulling me up and flipping me around on the chaise lounge so I'm on my knees, my hands going to the rolled back of the chaise to steady myself. My gaze goes to the handful of people standing there who had been watching the way Jerico just wrecked me. I quickly lower my face because I have no desire to see what would be reflected at me in their eyes, although I'll admit... the minute Jerico put his mouth on me, I didn't think once about the crowd around us.

I startle when Jerico takes my wrists and pulls them behind my back, causing my body to straighten as I'm forced to balance on my knees. My pulse goes crazy again when he starts winding his tie around them, finishing off with a secure knot that I test by trying to pull my arms apart. They are stuck tight.

It's not the first time I've been tied up, so I'm not concerned in the slightest. In fact, me being helpless at Jerico's hands makes me hunger for him more than ever. Wetness slides down the inside of my thighs, which is something that has never happened to me before. Proof perhaps that my body and sexual psyche were built for these types of experiences. I have no clue if it's because Jerico just gave me the best oral sex of my life or if it's because I'm doing this in front of other people, but I've never been so turned on or had stronger orgasms in my life.

Jerico's lips are on my shoulder, and he kisses me from behind before murmuring, "Hang tight just a second. Need to get a condom on."

My body starts to tremble as I know I am very close to having this man fuck my brains out. Closing my eyes, I try to regulate my breathing. I can hear him rustling his pants, the tear of the foil packet, and then a soft groan from Jerico, which I imagine came from the stroke of his own hand as he put the rubber on.

I can feel him shift behind me, and he slides an arm around my stomach to pull me back against his body. His erection presses into my lower back, and I can feel the rhythm of his pulse through it.

"Open your mouth," Jerico tells me.

I do as he commands and tilt my head to the side, assuming he wants to kiss me again. Instead, I cry out in surprise as Jerico pushes my panties into my mouth. He leans around me and brings his eyes, which are filled with mischief, to mine. I can't tell you how much I like that look. It makes him seem more human... less like a god.

"I don't want you to be embarrassed by involuntarily calling out my name over and over again," he teases.

I roll my eyes at him, but that's all I can do.

He laughs and presses his lips against my temple. His kiss is soft... gentle. He lets it linger, and that intimate gesture makes me dizzy as it's so unexpected from a man like him.

And then he's gone.

Back behind me with his hand to my neck, pushing my torso toward the cushion. When my cheek meets vinyl, he releases his hold on me and uses his hands to spread my legs apart. He adjusts my skirt to push it up my back, and then he's rubbing the head of his cock against my wet opening.

While I didn't get a look at him just now, I remember clearly how big he was when I watched that woman sucking his dick. My vaginal muscles contract in fearful anticipation. Jerico must sense it because he whispers, "Easy now. I'll take it slow."

I relax immediately, completely surprised I'm able to do so just because he tells me to. I don't know this man, so I have no clue why I have this innate trust in him right now. But this is the most dangerous, intimate, and crazy thing I've ever done in my life, and I can't imagine doing this with anyone but Jerico. It may have been that soft, gentle kiss, or the mischief in his eyes, but it tells me clearly that he's a man that wouldn't ever hurt a woman intentionally. It tells me he cherishes what we are about to do.

As he continues to rub his dick through my wet folds, I start to gyrate my hips, a silent plea—because my mouth is full of silk—to give me more.

I'm pleased to find he's not a merciless lover who likes to torture by withholding, because he gives a tiny push and slides into me just a fraction. I groan from the pleasure as I expand to accommodate him more. I don't have much leverage with my hands tied behind my back, but I have just enough to let me push my ass backward a tiny bit.

"Slowly," Jerico whispers, but I hear the amusement in his voice. He pulls his cock out of me and I cry out in distress, but it makes it no further than the bottom of my throat due to the silk impediment in my mouth. When he puts the head of it back to my opening, he tells me, "Let me do the work for right now."

I don't respond because I can't, but I am patiently waiting for him to give me what I need.

Jerico works himself into me with care. I am soaking wet so it's not a difficult entrance, but he is long and wide, so he's considerate of me. He takes his time so that my body can form to fit his cock and by the time he is fully planted inside, my entire body is on fire.

"Jesus... you're fucking tight," Jerico grits out as he rotates his hips against my ass. "Can't even imagine what your ass will feel like."

A shudder runs through me and I know Jerico feels it because he groans in response just before sliding out of me and pushing back in just a little harder.

I grunt. It's not ladylike, but it's appropriate. Jerico is the type of man who makes a woman grunt.

And then he fucks me.

He fucks me hard, deep, and fast. It's the motions of a man who wants to get off quickly. Jerico's breathing is harsh, his fingertips digging down into my hips so he can hold me in place while he pounds into me.

It feels so freaking good I think I'm going to lose my mind. My entire body feels like a live wire, electrified and ready to explode. I've never been able to have an orgasm without clitoral stimulation, but there's no doubt in my mind my body is going to give me that elusive treasure before too long.

Jerico slams into me a few more times, grunting with pleasure—same as me. Then he pulls back to the tip, holds for a brutally long moment, and then merely slides into me with gentle slowness.

The sound of protest bubbles up against the panties in my mouth as my brewing orgasm starts to fade. Jerico's hands smooth along my hips in a reassuring manner.

"Don't worry, Trista. I'm not done with you yet." I'm mortified Jerico knows he needs to reassure me. I don't like coming off as needy to anyone, and I sure as hell don't like depending on anyone for something. But God help my soul I need that orgasm I know he can give me. I'm convinced it's the type of orgasm I've never felt before.

Jerico's hands come down to the cushion by my head, his lips slide against my ear where he whispers, "Gonna try something a little different. It's going to be intense. Not sure if you're going to like it or not, but I really hope you do. It's not like you can tell me to stop with those panties stuffed in that beautiful mouth of yours."

He gives me another sweet kiss on my temple again and pulls back. My entire body tightens with fear and excitement. In my heart of hearts, I believe Jerico's words were meant to scare me… to heighten the pleasure factor. Still, I'm nervous and he knows it. I imagine Jerico is getting off on my uncertainty and fears.

That's okay, though. I'm getting off on them too.

Jerico pushes up. The next thing I feel is his hand grabbing my hair and wrapping it around his palm. He has a secure hold right at the nape of my neck. I know this because he tugs on my head and lifts me from the position I was in. This isn't the most comfortable feeling as I'm being pulled up by my hair without adding any strength of my own but he's holding such a large hank in his hand, it's not exactly painful either.

Regardless, it turns me on. It's a total caveman move, and I apparently have something inside of me that likes that.

When my torso is parallel to the chaise lounge and I'm suspended that way only by Jerico's hold on my hair, he shoves his cock back into me. My back arches downward even though it pulls on my hair more as Jerico holds my head up.

He doesn't move though. We're suspended there, connected by his dick lodged deep in my pussy and his hold on my hair. I imagine it looks much like he's riding a horse with my hair as the reins.

"Fuck me, Trista," Jerico demands.

For a moment, I have no clue what he means but then my body takes over. I tentatively lean away from him, feeling his dick slide out. Jerico gives me some slack in his hold so I can accomplish this. Before he can fall free from me, I contract the muscles in my thighs to easily push back onto his cock. A thrill of pleasure runs through me when I hear Jerico give a satisfied groan. I realize that even in this precariously held position, I have some power over him.

"Just like that," he praises me hoarsely.

I do it again. Pull away from him, feel the tension on my hair, then use my legs to pull myself back onto his cock. I do it again and again, each time going slowly so I can enjoy the sensations.

So Jerico can enjoy the sensations.

"Faster," Jerico growls at me.

Apparently, he wants to enjoy faster sensations.

I do what he wants because the first time I pull off and slam back onto him, I realize it is exactly what I need to fire my orgasm back up again. I fuck Jerico Jameson and I do it hard, deep, and fast, just as he did to me moments ago.

The only disappointing thing about this encounter is that I can't see the man whose cock I'm riding. But I can hear him. Grunting and groaning and panting and cursing.

Fuck, that feels good.

So fucking good.

That pussy is golden. I'm going to fuck it again and again.

I listen to all of this and that mighty "O" starts to brew. It's different than the first one. It's forming deeper in my belly and feels more substantial. Tangible, as if I could reach inside of myself and squeeze it. I can feel it rumbling, morphing, growing bigger. Every time the end of his cock hits my womb, it contracts inward and then grows a little bigger until it feels like everything from my belly button down is strung tight and ready for release.

I want to tell Jerico I'm close, but I can't. So instead I throw myself on and off his cock faster and harder, and this causes Jerico to hiss in pleasure or perhaps pain. I'm not sure and because I am so far gone, I'm not sure I really care either.

"Jesus, fuck," Jerico chants. "Fuck… going to come."

Those three words are apparently the key to unlocking that huge rumbling orgasm inside of me. It detonates just as Jerico releases my hair and grabs my hips so he can slam into me one last time. My vision goes black for a moment as my entire body convulses with pleasure. He quickly wraps an arm under my chest with his palm to my shoulder so I won't fall forward and grinds against my ass as he shudders and curses out his climax.

I cry out against the panties in my mouth. Before I know it, Jerico's pulling them out with his free hand. His chin falls to my shoulder and his other arm wraps around my lower abdomen. He holds me tight, his frantic heartbeat pounding against my back while I heave in as much oxygen as I can get. We stay that way for several long moments, heavily panting while we both come down off the orgasmic high.

I don't say anything because I don't know what to say. Jerico is silent as well. I notice that the crowd disperses, off to do their own thing, essentially leaving Jerico and me alone.

It's weird.

We're in a room having just engaged in public sex. There are people all around us having sex. Strange men held my legs apart while Jerico ate my pussy. And yet right now, both of us kneeling on a vinyl chaise lounge, his cock still deep inside of me and his arms wrapped tight, this feels so very private and intimate.

I mentally shake my head to chase that thought away.

This is just sex. That's what Jerico said, and that's what I need to believe.

CHAPTER 11

Jerico

I GLANCE AT my watch and then to Kynan as he tightens the last screw on the small camera he's mounted to the wall. It's small, black, and unobtrusive. I doubt Trista would notice it.

The installation of the camera was necessary because when I reviewed the security feed tapes of me fucking Trista in the orgy room last night, I was disappointed in how little you could see. While I made my choice to fuck her on a piece of furniture surrounded by lots of people so she could get the full effect of her exhibitionism, I picked probably the worst angle for any of the cameras to pick up. The video would not be usable and I would have to pay more attention to these things in the future.

"Need you to hurry up," I tell Kynan. "Trista will be here in about ten minutes."

Kynan gives one more twist to the screwdriver and backs away. Turning to me, he says, "You're all hooked up. Its motion activated and should catch everything you need."

I don't miss the censure in his voice, but I don't address it either. This is none of his business.

But apparently, he wants to make it his business because he says, "This may be the worst idea you've ever had, Jerico."

I cock an eyebrow at him. "Revenge is never a bad idea. You know that better than anyone."

"True enough," Kynan acknowledges as he puts the screwdriver back in a small toolbox he had brought with him. "But not if it stands to hurt an innocent."

I fucking hate that word.

Innocent.

Because that is exactly what Trista is. I may have introduced her to a sinfully erotic world that I intend to keep showing her, but she is innocent of anything to do with her brother's betrayal of me. While my plans are intended solely to strike at Jayce, I'm fully aware Trista could get hurt.

Having Kynan point that out to me definitely chafes, but it changes nothing. I fully intend to use Jayce's sister in every conceivable dirty way… and then I'm going to send him a lovely compilation of video and photographs to show him exactly how I made his sister pay back the money I gave her so his debt to me could be forgiven. I'm banking on this practically killing him, and that gives me enough solace that I can overlook the potential harm I would do to Trista.

"Trista will probably never even know I did this," I tell Kynan.

I'm banking on the fact that Jayce won't show this stuff to Trista after he receives it to spare her feelings. Fuck, I know if I had a sister, I would do anything to protect her. In fact, if I had a sister and a man sent pornographic videos of him doing the things to my sister that I intend to do to Trista, I'd kill the motherfucker. That's actually my hope in all of this. Not only will this strike at Jayce's heart, but it will enrage him to the point he'll come after me and I relish that thought. I didn't beat his ass hard enough the last time because I was pulled off by my men.

"You keep telling yourself she'll never know," Kynan says grimly. "But it's a big risk you're taking."

And I'm done with this conversation because it is not the way in which I wish to think about Trista. I don't want to think about how this constitutes a betrayal of the trust Trista put into me last night. I know how bad betrayal hurts, but it can be overcome. I wasn't lying when I said I'm past the betrayal of Michelle and Jayce. I'm just not over what they did after.

"Fuck off," I tell him half-jokingly but halfway seriously. "I've got things to do."

"No doubt you do," Kynan mutters as he walks out of my office.

I glance at my watch again, eager for the moment when Trista will be knocking on my office door.

A shocking realization came to me last night as I laid in my bed and thought about the amazing sex I had with Trista. It was fucking beyond amazing. I haven't had anything like that in a long time. I've done dirtier things and I've done kinkier things, but I sure as shit haven't orgasmed like that for as long as I can remember.

As I was thinking about that, I got hard and it necessitated me jacking off in my bed. But I realized if I'm going to use Trista to get back at her brother, I'm going to need to have her hooked to me in some way. I had told her very clearly that the ground rules included the realization that this was just sex between us. There is a damn good chance Trista won't be able to accept that, and I can't afford to have her cut me off until I'm through with her.

So after I jacked off last night, I sent her a text to appeal to her womanly inner need to be wanted. To believe a woman could be the center of a man's universe.

You were phenomenal tonight.

Yes, I had ulterior motives in sending that text to Trista, but it's also the fucking truth. It's probably why I can't get her out of my goddamned head.

I didn't have to wait long for her response. *There's not a word to describe what you were.*

Short, witty, and fuck if she didn't inflate my ego. I texted her back. *That wasn't a one-time only thing.*

Her response back was even shorter. *Relieved to hear that.*

I grinned as I realized Trista was willing to play this game with me. She certainly didn't know what my end goal was, but she clearly wanted more of what we both experienced. It seems she's on board with some casual and hopefully kinky sex in the club.

I texted back to her, *Be here half an hour before your shift starts. Meet me in my office. I'm ready for you to return the favor.*

I've been thinking about her sucking my dick pretty much from the moment I pulled out of her. Her offer to give that to me after I made her come with my mouth was beyond endearing. Most women just want cock between their legs, but Trista felt that what I gave her was a gift, and she wanted to give one back.

It was refreshing.

Trista's response was quick and short. *Okay.*

I look over at the camera Kynan just mounted and have a moment of hesitation. There is absolutely no doubt it's wrong and immoral to record Trista and me together without her permission. The fact I don't intend to use it for profit or gain really doesn't matter. That she may never know I did this, especially if her brother keeps quiet about it, really doesn't matter either. What I'm doing is wrong, wrong, wrong.

But when I think about Jayce and the pain he caused me, my fury rages and suddenly, I don't care if Trista gets hurt. I have to keep it always in the front of my mind that the revenge is more important than one beautiful woman who just happens to be a great fuck.

Who happens to be a woman I can't stop thinking about.

Fuck.

The soft knock on my door causes my heart rate to pick up. I give one last fleeting glance at the camera before I call out, "Come on in."

Trista walks in just as I'm shutting the drawer and my groin immediately tightens when I see her. She's dressed in regular street clothes, which she wears very well. Dark skinny jeans with a pair of ballet flats and a cream-colored shirt that hangs low on both shoulders, but not completely off. Her hair is radically different. It's her most beautiful feature by far, and she always wears it spilling all down her back in honey-colored layers looking windblown and just fucked. But tonight, she has it pulled up in a high ponytail on top of her head and it makes me realize how long and elegant her neck is. My lips could spend a lot of time on that neck.

Trista shuts the door and leans back against it as she smiles at me. "You done staring at me or what?"

"Never," I tell her with a wicked smile. "Because I very much like what I see."

Adorably, she lowers her eyes as if embarrassed by the compliment.

Even more adorably, she looks back up at me and plays coy. "You said you wanted me here half an hour before my shift started. What did you want to see me about?"

Chuckling, I push my chair back from my desk and start removing my belt. "I want to know why your mouth isn't on my dick yet."

Trista wrinkles her nose in distaste, but pushes off the door and starts walking my way. "Do you really have to be so crass and crude?"

I slide my belt free and drop it on the floor. My fingers go to the top button of my pants as I answer her with a nasally, nerdy voice. "Well, gee whiz, Ms. Barnes… I'm sorry. Would you kindly come over here and put your sweet mouth on my penis? I'd be much obliged if you would lick and suck it while you're at it."

Trista halts, staring at me blankly. And then her mouth widens into a brilliantly beautiful smile, and she laughs at me while shaking her head. "Oh my God… that was hilarious."

I waggle my eyebrows at her as I grin back. "I'm told my cock tastes really good too."

Trista is still chuckling as she walks around my desk and my dick gets harder the closer she gets. She comes to stop in between my legs, her amber eyes locked onto mine. When my fingers move to pull down my zipper, she whispers, "Don't."

My hands fall away and hers take over. She slowly lowers the zipper as she murmurs, "Let me do everything."

My cock jumps at her words, and the head starts to

weep as she pulls the front of my underwear down to free me from my confines.

"Lift your hips," she tells me.

Putting my hands on the armrest of my chair for leverage and so it doesn't roll out from underneath me, I plant my feet and lift my hips. Trista pulls my pants and my boxer briefs down below my ass to free me.

She stares at me in satisfaction and says, "There… now I have access to your balls so I can play with them."

I can't help the bark of laughter that pops out of my mouth. I've never found sex to be funny. Haven't found much in life to be funny with some of the terrible shit I've seen in my line of work, but I find I like Trista making me laugh. Apparently, my cock likes it too because it gets harder yet.

Trista kneels between my legs and wraps her hand around the base of my shaft. Her skin feels like fire on me, and I have to resist the urge to thrust into her fist. Leaning forward, she gives a light lick under the base of the head, which produces a drop of pre-cum at the slit. That does not escape her attention and her tongue darts out to catch it. I groan deep within my chest over the erotic sight of her closing her eyes as she tastes me.

When she opens them back up, she gives me a sly smile. "I want you to know, I'm really, really good at oral. Or, at least that's what I've been told."

While that is very good to know indeed, for some strange reason, I don't like thinking about the practice she's had.

But then all thoughts of her past are obliterated when she leans over me and takes me in deep. The woman has no gag reflex and when she pulls off, I thrust immediately back into her mouth so I can feel that again. Even though her mouth is stuffed full of my dick, I can feel her laugh at my eagerness. She gives me one long hard suck and pulls free.

With her hand back around my shaft, she looks up at me and asks, "What do you want? You tell me what to do, and I'll give it to you. Do you want me to get you off slowly with licks, nibbles, and gentle sucking, or do you want to fuck my mouth while I roll your balls in my hand?"

With every word that comes out of her mouth, my cock keeps getting impossibly harder until it's painful. I stare at her blankly for a moment, surprised she had those dirty words inside of her. Where in the fuck did she learn to talk like that?

She knows I'm surprised and grins at me as she shrugs. "I learned a few things since working here. Dirty talk is one."

I push up out of my chair, causing Trista to sit back on her calves for a moment. My dick hovers just above her as we stare each other.

I bring a hand to cup her cheek, rubbing my thumb just over the bone, and tell her, "I want to fuck your mouth. And I want to do it deep."

Trista raises up on her knees and takes me in her hand, but before she opens her mouth to give me entry, she winks at me and says, "Just the way I like it."

Trista is not a liar.

Certainly not when it comes to her bragging about her oral skills. She takes everything I give her and I swear when her eyes look up at me, she begs me for more. But I have her head held tight in my hands and my hips are practically jack-hammering against her face. I can feel the slight roughness of her tongue on the underside of my cock and the tightness of her throat as the head breaches her. She doesn't gag once, although I know it isn't easy for her.

It isn't easy for her. Involuntary tears start leaking from the corners of her eyes. My thumbs reach out to swipe at them, and I slow my movements within her mouth. She frantically shakes her head and within her golden-brown eyes, I see her telling me that she can take it.

In that moment, I don't think I've ever been more turned on in my life. Yet what I would really love to do is pull out of her mouth, drag her to the floor, and eat her pussy until she screams.

But then her hand is on my balls and she is indeed rolling them. Tugging them. Lightly pinching them.

I slam back into her mouth as she tortures my nut sack, and she purrs with appreciation that I'm giving her all I got.

My balls draw tight, and I never even have to wonder if she wants me to pull off. Anyone this good at oral wants to swallow.

It's when she lightly skims a finger behind my balls, headed straight across my taint, that I give a bark of surprised pleasure as I explode so quickly that my knees almost buckle.

I look down at Trista in utter amazement as she swallows and then swallows some more. She licks and cleans me off, all the while her fingertips gently stroke my spent balls. With one final lick to the tip of my softening dick, she looks up and says, "Told you I was good."

I grin down at her. "I'll never doubt you again."

Trista stands from the floor as I pull up my pants. She turns from me as she says, "I better get to work."

My hand shoots out and grabs her wrist. When she turns back to me, I tell her "After work… I want you again."

Her eyebrows furrow in confusion. "You mean… out there? In one of the rooms? But we'll be closed up."

I shake my head. "Just come back here in my office when you get off."

She stares at me a moment in contemplation and I can tell she's considering telling me "no". I brace for it, prepared to argue with her and perhaps even hold her job over her head, but then she smiles at me and nods her head.

"Okay," she says casually. "I'll see you back here."

It's not until Trista is gone from my office that I let out a huge breath of relief that I'm going to see her again tonight.

This relief concerns me.

Greatly.

CHAPTER 12

Trista

I STAND OUTSIDE of Jerico's office and nervously wipe my sweaty palms on my jeans. Glancing at the locker room door, I pray none of my coworkers come out to see me standing here. While I found out tonight that every single one of them had heard about Jerico fucking me in The Orgy Room, I'd also been assured by more than one female coworker that he doesn't do repeats, so the encounter was easily dismissed by most.

Because of this, I do not want anyone to see me standing outside of his office. They'll either know Jerico is asking for a repeat or think I appear desperate for his attention.

Before I can change my mind, I rap my knuckles against the door three times. To my relief, I hear Jerico's voice calling me in. I quickly open the door and step inside, surprised to find my nerves have quieted a bit. I'm thinking I was more nervous someone would see me than I was about what Jerico and I might do tonight.

Jerico stands from his desk and grabs his suit jacket that had been draped over the back. "Are you tired from your shift?"

"A little." Truth of the matter is I'm physically fatigued to the point if I could lay down on the floor and go to sleep, I would. Walking around in high heels for hours on end with a heavy tray strapped to my shoulders isn't for the weak.

"Little liar," Jerico chides me as he rounds the desk. He walks up to me and places his fingers under my chin so I'm forced to look up at him. "You look exhausted. Do you want to go home?"

I lift my chin a little higher and turn my face so that his fingers fall away, giving him a smirk. "That depends on what you have planned. If you want to run a marathon, count me out."

Jerico's eyes go bright with amusement, and he chuckles as he reaches down to take my hand in his. "No marathons tonight. But you won't be going to sleep soon."

"No worries. I don't have to be at work until seven PM tomorrow so I can sleep as late as I want."

It was approaching almost three AM as the club closes at two thirty. I could technically stay up for several more hours and still be fresh for work tomorrow. Just the thought of Jerico spending hours on me causes a thrill of excitement to jolt up my spine, and I feel slightly energized.

Jerico doesn't walk us to his office door, but instead heads to a door at the back of his office. I'm imagining it might be his secret playroom, but I'm utterly surprised when he opens the door and we step into a kitchen. Correction… as I look around, I see we are inside of an apartment.

"You live here?" I ask as he drops my hand and I walk through the kitchen toward the wall made of glass that looks out over Vegas.

"It's convenient," he says.

I look over my shoulder at him and give a sardonic grin. "I can just imagine."

Jerico comes up behind me and my pulse races when he brings his hands to my hips. "What do you mean you can just imagine?"

I shrug my shoulders. "I'm just saying… you want to bring a girl here, it's quite convenient."

"What if I told you I've never brought a girl here before?"

This surprises me, and I turn to face him. His hands don't fall away from my hips but merely circle around to clasp at my back before he pulls me into him. I look up and try to gauge whether he's kidding me.

"You've never brought a girl here before me?" He cannot mistake the sarcasm or skepticism in my voice.

Rather than appease my curiosity, he merely gives me a secretive smile and says, "I guess it doesn't matter what my answer is because I can tell by the tone of your voice you wouldn't believe me if I told you that you were the first."

I decide to leave that subject alone. It's too confusing to me, especially since Jerico laid the ground rules out, which included a very clear indication that we would not be monogamous, nor would we succumb to jealousies if the other person fucked someone else.

"You're right," I tell him nonchalantly as I slide my palms up his chest, over his shoulder, and lace my fingers around his neck. "I wouldn't believe you."

I don't miss the flash of annoyance in Jerico's eyes, but he doesn't respond. Instead, his head tilts to the side and he runs his lips along the side of my neck. When he pulls away and looks back in my eyes, I see nothing but pure longing.

"Would you believe me if I told you I've been thinking about you all day? Or that I've run through a dozen different scenarios of what I want to do to you tonight?"

"Technically, it's morning," I say breathlessly.

Jerico's eyes smile at me with amusement, and he shakes his head. Taking me by the hand, he turns and leads me through the living room toward a hallway. While he doesn't address me directly, I clearly hear him mutter, "I swear I think I could actually sit down and have an actual conversation with you."

I smile. It's big and bright and he has no clue I'm smiling since he's walking ahead of me. While the sex we had last night was beyond anything I could have ever imagined, and the blow job I gave him today was my best work, and I have been thinking about him all day as well as a variety of scenarios we might participate in, I think I am most pleased in this moment to know Jerico views me as something slightly more than a convenient fuck. His statement just now tells me a lot about him, but most particularly that he doesn't have any female friends, nor does he have any close female relationships. I have no clue what it is about me that makes him feel like I'm worthy enough to talk to, but that is a conversation for another time.

That's because Jerico walks me into the most sumptuous bedroom I've ever seen in my life. A massive four-poster king-size bed that is ornately carved takes up one wall. It's covered with a navy blue and gold brocade comforter with gold braiding along the edges and gold tassels at the corners. A long dresser takes up another wall with a mirror above it. Both pieces having the same carvings as the bed. The walls are done in what appears to be silk of the same navy color that matches his bedding but with a subtly darker pattern within. A plush and expensive-looking oriental carpet done in golds, blues, and whites covers most of the hardwood flooring. To add final complement to the elegant decor, there's a massive brass chandelier that hangs from the center of the ceiling with what looks like hundreds of candelabra lights.

I would consider Jerico Jameson a sophisticated man,

but I had no clue his style ran so traditionally. It adds complexity to the man I am still learning about.

Jerico tosses his suit jacket on a gold brocade bench that rests at the foot of his bed and starts to unbutton his shirt sleeves as he walks toward what I believe to be the master bathroom.

"Get naked," he says with his back turned to me. "Then get on the bed. I'll be just a minute."

He's barely over the threshold to the bathroom when I retort, "Your foreplay sucks."

Jerico turns slowly around and stares at me impassively. I stare stonily back at him and cross my arms stubbornly over my chest.

The corners of his mouth turn upward, and Jerico shakes his head as he walks back toward me. His palms come to my cheeks and his mouth comes to mine for what I thought would be a deep, hot, and wet kiss that was worthy of the term foreplay.

Instead, he feathers his lips briefly against mine before pulling back to smile at me. "You are going to be begging me to stop my foreplay, Trista. It hasn't started yet, but it's going to drive you crazy. Now I'm going into the bathroom to get a few things that we'll need and I would appreciate it if you would save me the time of undressing you or even possibly saving your wardrobe because I want you so badly I could see me tearing your clothes off."

I blink at him. My mouth parts open in surprise.

Jerico grins at me. "Any questions?"

All I can do is shake my head, which satisfies Jerico. He returns to the bathroom, and I take off all my clothes before crawling into the middle of his bed to wait for him.

♦

"PLEASE STOP," I beg Jerico as he continues to lick between my legs. I've had three orgasms so far, and I am going crazy with the need to have him inside of me.

Jerico chuckles against me and I have to struggle not to slam my knees against the sides of his head in retaliation.

Fucker.

He was absolutely right. I am begging and pleading for him to move past his foreplay.

To my relief, Jerico pushes up and crawls backward off the bed, using his forearm to wipe the back of his mouth, which is shiny with my juices. I've never known a man like Jerico who enjoys pleasuring a woman orally so much. It's with a little bit of melancholy that I realize once this thing runs its course with us, I'm probably never going to have it as good as I've had it with him again.

Reaching a hand out to me, Jerico says, "Come off the bed."

I clasp his palm and let him pull me up. When my feet hit the rug, my toes sinking down into its decadence, my legs feel like they're going to buckle. Jerico turns me around with his hands at my waist and sits down on the edge of the bed, pulling me in between his legs. Leaning toward me, his mouth closes over one of my nipples and he gives it a hard suck before letting it pop free from his mouth. I groan from the sensation and wait for him to do the same to my other breast.

Instead, his expression turns intense as he tells me, "We're going anal."

I jerk and try to step backward, but his hands are on my hips to hold me in place.

Shaking my head, I whisper, "There is no way your dick is going to fit in my ass."

Jerico laughs lightly and squeezes my hips with affection.

Yes, that was affection from the self-proclaimed hedonist.

"I'm going to start the process of getting you ready I should have said," he amends.

Jerico leans to the side and grabs something off his nightstand. When he straightens back up, he holds an object up for me to examine.

"So you're going to use a butt plug?"

"A small one," he clarifies with a wicked smile. "I promise you it will feel good."

I study the glass plug, which is no thicker than his index finger and I have to admit, it doesn't intimidate me. I don't know if the fact I was able to have dirty sex in front of complete strangers with a man who is a virtual stranger broke something open within me, but I feel this adventurous spirit… Almost as if I've been freed from some sort of intangible shackles.

My gaze goes from the plug to Jerico's eyes, which seem brighter than normal. "Okay. Let's give it a try."

Jerico's hand shoots out to grab me behind the neck. He pulls me roughly to him for a hot, possessive kiss. When he releases me, his voice sounds like pure sin as he says, "Turn around and grab your ankles."

Adrenaline, fear, excitement, and plain old giddiness course through me.

I turn around, bend at the waist, and grab my ankles.

CHAPTER 13

Jerico

TRISTA ISN'T THE first woman who's bent over and grabbed her ankles at my command.

But she is the first to induce a wave of lust so shockingly powerful, my balls tighten up in anticipation of an orgasm.

Drawing in a silent but deep breath, I smooth the palms of my hands over Trista's ass to collect myself. The silkiness of her skin turns me on even more. As I slide one palm down the back of her thigh, I contemplate what it is about this woman that is affecting me differently than others.

There's no doubt the two orgasms I've had with her have been spectacularly better than anything I've experienced in a long fucking time. But the question is why?

Trista is beautiful, but that alone isn't the cause. I've had women just as beautiful, if not more so.

Perhaps it's because of the very thing Kynan pointed

out to me.

She's an innocent.

Not so innocent she's a virgin, but the world she has stepped inside of is sordid and depraved, and for every experience she has inside The Wicked Horse, a little more of that innocence is being scraped away. I'm a fucker for thinking it, but I might be getting off on teaching her how to push past her normal boundaries.

Trista's entire body trembles under my touch, I'm sure with a mixture of fear and excitement. I bet she's the type of girl who would bungee jump off a bridge or go skydiving for the rush. Fear definitely enhances pleasure if it's done right, and the fact she jumped off a pretty tall bridge by having sex with me in The Orgy Room last night tells me that her adventurous spirit is only growing bigger.

Bringing my palms back to her ass, I use my thumbs to spread her cheeks, lightly stroking the sensitive skin there. She lets out a tiny moan, and I can't help the smile that comes to my face.

"This won't hurt," I tell her softly as I graze the pad of my thumb right over her tight opening. She jerks forward slightly and then pushes back. "But I think you can figure out it will be intense."

"I can take it," Trista reassures me.

"I don't doubt it. But just so you know, all you have to do is say stop at any time and I'll take it out."

She whispers just one word. "Okay."

"Okay," I mimic her, leaning to the side to grab the lube from my nightstand.

With a practiced and efficient flick of my thumb, I open the tube. Rather than drizzle it over Trista's exposed ass, I pour it in my palm and rub it together so it becomes warm. Then I use my fingers in between her ass cheeks to massage lightly over her pucker, taking great satisfaction as Trista moans in pleasure.

I take the butt plug, give it a squirt of lube, and then command Trista, "Let go of your ankles and spread your ass for me."

"Oh, God," she mutters softly with clear embarrassment but immediately complies.

"Good girl," I praise her. "I'm going to insert it now, and I'll go very slowly. Tell me if you want me to stop."

She doesn't say anything, but I can see her shaking her head in the negative. What little I've come to know about this woman, I know the word "stop" will not push past her lips because I'm not hurting her, nor will I.

I place the tip of the plug right at her opening and push it forward just a fraction of an inch. She immediately tightens up.

"Deep breath," I instruct her. "It helps if you want to push against it."

Trista does exactly as I tell her, taking in a lungful of air. As she blows it out, I push the plug in about an inch.

"Oh, damn," Trista groans.

"Good?" I ask with a smile, but I can tell by the

nature of that groan what her answer will be.

"Really, really good," she murmurs as I push the plug in slowly all the way to its hilt. "Oh, Jerico... yes, that feels so good."

"I knew you'd like it," I tell her with confidence. I know this because there isn't a woman who I have done this to who didn't like it. But again, something about Trista taking pleasure from it is more rewarding than what I've experienced.

"Go ahead and stand up," I tell her gently.

She does with a soft moan and turns to face me. I spread my legs a little further. She steps in closer to me and my palms go to her ass, where I start deeply massaging the muscles of her cheeks.

Trista's head falls back in ecstasy because I know this is moving the plug around slightly inside of her, connecting with sensitive nerves and ramping up her pleasure.

I tap the flat end of the plug lightly, and her head flies back up as she looks at me in surprise. "This is what keeps the plug secure, but I just want to give you a head's-up you're going to feel it move a little while we're fucking."

Trista gives me a sly smile, her eyes glazed over with extreme pleasure. "I can tell you without a doubt I'm glad to know that."

Taking stock of the mixed emotions of amusement and lust I have coursing through me, I grab Trista and haul her onto my lap so she's straddling me. My cock is thick and hard and completely ready for her.

But first…

"Kiss me," I order her.

Her eyes flare wide with surprise, but then her lids lower with unrepentant desire that I've asked for something so intimate. She places her palms on my face and leans forward to press her mouth to mine.

Gently, with absolutely no hurry, she uses the pressure of her lips to get me to open up. I follow her lead, content to let her mouth move over mine in a lazy way. You would think the fact that my cock is hard because I just ate her pussy and shoved the butt plug up her ass, it would start to wane a little with this slow, sensuous kiss she's giving me, but I've always found the mouth to be so erotic with the things that can be done with it. If anything, the care and gentleness within her kiss is making me harder and hornier.

With no hesitancy but still a tender touch, her tongue slides along mine and we deepen the kiss. My fingers squeeze into her ass cheeks, and she moans into my mouth.

Reluctantly, I pull away, giving her a tiny brush of my lips before I reach once more to the nightstand to grab a condom. Trista immediately takes it out of my hands and says, "Let me."

So I let her.

Putting a condom on has never been anything more

than a function of practicality and safety. But Trista makes it a sensual delight as she slowly rolls the sheath over my dick, giving me a hard squeeze at the base. I have to practically bite down on the inside of my cheek not to make noise when she does this. It's not that I can't get loud in the throes of passion, but I don't like showing my hand so early in the game. I certainly don't want Trista knowing how good it feels just having her hand squeeze me.

Holding her firmly by the hips, I lift slightly from my seat on the bed and push backward before lying flat on my back. This allows Trista to place her knees on the mattress at my hips and sends a clear message of what I want. She places her hands on the bed next to my shoulders, hovering over me on her hands and knees with her face inches from mine.

Yes, the message is clear what I want, but Trista gives me a coy, innocent smile. "Whatever do you want me to do in this position?"

A sharp slap right in the middle of her ass is my answer, my palm coming in direct contact with the end of the butt plug. Trista yelps and then glares at me. I merely grin back up at her.

"You know what I want," I say as I rub my hand over her warm skin.

Trista cocks an eyebrow at me as she sits up while straddling the tops of my thighs. She places the tip of her finger at the corner of her mouth and says, "Hmmm. I'm pretty sure you want me on top, but I have to say that slap felt pretty damn good to. Maybe we should concentrate on that."

I grit my teeth, not from frustration but so I don't start laughing at her antics. Reaching down, I grab my erection and growl at her, "I want you on my cock, and I want you there now."

Trista grins at me but she doesn't make me wait, crawling forward just a bit and hovering her pussy right over the tip of my dick. I hold it steady as she starts to slowly sink down on me with no hesitation. She is good and relaxed, completely worked up from the multiple orgasms I gave her prior as well as the plug in her ass. When she climaxes, it might even destroy her. I'm looking forward to that.

Trista's eyes flutter closed. She has a serene smile on her face as she just holds still and feels the fullness within her. I am anything but feeling serene at this moment and need her to move.

My hands go to her breasts, squeezing them roughly. Trista's eyes fly open and she watches as I pinch her nipples. This causes an immediate reaction and her hips start to gyrate.

Not enough though.

"Ride me, baby," I growl her.

"Like this?" she breathes out in a raspy voice as she starts to raise and lower herself on my cock in a slow, methodical way.

While there are many times I love to take the time to get off slowly, this is not one of them. For Trista to fully appreciate that plug in her ass, I need her to move.

Putting my hands on her hips, I spread my fingers wide to curl around her back. She looks down at me curiously as I use my hands to move her up and down, still letting her set the pace for a few more moments.

I can tell by her shallow breaths, the blush across her neck and the tiny moans she makes when her ass presses down on me, that she's feeling the plug. But I want more than her just feeling it. I want her consumed by it.

"Do you know what riding cock means? I ask her.

She shakes her head as she continues to move up and down slowly.

"It means," I tell her as I use my hands and my physical strength to pull her up my shaft and then slam her back down onto me, "that you should be bouncing, your tits should be jiggling, and you should be screaming at the way that plug is pounding into your ass."

Trista's eyes flare wide and look stunned, and I find I like doing that to her.

"Ready?" I asked her with a grin.

Eyes still round as saucers, she gives me a short nod.

"Then let's get at it, baby. I want you to fuck me hard."

Before I even have a chance to help assist her in the movements I want, Trista raises herself up before falling back down onto my shaft. Before a groan can even tear free from either one of us, she's already lifting back up again and slamming that tight pussy back down again.

This time, she screams. Not in pain, but in pure pleasure from that plug as well as my cock based on the rapture across her face. She starts to go faster and harder, to the point where my balls are starting to take a pounding.

Since I don't want to interfere with her enthusiasm, I don't try to get her to change her pace.

Instead, I tell her, "Turn around."

"Turn around?" she asks in a daze as she slowly gyrates to keep some friction going. She is completely lost to sensation.

Using my hands, I pull her off my dick. "Turn around. Ride me reverse."

Trista scrambles to turn herself around over me, and she immediately has her hand on my cock guiding it back into her. I love this position. Love watching that ass as she bounces up and down, and that's exactly what she starts doing right away. When I told Trista to ride my cock, she took me very seriously.

I don't put my hands back to her hips, but content myself to just watch her for a few moments. She's magnificent from this angle. Granted, I can't see those fantastic tits bouncing up and down but her ass and that plug sticking out more than makes up for it.

"I think I'm going to come," Trista mutters as she picks up the pace.

That makes my balls tighten up in anticipation, my hands coming to rest lightly on her hips.

"That's it, baby. Let go. I want you to come all over me."

Trista only pulls up and slams down one more time before her back arches so deeply her ponytail touches the top of my chest. The corresponding scream that tears out of her throat causes my own climax to fire in my hips as I thrust upward into her. My hand goes to the plug in her ass, and I tug it out slowly as she's orgasming. This causes Trista to scream again, which makes my orgasm seem to magnify. Her scream dies to a groan, then finally a soft mewling as she falls face forward onto my legs in complete exhaustion.

I can feel tiny quakes running through her pussy as my dick continues to jump inside of her. Taking a deep breath, I look down my body at her and ask, "Are you okay?"

She nods her head and groans with her cheek resting on one of my shin bones.

Yup, I think she's destroyed. And I like that a lot.

Long, long moments pass as we lay there in silence. My cock softens and slips out of her, and she continues to lay like dead weight on my legs. Eventually, she stirs and pushes herself up before swinging a leg over me. She continues to roll right off the bed as she asks," Can I use your bathroom?"

I start to peel the condom off me as I answer, "Of

course. Help yourself to anything in there."

Trista surprises me by picking up her clothes and carrying them with her to the bathroom. Before I even know what I'm doing, I tell her, "Don't put your clothes back on."

She turns around to look at me in shock. Her gaze cuts down to my softened dick and back to me. "You want to go again?"

This is a first for me. I don't do women in this apartment. There's no need when I have a sex club within walking distance. But even before that, I didn't like having women in my personal space. Once Michelle betrayed me with Jayce, I closed myself off tight, which means I don't go for second rounds or sleepovers.

Obviously, I am not acting quite myself where this woman is concerned. This should scare the shit out of me... particularly because I have ulterior motives where she's concerned. And yet, I want her again, and I want her to stay. Despite the fact I have no cameras in this apartment and what we are doing is no use to my scheme, I just want her again, and I usually get what I want.

"Yes, I want to go again. And maybe again after that."

Trista stares at me for a moment, weighing her options. She could go home to an empty—I assume—bed, or she could have more fantastic, mind-blowing orgasms. It doesn't take her long to make her decision. She drops her clothes to the floor as she turns to the bathroom. "I'll be right back."

I smile to myself and roll off the bed to dispose of the condom. On the way back, I grab two more and then pull the covers back. By the time I'm settling onto the mattress, Trista is walking back out of the bathroom. She has let her hair out of her ponytail and looks like a goddess as she walks my way.

As it turns out a few hours later, I needed three more condoms rather than two.

When we both come down from the last round of orgasms, Trista once again starts to roll out of the bed.

"Where are you going?" I ask as I turn to my side to watch her.

She stands up and turns to look at me. "Going home to get some sleep. Otherwise, I'm going to feel like shit tomorrow."

I'm pretty convinced I might be possessed by some type of malevolent spirit because before I know it, my hand is patting the mattress and I tell her, "Get back in bed. Stay the night here."

Trista has come to know enough about me, particularly with my ground rules, that this is not something I normally do. She merely cocks an eyebrow at me in skepticism.

I pat the mattress again and tell her with complete nonchalance, "I feel compelled to walk you to your car since it's so late and the security is not the greatest at this time in the parking garage. I'm too lazy and sated to do that. So do me a favor and come sleep in my bed. You can leave when the sun comes up."

Or stay for hours until you you're ready to wake up. I'm cool with that too.

Trista rolls her eyes at me either because she knows I'm full of shit or she's not the type to be flattered by chivalry, but regardless, she crawls back into the bed. I pull the covers over us.

The malevolent and completely bat-shit crazy spirit that must be residing inside of me then pulls Trista into my arms. Within moments, I fall asleep.

CHAPTER 14

Trista

I KNOCK ON Jerico's office door, wondering what he could possibly want. He'd sent me a text and asked me to just swing by for a few minutes before I started my shift.

That means he doesn't want sex because there's no way you can have sex with Jerico Jameson in just a few minutes.

He calls for me to enter and I do, shutting the door softly behind me.

"What's up?" I ask casually.

As usual, he looks elegant, gorgeous, and domineering, three traits I find to be very appealing. He's wearing a charcoal-gray dress suit with a white shirt and a lavender tie. Again, his clothes are clearly custom made to fit every angle, hill, and valley of his body. And he has a lot of those I can attest to as last night, over the four different times we had sex, I was able to explore pretty much every inch. The same could be said for Jerico and my body.

Jerico sweeps a hand toward one of the guest chairs opposite where he sits behind his desk. "Take a seat."

I do as he asks, but I can't help but quip, "I feel like I'm in trouble and been sent to the principal's office."

Jerico gives me a wicked grin. "If you were in trouble, you'd already be bent over my desk and getting a nice paddling."

I press my legs together tightly to try to alleviate the ache that has suddenly sprung up there.

Glancing at my watch, and then up to Jerico, I prod him. "I've only got about five minutes before my shift starts so what do you need?"

He laughs at me. "I think you can afford to be a few minutes late."

"I thought you said you didn't give preferential treatment to your employees, especially the ones you were fucking," I remind him.

"Trista," he says in almost a patronizing tone. "I don't know if you realize this or not, but I really don't need you working for me. You're actually an extra employee I don't need, but by giving you the job here, I've enabled you to pay back the money I gave you."

I just blink at him.

He gives me a wry smile. "Although I do have to admit, I enjoy watching you prance around in your little black thong. I equally enjoy having you close by so I can fuck you when I want to."

My eyebrows shoot up. "So this whole repayment thing is really about sex and not because you need somebody to work at the club?"

The smile slides from Jerico's face as he gets a hard glint in his eye. "It's not just about sex. You can tell me 'no' whenever you want to. The question is, do you want to say 'no' to me? Do you want to call an end to our sexual relationship right now?"

My immediate and initial gut reaction is to hastily reassure him that I do not want to end the sexual relationship because I've not learned all I want to learn. I clearly have not had enough of Jerico.

But for some reason, I'm having a hard time admitting that to him because not only did we have sex four times last night, but we also had conversation. Granted, it wasn't heavy conversation and most of it was casual and impersonal. But I got a slight peek at what lies underneath the starched suits of the intimidating businessman who owns a sex club, and what I saw I can say I honestly liked.

Sadly, I'm letting some of my womanly insecurities surface. Jerico's ground rules seemed acceptable to me at first, but I can't help some slight feeling of jealousy at him being with someone else. I don't know he's been with anyone else since he started sleeping with me, but how would I? Most nights I work, I don't see him. I'm stuck in one room. For all I know, he could be in one of the other rooms fucking out his heart's desire.

On the flip side, I could be doing the same thing. He gave me free license to do what I want inside this club. And I've had some offers, a few of which were appealing. Ultimately though, I declined, not because I owe Jerico any loyalty but because I just can't have casual, anonymous sex in a sex club in front of other people. Yes, Jerico was a stranger to me, but I reasoned that we had at least a connection. He's friends with my brother Jayce, although I get the impression they have drifted apart. I also know they served in the military together, so in my mind that made Jerico more trustworthy.

"Trista," Jerico says to get my attention. "Do you want to say 'no' to me?"

I don't know if I hate myself or not, but I shake my head. "At this point, I wouldn't say 'no'. I could feel differently tomorrow, though."

I felt the need to add that last little bit on so he knows I'm playing by the rules of casual sex.

Jerico gives me a curt nod and while I don't think he looks overly happy at what I just said, he brushes past it by changing the subject.

"I want to ask you about something you and I talked about last night," Jerico says.

I tilt my head in curiosity. We talked about a lot of stuff, most of it inane, some of it funny, and of course, a lot of it was sexual. That usually led us into the next round of sex.

"What in particular?" I ask.

"We talked about fantasies last night," he reminds me.

I nod because those talks had me blushing, as well as wet between the legs. One of the things I had found out was that Jerico has indulged in most of his fantasies. It was with no small amount of shame that I admitted to him I didn't have many fantasies, but he'd already fulfilled one of them that first night in The Orgy Room.

"You told me that one of your fantasies was to be with multiple men at the same time," Jerico reminds me.

I flush hot all over, but I nod at him.

"Do you want me to make it happen?" he asks me.

My body tightens up with tension even as my pulse races with genuine curiosity. "Would you be involved? I mean… would you be one of the men?"

"Of course. And I would only choose men I trusted."

I start to nibble on one of my fingernails, considering this. I'm wildly intrigued, woefully unprepared, and totally scared. "I honestly don't know if I can handle it."

"What do you mean?" He looks genuinely befuddled.

"I mean…" My voice lowers to a whisper because this embarrasses me, "I don't know if I can take a man in every single one of my openings."

Jerico's eyes sparkle with amusement as he understands my fear, but he spares me genuine laughter. "Trista, a multiple can be anything you want to be. It's your fantasy."

"Really?"

Jerico nods at me with a reassuring smile. "If you want this, I suggest we start you very slow and with only one other man in addition to me. You will have all the control and tell us what you want from us."

Okay, this has some real potential. I think I might orgasm just thinking about the prospect. And why shouldn't I take advantage of this opportunity? Let's face it… this isn't going to happen to me again.

But I still have some reservations. "Who would you choose?"

"Kynan would be my first choice. But I have a few others I would trust."

I nod in understanding and ask, "And when would we do this?"

"Whenever you wanted. Kynan's on a break from work."

I take a deep breath and make the only decision I can because I bet I'll regret it if I don't. "Okay. I'd like to try that. Set it up whenever it's convenient for both of you."

Jerico gives me his patented wicked smile, and my nipples tighten in response. I start to stand up from the chair, but he gives me pause when he says, "I've got one stipulation."

I swallow hard. "What's that?"

"We do it in The Silo in one of the glass rooms so people can watch," he says with a silky voice that holds a sinister tone underneath.

I take a quavering breath and decide to go all in. "I'll

probably die from embarrassment but after I finish my service here with you, I'll at least take comfort in the fact I'll never see any of these people again."

Something flashes on Jerico's face that I might peg as annoyance, but then my attention is taken by my cell phone ringing in my purse. I immediately recognize my mom's ring tone and given the circumstances of Corinne's medical condition, I can never ignore it. Even when I'm on duty, I have one of the bartenders watch my phone in case she has to call with an emergency.

After fishing my phone out of my purse, I connect the call and say, "Hey, Mom. Is everything okay?"

My mom's voice is brittle and shaky. "It's Corinne. She was having some chest pain and trouble breathing. I called an ambulance. We're on our way to the hospital now."

An immediate and monstrous wave of fear crashes over me but as soon as its tide recedes, I kick into this weird mode where I become utterly calm and collected. It is something I was forced to learn how to do when Corinne became sick and it was obvious I was the only competent one who had a strong enough backbone to handle it. While I love my mother beyond reason, she has never been a strong woman. It's why Danielle and Jayce have always walked all over her, and it's why Danielle has taken off and abandoned Corinne to my mom's care, which means my care, too.

"Are they taking her to Mercy?" I ask. Her heart

surgeon practiced there.

"Yes," she says, and I can hear tears in her voice. "At first, they didn't want to because it was further away, but I insisted."

"That's wonderful, Mom," I praise her as I know that will go a long way toward calming her down somewhat. "Hang tough. I'm on my way there now and should see you very soon."

"Okay," she whispers, and then lets out a tiny sob that breaks my heart. "But hurry please."

"I'll bust all the speed barriers," I assure her lightly, and getting a laugh from her, which was my goal. "I love you, Mom. Tell Corinne I love her and I'll be there soon."

I push out of my chair as I disconnect the call and give an apologetic look to Jerico, all conversation about having a threesome with him and Kynan completely obliterated from my mind. "I'm really sorry. But I can't work tonight. If you want to tack it onto the end, that would be fine."

I turn away and walk quickly toward his office door. As my hand reaches out for the knob, I'm completely stunned to see Jerico's hand there first. I didn't even realize he had followed me there.

"What's wrong?" he asks, his voice laced with concern.

While I find that very sweet, and a new side to Jerico, I don't have time to get into it. "My niece is at the hospital, and I have to go."

"Is everything okay?" he prods me.

I push his hand away from the knob and grab it myself to open the door. There's frustration in my voice at being delayed and I don't have time for politeness. "I don't know, Jerico. I hope so. But I won't know until I get there."

He gets the hint, stepping back from his door so I can walk through.

"If you need off more than one day, it's not a problem," Jerico says as I step into the hallway.

I don't even look back at him, but I do call, "Thank you," over my shoulder.

Then he's forgotten and all I can think about is Corinne.

CHAPTER 15

Jerico

I STARE AT my phone and it's like watching water boil waiting for a response from Trista. I sent a text to her about an hour after she'd hurried out of my office to go to the hospital, asking if everything was okay with her niece. That was two hours ago, meaning I've been wondering what the fuck is going on for three hours.

Of course, I didn't know she had a niece because our time together has been spent mostly fucking, and the talks we've had never got personal enough to talk about family. It makes me realize I don't know much about Trista at all, and normally, this would not bother me because all I need to know from a woman is whether she came.

But there's something about Trista that's gotten under my skin a bit. Yeah, the sex is downright amazing, and it's because she's innocent yet adventurous and I'm enjoying showing her things. The thought of what Kynan and I could do to her in The Silo while people watch is enough to give me a hard-on even though I'm more worried about Trista right now than anything.

This I don't understand, because as I said, I don't know much about the woman.

But here is what I do know.

Trista is the sister of the man I hate most in the world, and she's collecting on a favor I unequivocally owe him.

She's gorgeous and sexy and funny and smart, and since I first put my mouth between her legs, I haven't looked at another woman.

She also has family she cares about... a niece who is in the hospital, and by what I could glean from listening to Trista's end of the conversation, it wasn't the first time. I know it was her mom who called her because she kept saying it, but I don't know whose kid it is. It must be another sibling of Trista's... a sister or brother who has a child. It's not Jayce because that fucker hated kids, and I doubt that's changed over the years.

I'm not sure why Trista having a sick niece bugs me so much, other than it's making her more of a real human and that's creating some guilt issues for the way in which I'm using her.

The thought of just going to Mercy hospital crosses my mind briefly. I can be impetuous at times, but I doubt Trista could find fault with me seeking her out because I'm say... worried about my employee, right?

But I quickly quash that because of two very important things. First and foremost, I doubt this niece is Jayce's, but there is a chance he could be at the hospital. I don't want to be anywhere near that bastard ever again because I might kill him. More importantly, however, I cannot give credence to any thought that Trista is anything but a good lay I'm going to continue fucking until her time here is up. If I reach out with an ounce of interest in her personally, it could dissuade me from my plans for revenge against Jayce, and I'm not willing to give that up no matter how intriguing the woman is.

There's a short knock on my door, and then Kynan walks in. He looks mellow and relaxed, and if I had to guess, he just got laid nicely. He flops down in one of the guest chairs, stretching his legs out in front of him and settles his clasped hands over his belly.

"What's up?" he asks.

"Not much," I tell him as I glance down at my phone again. I know a text didn't come in because I would have heard it, but just in case. "What are you up to?"

"Just got an amazing blow job from some tourist chick visiting from Nebraska or somewhere like that," he says with a wide and very pleased grin. "She's here for a bachelorette party. In fact, there's a group of about twenty of them if you want to get in on that action."

"Not tonight," I say brusquely as I pull some papers out of my lateral file drawer so it looks like I'm busy. "Got too much to do."

"Bullshit," Kynan says, and his sparkling eyes say it all. Still, he makes sure to rub my face in it. "You've only got one girl on your mind. I noticed she's not here tonight."

Kynan sounds way too confident to make that assertion, so I ask, "What makes you think that?"

"Lydia at the hostess stand heard it from Carma who heard it from Jose that he saw her coming out of your apartment this morning looking thoroughly fucked and satisfied. And this is big news, of course, because everyone knows you never take women into your apartment and you don't do repeats."

"Jesus," I mutter as I rake my fingers through my hair in agitation. "Don't the people around here have anything better to do than gossip?"

"Not when you're like the most wanted man around here," Kynan says with a chuckle, "as well as being the most elusive."

"So I like to fuck her," I say with a shrug. "What's the big deal if I was super horny last night and wanted to go several rounds?"

"Because you've been super horny before and gone several rounds with a variety of women all in a single night in your club," he says, further rubbing my nose into the fact I've really stepped outside my boundaries.

The "whooping" sound of an incoming text takes my attention and I grab my phone, relieved to see a text from Trista. *All is fine. Headed home from hospital and will be in to work tomorrow at regular time.*

I want to text her back and tell her to come here instead of going home, but that's selfish. She should be with her niece or getting rest at least. I merely respond, *See you tomorrow.*

"What's up?" Kynan asks as he nods toward my phone. "You look agitated and relieved at the same time."

"Trista's niece was in the hospital and she had to leave," I say as nonchalantly as I can. "She was just telling me she'd be in to work tomorrow."

But the fucker was right. I was agitated I wouldn't see her, but relieved nothing serious was going on. The knowing look in Kynan's eyes says he is amused by my reactions. He was a human intelligence officer with the Royal Marines, and he knows how to read body language and facial expressions. He could have an entire conversation with me without me opening my mouth to stay a word.

So to knock him off his high horse a bit, I tell him, "I want you to do a three-way with me and Trista."

I take immense satisfaction when his jaw drops open. "A three-way? With you and Trista?"

Trying not to sound too smug, I tell him, "Just because I've fucked her exclusively for a few days doesn't mean we're exclusive."

"And she's on board with this?" he asks skeptically.

Not about to tell him it's her fantasy. I'm doing this

because I want to indulge her in something she'd probably never have the guts to do. While I've shared plenty of women with Kynan before, I can't say as I'm overly happy about it, but if I had to choose one man, it would be him. I go vague when I say, "I mentioned it to her last night and she's interested. Are you?"

"I'm interested if you say it's okay for me to be interested." The hesitation in his voice causes my eyebrows to narrow.

"Jesus Christ, Kynan," I say with frustration, and even though I know this is probably a lie, I tell him emphatically, "She is nothing to me right now but a really great piece of ass. One I'm offering to share with you. If you don't want in, just say so."

Kynan never hesitates. "Oh, I want in. She's sexy as hell. I've wanted a taste of that since you had me hold her for you the other night."

I have to grit my teeth and clench my hands into fists not to leap across the desk and pop him in the face. This emotion, which I peg as jealousy, surprises me because I've not ever quite felt it before. I mean, sure... when I found out Michelle was screwing Jayce, I went apeshit with anger, but I didn't have this ugly, dark sensation inside of me I'm feeling right now over Kynan's clear interest in Trista.

Regardless, I push it down. I don't acknowledge it because to do so might make it real. Instead, I say, "Tomorrow night then. The Silo. Around ten?"

"I'll be here," he says, but he doesn't move to get up. His expression turns serious, his eyes hardening slightly. "Are you still going through with your plan to use Trista to get back at Jayce?"

My stomach tightens, but I don't hesitate. "Of course I am. Like we discussed before, she'll probably never know. And just so you know, I'll be using video of us tomorrow night as part of my 'care package' I'm going to send to Jayce when this is all over."

Kynan grimaces, not because he objects in general to being videotaped as we've done that together before too, but also because he thinks I'm a fool for using Trista like this. He's probably right, and yet I refuse to be deterred. I can't let go of probably the only opportunity I'll ever have to cause Jayce some pain. Nothing like what he caused me, but still—

"Jerico," Kynan says in a faint voice laced with censure. "It's not the way—"

"Don't tell me about how I should or should not choose to exact revenge on that bastard," I snarl at him as I come up from my desk and slam my fists down on it. "You know this goes beyond just the anger and humiliation of betrayal. It goes far beyond that."

"But using Trista—"

"He fucking killed my kid," I roar at him, and Kynan's eyes soften with shared pain. He'd been by my side for weeks when I'd been a walking zombie. I'd been so mired in despair.

It might be a bit dramatic to say Jayce killed my child, but when it's boiled down, it's what he did. He fucked my fiancée behind my back. She fell for that fuckwad although for the life of me, I can't imagine why. She'd been carrying our child at the time. Had been just six and a half weeks pregnant when I caught them together.

Being the hot tempered and mean son of a bitch I am, I kicked Jayce's ass good and moved out of the house I shared with Michelle. She tried desperately to try to work things out with me, but I don't take betrayal well. I cut her off emotionally—the only tie I wanted with her was my child. I can still remember vividly when I realized that tie had been broken.

Destroyed, actually.

After a few weeks had gone by, I called her to see if we could work out something where I could still be involved with her prenatal appointments. From the moment she opened her mouth to speak to me, I knew the baby was gone.

"Jerico," she'd said in a voice that was laden with so much fake sorrow that bile rose in my throat. "I was going to call you, but I wasn't sure how to tell you... I lost the baby a few days ago."

She even sniffled, but I could tell it was contrived.

I could have asked questions. Tried to narrow down exactly what her lie was, but I had better resources than trying to figure out the line between deceit and honesty when it came to Michelle.

I put one of my best hackers on it, and within just six hours, he'd been able to pilfer her medical records from a local OB/GYN's office in Vegas. One that was known for performing abortions, and I've never felt such devastating pain as I did at that moment when I read through the documents showing Michelle terminated my child. The icing on the cake was that the transaction was paid for by Jayce.

It was the one and only time in my life I've ever put a hand on a woman in anger with the intent to harm. I drove straight to her house. When she opened the door, my hand was on her throat, backing her up into her foyer, where I slammed her up against the wall. I could tell by the fear in her eyes that she knew that I knew.

"You fucking killed our baby," I roared at her, my fingers squeezing her slender throat. For a moment, I envisioned myself strangling her, but then self-preservation triumphed over my personal pain and I released her. She slumped down to the floor, coughing and gasping.

She looked up at me with tears in her eyes, and I asked her just one question, "Why?"

"Because Jayce doesn't want children," she whispered, and it took everything within me not to kick her in the face while she was down. "He insisted."

Instead, I turned toward the door but before I left, I turned to her and told her with deadly menace, "If I see either one of you again... if either of you cross my path... I will kill you. That's the only warning you get."

I stormed out of her house. I didn't know if she believed my last warning. They were empty words, of course, because as I said... I wasn't about to go down for murder. Instead, I'd just have to deal with the pain and move on.

Kynan was there for me. My closest friend. He helped pick up the pieces after I went for weeks on a drunken bender. He'd bailed me out of jail once and prevented me from getting in several bar fights. He watched as I fucked women without emotion, sometimes picking one up in a bar and just doing her up against a wall outside without even seeing if she was wet or not. He helped me through it and when I was ready to move on, he was by my side at The Jameson Group. He's been there the entire time, as well as spent some quality time here at The Wicked Horse, and there's no one's advice I trust more.

Except when it comes to this issue with Trista. I've not seen Jayce since the day I caught him with Michelle, but having an opportunity to cause him pain—even if it's nowhere near the same type—is just too much for me to pass up.

Kynan stands up from the chair and shoves his hands in his pocket. "I'm sorry, man. Sorry this is still eating at you."

"Then you understand why I'm doing it," I mutter.

"Yeah," he says. The tone of his voice implies he's

not going to broach it with me again. He may be against this idea, but Kynan will always have my back. "Don't like it, but I understand it."

We're silent for a moment, but then I pin him with a guilt-laden look. "I don't like it either, buddy. But I have to do it."

"Then I'll see you tomorrow evening," he says as he heads for the door. When he reaches it, he turns back. "Any hard limits?"

"No anal," I say distractedly. Trista's not ready for that. "Frankly... it's whatever she wants."

"You mean make all her dreams come true?" Kynan asks with a grin, and I feel the burden weighing me down lift a little. Trista's going to come so many times tomorrow that she's not going to know what hit her. I maybe have a very deceitful intent about what I'm doing to her, but I also intend to give her pleasure like she's never known.

CHAPTER 16

Trista

"MR. JAMESON ASKED me to send you to his office," Belinda says to me as I stand behind the hostess stand. She's one of the cleaners and why she's delivering this message is beyond me.

But then again… Jerico has me off-kilter tonight. When I arrived, there was a note on my locker that I was going to attend to the hostess stand in The Social Room, along with a black dress on a hanger he wanted me to wear. No other explanation and I haven't seen him all night.

The dress was simple but sexy, form fitting, and came to just above my knees with a plunging neckline. It was the same type of dress the other hostesses wore, so I didn't feel out of place or anything.

But I'm not sure why Jerico wants me here. He seems to have settled me into the role of a condiment tray girl because he told me he enjoyed watching me walk around half naked.

I smile at Belinda and turn to Marcy, the other hostess on duty with me, and say, "I'll be back in a minute. Mr. Jameson asked me to go to his office."

Marcy rolls her eyes at me. "Of course you'll be back in a minute."

"What's that supposed to mean?" I ask, my hackles raising up.

"Doesn't mean anything," she says with a shrug. "But really… you should call him Jerico, not Mr. Jameson. You know, seeing as how close you two are."

This is said with such cattiness that I get more angry than embarrassed that I'm being called on the carpet for my relationship with Jerico.

"Is that jealousy I hear in your voice?" I ask sweetly.

Marcy narrows her eyes at me. "Of course not. But don't get too comfortable in his arms. He's not a one-woman kind of man."

"And why should you care to even warn me about that?" This, I'm genuinely curious about. If Jerico doesn't do repeats, then he's never going to give Marcy a taste again, assuming he's had her. And why wouldn't he? She's beautiful just like everyone else here.

Or because he's been with me more than once, now the other women have hope he's broadening his horizons and will be back to them at some point.

God, I hope not. Our agreement is for sex-only, but I really don't want to see him with one of the staff. As well as I've done trying to shield myself, I still know it's going to hurt.

"Look, Trista," Marcy says, her voice actually soft. "Woman to woman… don't get caught up in what he does to you. He does it to everyone he's with. He loves it so much he's going to do it with a lot more women before he dies. That's just the type of man he is."

I can't tell whether she's being sarcastic or genuinely polite, so I just nod and walk away. I don't want to get into a further discussion with her about Jerico's sexual habits.

When I reach his office, I knock on the door and wait for him to invite me in. When he does, I give a quick swipe of my hands on my dress—nervous habit because of periodic sweaty palms—and open the door.

As soon as I see Kynan sitting on one of the guest chairs and Jerico's wicked smile, my palms go wet again.

My voice practically croaks. "You wanted to see me?"

Jerico stands up from behind his desk, rounds it, and comes up to me. His gaze rakes down me briefly before he takes my hand and leads me to the other chair beside Kynan. I sit down and clamp my legs together nervously, tugging at the hem of my dress. Kynan just gives me a genial smile, but my head snaps back to Jerico when he says, "We both want to see you."

He's leaning against his desk, his ass perched on the edge with his hands casually tucked into his pockets. The look in his eyes is almost predatory, and I can feel lustful vibes coming off him. I turn to look at Kynan again, but gone is his friendly look. His eyes are dark with desire as well.

I look back to Jerico and try to square my shoulders. "This is it, huh?"

"This is it," Jerico says with a smile. "If you still want it. I know we talked about it the other night, but there's no pressure. You say 'no', we go about our business for the night."

I wonder what that means? Does it mean Jerico and Kynan will find another woman to share? Or not that I really care about what Kynan does, but will Jerico?

"Will we be here?" I ask tentatively, thinking the desk looks solid. "Or your apartment?"

Jerico shakes his head, his eyes glinting with dark mischief. "The Silo, Trista. I told you I want people to watch you get pleasured by two men."

"Oh, God," I mutter as my gaze drops to the floor, and then pops back up to Jerico. "Oh, God. I don't know. I mean… I want to. God, I want to. But I'm scared, and nervous and embarrassed, and I wouldn't even know what to do, and really… do we have to do it in The Silo for my first time? Can't we just do this in privacy?"

Jerico just shakes his head, cutting off my rant. "Push past those boundaries, Trista. Dare yourself. Trust me… it will be so much better."

I swallow hard and just stare at the gorgeous man who is telling me to take a walk on the wild side and get naked with him and Kynan in front of not only just strangers who come to the club, but hell… my coworkers now. I know it's probably not a big deal as most of them practically live here when they're not working but still… this is a big deal to me.

"That's easy for you to say," I murmur. "You've done everything you can think of. I'm sure Kynan has too."

"We're adventurous," Kynan says with a grin. "And come on… it's sex. It feels great. You really can't lose if you know what I mean."

"There's nothing to fear," Jerico reassures me, and something strikes me from our conversation that night when we were talking about fantasies. I asked him if he'd ever been with a man. This was after he told me how two women together was like every man's spank bank go-to.

Jerico had chuckled as his finger ran down my arm. We were on our sides, lying in the bed and facing each other. "Every person has their limits, Trista. I guess mine is that I don't do guys."

Made sense to me, so we'd moved on to a weird conversation about BDSM. I'm not into it and thankfully neither is Jerico, but he knew a lot about it since so many patrons practice it.

I narrow my eyes at Jerico. "You want me to push past my boundaries, huh?"

"That's right," he says smoothly. "Piece of cake."

My lips curl up and they do so in such a way that Jerico's smile slides off his face.

"Okay, then," I say as I relax in my chair and cross one leg over the other. "You told me this is my fantasy, right?"

Jerico nods and Kynan leans forward in his chair, sensing from the vibe in the air that this is going to get interesting.

"Then I want you to push your boundaries too," I say smugly.

"What did you have in mind?" he asks tightly.

I jerk my head toward Kynan but never take my eyes from Jerico's, which are looking slightly unnerved right now. "I'd like you and Kynan to fool around with each other to start. Get me a little worked up that way."

"Fucking Christ," Jerico mutters. He looks to Kynan with a very clear and simple plea for him to say "no" to this idea.

Kynan shrugs and grins. "I'm in. I'll try anything once."

"Bastard," Jerico mutters again, and then points out to Kynan, "This wouldn't be a first for you."

"It would with you," he says back with almost a cackle of a laugh, and I'm in awe as Jerico goes red in the face.

Very interesting. Kynan swings both ways apparently, and Jerico seems as nervous about Kynan touching him as I am about being with the two of them in The Silo.

I think I might be able to get my way after all, so I

stand up from my chair and walk up to Jerico. Placing my hand on the knot of his tie, I give it a playful tug. "I'll let you off the hook and won't require any hanky-panky with you and Kynan if we can do this in the privacy of your apartment."

Kynan chuckles behind me, but my eyes are pinned on Jerico's. His jaw hardens as he considers my offer, and then my stomach clenches when his lips curl upward. "Tonight's about pushing boundaries. Guess I'll push one of my own too. Let's get your pretty ass over to The Silo so we can get started."

My knees start shaking and my heart hammers within my chest. My panties go wet. I realize not only is this going to happen, but it's going to happen publicly and it's also going to involve some Kynan-on-Jerico action.

Jerico takes me by the elbow to escort me to The Silo with Kynan following right behind.

♦

THE MINUTE I step across the threshold of The Silo, I figure the only way I'm going to get through this is to shed Trista Barnes completely and step through as a new person without any inhibitions. I vow I won't look at another person in the room because ignorance is bliss. If I can't see them, then I can pretend they aren't interested in me.

So I become just an anonymous girl looking for a wild ride with two gorgeous men. I prefer to think of us as strangers. After tonight, things will go on as usual. I won't be ridden with any guilt or embarrassment, and I might even come away with a little pride in myself for being so daring.

Jerico leads me to a door that goes to a hallway that wraps around the perimeter behind the glassed rooms. The wall that separates the rooms from the hall are solid, so this is the only place where there's a measure of privacy. When we reach a door I assume is our destination, Jerico stops and turns to me. "You okay?"

I nod and hope it's enough because my throat seems constricted.

But I can't help the long, wet moan that comes out when Jerico grabs Kynan by the wrist and pushes his hand between my legs. They spread involuntarily as Jerico orders him, "Check to see if she's wet."

Kynan's fingers only rub over the crotch of my panties in a gentle move, but a rumbling sound of appreciation from him proves I'm wet. My cheeks flame hot, but I manage to whisper, "What can I say... the prospect of watching you two together really turns me on."

Jerico grunts in acknowledgment, but I can tell he's not liking that part. I can't wait to see what happens.

We enter the room, and I refuse to look at the glass wall that faces the interior of The Silo. I pretend no one is out there and it seems to work. My nerves are in check and I look around the room, noticing it's the one with the raised bed with silver satin sheets tonight.

When the door closes, Kynan says, "This is your fantasy, Trista. Tell us what to do."

My gaze goes to Jerico. Even though he's on edge over what I might have him and Kynan do, he's also radiating pure lust as he looks at me. I turn to look at Kynan and appreciate his magnificence as well. He's about an inch or two shorter than Jerico, and he's the light to Jerico's dark. His hair is sandy blond, cut short, and he sports a goatee that's just a shade darker. His eyes are deep brown, but warm and always seem to be filled with easygoing humor, whereas Jerico always looks so intense and ready to do battle with the world.

I give a slight cough to clear my throat. "I want you two to undress first, and if you wanted to… you know… sort of help each other, that wouldn't be an undesirable thing."

Jerico curses under his breath and his hands bunch into fists, but he looks resolved. Kynan looks amused.

Me?

I'm quivering over this, deciding to get a front-row seat to watch. I'll never again have this type of power over two men at the same time. Hell, I'm not even sure I want this power again, but while I have it, I'm going to enjoy it. I crawl up onto the bed and perch myself with my back resting against the headboard. My legs stretch out, cross over each other, and I settle in to watch.

Both men first dispense with their shoes and socks,

which I appreciate. Nothing worse than a sexy striptease with awkward hopping around to get the shoes off.

Jerico doesn't wait for Kynan to make a move, but instead works on his own shirt. It hits me suddenly that he's not in his trademark business suit, but rather dressed in a dark gray T-shirt with a V-neck and jeans. He's got on a worn, black belt that's seen better days. I had no clue Jerico could be so casual. My tongue almost falls out of my mouth as he pulls the shirt over his head. That chest, his abs, the light dusting of hair… he's all man and I start to ache for him.

Kynan takes his shirt off as well. It's a button down and he takes his time with the task, watching me the entire time. He's built a little bigger than Jerico even though he's not as tall. As he's revealed to me, I suck in a breath because his body is beautiful in a different way. It's covered from collarbone to waist in tattoos and they run down his arms as well. There is well-defined muscle, meaning this guy works out seriously hard, but the tattoos… I've always been a sucker for them. Add on the British accent and well… this is just freaking awesome.

Dropping his shirt to the floor, Kynan turns to Jerico and says, "Give the lady something, dude. Take my jeans off."

Jerico again curses under his breath, but he doesn't hesitate. And more importantly, he doesn't rush through it either. This may be pushing his boundaries, but he's going slowly so I can savor this and for the first time since knowing Jerico, I feel a rush of genuine affection for him.

Kynan's belt comes off, and Jerico's big hands work the button and zipper. Kynan's head is bent, watching what Jerico does. His abs flex and relax as the zipper is lowered, then flex hard again, showing he owns a six pack as well when Jerico's thumbs go into the waistband of Kynan's briefs so he can pull them down with his jeans.

My breath catches as Jerico slowly lowers his body along with the clothing as he drags it down Kynan's muscular legs, which I give a passing glance to, but my eyes go back to what's in between those legs. He's semi-hard and a big boy. If I take him and Jerico tonight, I'm going to be sore for sure tomorrow. Kynan steps out of his jeans and briefs. As Jerico starts to rise, Kynan takes his cock in his hand and starts to stroke it. Jerico doesn't spare him a glance, but his mouth comes awful close to the tip of Kynan's shaft. Kynan did that on purpose to make him uncomfortable. He's getting a kick out of this going by the devilish gleam in his eyes.

"My turn," Kynan says, his voice husky which I'm sure is deliberate. He takes the same care in removing Jerico's jeans and boxers, squatting down at his feet as he sheds out of the clothing.

Cutting his eyes to me briefly, Kynan gives me a wicked grin. As he starts to stand up, he wraps his big hand around Jerico's cock, which had also been half-hard.

Jerico jumps in surprise as he says, "What the fu—?"

But then his head falls back and he releases a guttural moan as Kynan starts to stroke him.

Oh, wow. Just… wow, wow, wow.

I raise quickly to my knees and crawl down the bed to get closer to the two men. Sitting back on my calves, I watch as Kynan roughly strokes and squeezes Jerico's dick. It grows, lengthens, and then starts to leak at the tip. Jerico's eyes are closed tight, his mouth parted and his chest rising and falling quickly. A terrible pulse of yearning hits me square between my legs, causing me to squirm.

My gaze turns to Kynan to see his eyes are burning with lust. Not a true and genuine interest in Jerico's body, but because he's doing something unbelievably dirty and taboo, and that's mainly because they are best of friends and coworkers, and oh yeah… Jerico is as hetero as they come.

Suddenly, Kynan reaches out to grab my forearm and he drags me forward a bit, pushing my hand against Jerico's cock.

"Take it," he says gruffly. I do as he says, forgetting this is my fantasy and I'm in charge. When I give a tentative stroke, Jerico's hips push forward to thrust into my fist. At the same time, Kynan goes to his knees. Before I can even drop my mouth open in astonishment or Jerico can protest, he opens his mouth and takes

Jerico's cock deep inside.

"Jesus fuck," Jerico groans and I can't tell whether he likes it or not. I drop my hand away and Kynan pulls him into his mouth deeper, his own hands going to Jerico's ass where his fingers dig into the muscle.

I lean back on my calves and watch, completely fascinated, thoroughly titillated, and wondering what will happen next if I don't tell Kynan to stop.

CHAPTER 17

Jerico

I'M GOING TO motherfucking kill Kynan after this is all over.

"Goddamn, that feels good," I mutter as he sucks hard.

Maybe I won't kill him, but I'll lay into him for sure. I don't do dudes.

Except apparently right now because Trista wanted it, I'm letting my best buddy blow me and everyone in The Silo is watching through the glass windows. This is definitely something they've never seen me do before, and they better get a good eyeful because I won't be doing it again.

Soft hands touch my shoulders, then one goes to my jaw. It's Trista turning my face toward her. Her mouth comes to mine for a feathery kiss over my lips, and she whispers, "You breaking boundaries is beautiful to watch."

I groan again as the tip of my cock punches into

Kynan's throat, and while it feels fucking amazing, I want to move on to the part where we both give Trista pleasure.

"Baby," I rasp out. "Let's move this all to the bed, okay?"

She pulls her head back a bit and looks at me, and I know she can see it in my eyes. This feels good, but I don't want to blow my load right now. Kynan will never let me live it down.

Offering me a smile, she reaches a hand down and threads her fingers through Kynan's hair as he bobs in front of me, clearly getting into it. "Kynan... that's enough."

He makes a sound... a chuckle or maybe a rumble of regret, but he pulls off me in one long stroke and licks his lips. I'm fucking hard as a rock and never in a million years would I have thought another man could do that to me.

"Undress me," Trista murmurs, and I turn to her. Kynan stands. As I work the zipper at the back of her dress, Kynan pulls the material up her body and over her head. She kneels before us on the satin-covered mattress in a simple black lacy bra and panties. And, of course, some killer high heels we may take off later but not right now.

Trista isn't the first woman Kynan and I have shared, and it's probably obvious by how well we work together. Kynan removes her bra and I pull her panties down her legs, letting her lie back so I can pull them free.

Then she's before us, gloriously naked except for those sexy-as-fuck shoes and a lovely blush across her cheeks and the top of her breasts. My cock is still amazingly hard. A quick glance at Kynan tells me he's locked and loaded as well. He reaches down to his pants and pulls out a few condoms, tossing them on the bed.

I bend over and run my hand up the inside of Trista's leg, stopping before I get to the apex. "What do you want, Trista?"

She stares at me a long moment, her amber eyes filled with uncertainty and longing. She worries at her lower lip with her teeth, and I can tell she's stalled somewhat now that she's laying down naked and vulnerable.

"What me to lead?" I ask her gently, moving my hand and brushing my fingers through her swollen folds. She's wet as I'd expected because I know she was totally turned on by Kynan sucking my cock.

She nods her head, those eyes going lighter and her smile turning grateful.

"Get up on your hands and knees," I tell her. "I'd like your mouth on me as it's way softer than Kynan's."

He grins at me as Trista does what I say, crawling down to me at the end of the bed. Kynan winks at me as he walks toward the headboard. "That was the best blow job you've ever had."

Yeah, pretty sure it wasn't. It was nice, felt fucking phenomenal, but it wasn't the best. Certainly was plain dull compared to what Trista can do with her mouth.

My hand goes to my dick, and I hold it for Trista as she reaches me. She opens her mouth, eyes turned up to capture my gaze as she takes me in deep.

"Mmm," I moan out a praise as she pulls off before sucking me back in. "That's it."

I look up briefly at Kynan, and his head tilts toward Trista's backside in question. I give him a nod, giving him clearance to work on her from that angle.

Fingers threaded deep in Trista's hair, I let her move slowly on me, feeling the warmth of her mouth and the slight rasp of her tongue on the underside of my cock. She's working me a bit faster now, completely into it, and I know she wants me to come, but fuck if I'm ready. Kynan puts a knee to the bed, then another, and his hands go to Trista's hips. She jerks slightly, and then moans long and hard as his hand goes between her legs to play with her. I can't see exactly what he's doing, but it's thrown her off pace. For a few moments, her mouth just opens wide as she moans and my cock slips out.

"Jerico, man," Kynan says thickly, his hand making a pumping motion. "She is fucking drenched."

Trista arches her back as Kynan does something to her, and she cries out in pleasure. I'm guessing he hit her clit and I just watch as he works her over, bringing her to a quick orgasm with just his hand.

Trista huffs and puffs, her head hanging low and her hair falling forward. But then she raises back up and looks at me. "Give me your dick again."

So I do.

Slide it right back into her mouth and let her set the pace.

Kynan busies himself with suiting up, easily getting a condom on. The dude certainly likes foreplay but I think after blowing me for a bit and then getting Trista off, his balls have to be turning blue.

Crawling closer to her on his knees, he takes his cock in hand and starts to push into her from behind. Trista goes still, holding my dick in her mouth as she rotates her hips a little. Kynan makes short pumping movements with his hips, and Trista grunts in response as he goes deeper each time. It is sexy as fuck watching her take it from Kynan while my dick is just sitting in her slack mouth.

When Kynan thinks she's ready, he slams his hips forward and buries himself into her deep. She cries out, the vibrations of it rumbling through my cock. My hands go to her head, tilting it so she looks at me. Her eyes are glazed over, and she's in the throes of passion right now.

Giving her a smile, I start doing the work for her, fucking her mouth slowly while Kynan pounds her from behind. I take my time, sometimes pausing so Trista can relax and just feel Kynan's dick. When he slows down a bit, I push into her throat a time or two. Kynan and I make a dynamic duo fucking her at both ends. When my balls start to tingle, I pull all the way out, not wanting to spend that way. Instead, I merely watch as Kynan fucks my girl.

Wait!

What?

Our girl.

Anyone's girl.

Not my girl.

And even as I struggle to figure out why my mind went there, I start to feel a little kernel of jealousy as I watch Trista completely lose herself to Kynan's dick. He's taking her thoroughly, even dropping a hand to rub in between her legs and Trista starts thrusting back onto him.

Kynan's close. I can tell by the way he's practically lurching into her body. Trista throws her head back, her hair beautifully cascading against her back as she screams out another climax. It sets Kynan off. He falls onto her, ramming in deep and grinding against her ass as she lays beneath him on the mattress. He comes silently but his face tightens in ecstasy, so I know it feels good to him.

Even as Kynan's grinding and Trista's panting under him, I'm wanting my turn.

Wanting to stake the final claim.

I put a condom on and walk around the side of the bed. Giving Kynan a poke in the ribs, I say, "Roll off her, brother. It's my turn."

"Yes," I hear Trista whisper and with a groan, Kynan

rolls in the opposite direction of me, pulling the condom off his spent dick.

I waste no time. After I climb onto the mattress, I pull Trista's hips up and position myself. I give her a moment to come up to her hands, but then I slam into her. She cries my name out, and my chest expands with pride. She didn't do that when Kynan entered her.

She fucking feels so good, is taking a double fucking like a champ, and she's already come twice. I want her to come again. I have to make her come again.

I slow my pace a bit, rolling my hips and rooting myself to the hilt each time. Trista moans in frustration, wanting it harder. The girl loves harder, and I love that too. I love rough, raunchy sex that is bound to leave bruises and bite marks, but I need to get her worked up again. When I pull out of her, she growls at me, "Don't stop."

"Shh," I tell her gently as I bring a hand between her legs. She's wet, swollen, and so fucking warm. I press two fingers into her, collect her juices, and then make pressing circles around her clit. I do this repeatedly until she's thrashing under me and I know she's close. Twisting my hand, I stick my thumb into her wet cunt and press against her inner wall while my fingers massage that tight bundle of nerves.

"Oh, God. Jerico… I'm so close," Trista chants. "So fucking close."

That's what I wanted to hear. My hand is gone, my

cock is slamming back into her, and because I want to get down and dirty with this beautiful, adventurous creature, I push my thumb into her ass.

She detonates and by that, I mean she screams and her pussy contracts on my dick and her ass on my thumb. As her orgasm rumbles through her, I fuck her harder than I've ever fucked a woman before. My balls ache as they swing back and forth. The front of my thighs sound like thunderclaps as they crack against the back of hers. I pull my thumb out, push it back in again, and Trista clenches harder around me, crying out in relief, pleasure, and perhaps even misery over how good it feels.

And that does it for me. Knowing I did that to her, my balls pull up. They feel like they're boiling with a need to burst. I slide deep into Trista, rotate my hips, and start to come.

Hot jets burst out of my dick, filling the condom. I'd give anything to have filled her pussy up instead. Yes, I want to fuck her bare and in every hole she'll take my dick. As I grind against her ass, shuddering my pleasure, I want to coat her skin with my semen. I want to come on her ass, then use it as lube to fuck her there. Or come on her pussy and make her rub herself to orgasm using it as lube.

"Fuck," I mutter to myself over these goddamn insane thoughts. Who thinks like this? Who wants to fucking mark a woman with their spunk?

I think I'm losing it, and maybe Trista is a fire I shouldn't be playing with. But as she sighs in pleasure underneath me and I can still feel my cock thumping inside of her, I'm pretty sure I'm willing to get burned to see where this goes.

"Can you close the curtains?" Trista mumbles, but it's loud enough that Kynan moves across the expanse of the room toward the glass wall and pulls them shut. Most of the people who had been watching had already dispersed, and I wonder what Trista thought of them.

Reluctantly, I push off her and pull out, hating the loss of warmth. She rolls onto her back, drapes her arm over her forehead, and grins at me. "That was wild."

I grin back at her, my chest loosening. I hadn't realized I'd been tense wondering what her reaction would be once it was over. "It didn't bother you to have all those people watching you get thoroughly fucked by two men?"

She grins back at me. "Did it bother you as they watched Kynan suck your dick?"

"Nope," I tell her, because while that shit was as uncomfortable as it felt good, I've never been embarrassed about showing my sexuality. It was nothing those people haven't seen before, although I might get hit on by some men now, I guess.

"Well, I didn't look out that glass wall once. I just pretended no one was there, and I'd like to keep it that way," she says as she raises up to her elbows, her fabulous breasts, which had been sorely neglected, thrusting outward. I reach out to pluck at her nipple, and she sucks in a breath.

"Stay with me tonight, okay?" I ask her softly. Not soft enough, as Kynan lets out a bit of a cough and moves over to his clothes to start dressing again.

Trista cocks an eyebrow at me. "You want me to stay the night with you again?"

"I'm not done with you yet." Going to my hands and knees, I hover over her. "I loved watching you take two men at once. With that image in my mind, I think it's going to be another long night for us."

She raises her eyes and looks off to the side, contemplating loudly with a "hmm" and a finger touching her chin. Looking back to me, she says, "Okay. I can do that."

And my dick gives a little jump of excitement. It just emptied my nuts less than five minutes ago... but it wants her again already.

CHAPTER 18

Trista

IT'S AS ODD laying in Jerico's bed tonight as it was last night. Maybe even more so since I'd fucked two men tonight. At the same time.

And then Jerico had to invite me to stay with him, because, of course, he wanted more sex. I was down with that. I wasn't reading anything into the invitation to his apartment, even knowing he could have me a million different ways within the club.

Well, I wasn't reading anything into it until the first words Jerico spoke as we entered his apartment were, "Let's get the smell of Kynan off you first."

He then dragged me into the shower where he thoroughly washed every nook and cranny of my body and gave me an orgasm along with it. While I was still trembling, he pulled me right out of the shower and spent a thorough amount of time drying us off before picking me up and carrying me to the bed.

And then?

Well, he's Jerico Jameson, a man I've quickly learned knows practically everything there is to giving and taking pleasure. Hell, even the missionary position with him is crazily erotic because he rolls his hips a certain way with one hand planted on the mattress and the other holding one of my legs under the knee. Hovering his face right over mine and growling the filthiest words I've ever heard in my life, well... I detonated two more times before he got his happy.

And the weird part is now.

Same as last night, I make a move to roll off the bed, intent on dressing and going home. Again, I've not forgotten Jerico's rules and by the fact he had no qualms about sharing me tonight, I know he's only in it for the sex.

But that's okay. I'm in it for the sex, too, and why shouldn't I be? It's freaking fantastic. I get the money to pay off Jayce and in return, I stand at a hostess desk, and on top of that, Jerico fucks me silly each night. It's like I'm working but on vacation. Or I'm living in an alternate reality, but I know I'll have to go back to the real world soon.

Surprisingly, Jerico's arm tightens on me and I'm held firmly in place.

"Want any more water?" Jerico asks squeezing me tighter so there's no more thought to me rolling out of bed. I've got my head on his chest as he's semi-propped up against the headboard. One arm around me, the other holding the bottle we'd been sharing. I shake my head.

Jerico leans slightly to the left to put the water on the nightstand, and then scoots down in bed so his head is on the pillow, rearranging my body so I turn more into him and my legs thread with his.

Without thinking about it, mainly because I'm wrecked from so many orgasms, my fingers run lightly over the hair on his chest while my mind wanders. I think about how ordinary my life was before coming to The Wicked Horse, and how maybe losing my job and getting into this predicament was supposed to happen for a reason. I'm not a religious person, but I consider myself spiritual and maybe there's something bigger at play here.

"What's the deal with your niece?" Jerico asks and his deep voice cutting the quiet causes me to jolt slightly.

But then I settle back down, continuing to rub my hand over his chest. His own hand is curled around my hip and his thumb is stroking my skin. "My niece is six and had heart surgery almost two months ago. She was having some chest pain and dizziness, so my mother rushed her to the emergency room."

"I'm assuming she's okay or you wouldn't be here."

"She's fine," I murmur, my heart squeezing when I think about what the doctor told us. "It was actually anxiety causing her issues. Her mom left about six months ago and Corinne's obviously having a tough time dealing with that and then of course, having a major surgery."

"Why did she need surgery?"

"Long story short… she got rheumatic fever and that damaged the mitral valve in her heart. They had to do surgery to repair the valve as well as a remove a large blood clot that had formed."

"Jesus," Jerico mutters in sympathy. "And only six years old."

"And her mom abandoned her," I add in case he missed that part. The bitterness in my voice is obvious, but what can I say? I'm pissed at Danielle for abandoning her daughter in her greatest time of need.

"Are you her guardian?" he asks.

"Sort of. She lives with my mom and me. My mom moved back to this area to help care for Corinne when Danielle left. We've not been able to get formal guardianship papers done yet because money has been tight with the surgery and all. Luckily, Danielle gave me a medical power of attorney for Corinne when she left."

"She knew she wasn't coming back?" Jerico asks. "Did you know that?"

"I thought she was going on vacation to Montego Bay with her new boyfriend." The acrimony in my tone is almost laughable.

"And she just never came back?"

"I'm going to kill her if she ever does for the pain she's put Corinne through," I snarl as my anger level starts to rise.

"Easy there, tiger," Jerico says gently as his hand starts stroking my back. "How do you know something bad hasn't happened to her?"

"Because she calls to check in." I raise my head, shifting my body so I can look at him. "I think she's on drugs or something. Sounds half out of her mind, but at least she calls to check on Corinne. If she sounds sober, I let her talk to her for a little bit."

"You care for her a lot," Jerico observes. "I saw how you reacted when you got the call. You were calm, but I could see the fear in your eyes."

"There isn't anything I wouldn't do for that little girl," I say softly as I turn my head and lay it back down on his chest. "She's mine for all intents and purposes."

Jerico doesn't say anything for a moment, but then I feel his body go tight under mine. He surges upward, bringing me with him. One arm goes around my waist and his eyes narrow at me, "That's why you needed the money from a loan shark, isn't it?"

"I told you it was a family emergency," I remind him.

"So Corinne doesn't have insurance?" he asks.

I shake my head. "And to do the surgery, the hospital wanted a deposit, although the surgeon was very nice and agreed on a payment plan. I had some money in my 401K I was able to pull out, but it wasn't quite enough."

"By thirteen thousand dollars," he says in a deep, rumbling voice that's filled with anger on my behalf.

"And that turned into the twenty-five thousand that you owe."

I shrug. "I'd do it all again under the same circumstances. She had to have that surgery. It wasn't elective. If she threw that blood clot, she would have died."

Jerico's eyes go a little flat, his voice sounding slightly dull when he asks, "What about Jayce? He couldn't help?"

"We're not all that close," I tell him honestly but without elaboration. I'm not about to tell him that Jayce doesn't give a shit about his niece, and he most certainly doesn't for me as evidenced by the bruise he left. I'm not quite sure what the nature of the relationship was between Jerico and Jayce, but I'm afraid if Jerico gets pissed at Jayce for any reason, he may decide he doesn't owe that favor after all and then I'm screwed.

Before Jerico can ask more questions, I turn the tables to satisfy some of my own curiosity. "You just got some personal information from me so I want some quid pro quo."

Jerico gives me a fiendish smile and tries to push me down onto the bed, his thoughts now controlled by his dick I'm sure. But I stand strong and keep my seat, pushing his hands off me. "It's only fair."

I wait to see if this will piss him off, but he just shrugs and lays back on the pillow. He puts his hands behind his head. The sheet just barely covers his pelvis. My eyes slide up his body—over those amazing, impeccably defined abs and up to his face where he's grinning at me. "What do you want to know?"

"Well, for starters—"

I gasp as Jerico's hands come to my hips and in a suave but forceful move, he pulls me over his lap so I'm straddling him.

I'm a bit self-conscious so I start to pull the sheet over to at least cover my lap, but his hand grabs a hold of it and he shakes his head. "You want answers, you have to sit on me like that with your legs spread wide."

I swallow hard as his hands come to my thighs, and then I get all squirmy when his gaze drops to my pussy. My breath freezes in my lungs when he gently runs a finger up my center and comments, "Look at you… all swollen and even a little red. Are you sore?"

When he raises his eyes for my answer, I shake my head, even though I am a little.

He smiles at me, his face saying he knows I lied, then he moves his hands back to my thighs. "Okay… you got ten minutes to ask me whatever you want, then I'm going to have you sit on my face and I'm going to give you a very gentle orgasm. Sound good?"

I croak at him, "Uh-huh."

And I pray I don't start leaking all over him just from his promise.

"Clock's running," he teases as he grips my thighs a little harder.

I cough, clear my throat, and say, "Tell me about

your family."

Jerico's eyes get a tinge of sadness as he says, "My parents are dead. My dad in a motorcycle accident, my mom from cancer. Didn't have any siblings. Have a few aunts, uncles, and cousins back East where I'm from, but that's about it."

"Back East?" I ask.

"New Hampshire."

My hands go to his chest. "I'm sorry about your parents."

He's eyes get even sadder, but his smile is very fond. "They were good people."

That's all he has to say for me to know... he's a family man. He may not have them now, but what he had was good, and I think it was passed to him. Otherwise, he wouldn't have just handed over that type of money to me with such a ridiculously easy repayment. Let's face it... he is practically giving me that money.

I want to know more about his family, but I also want to lighten the mood.

So I switch curiosities. "Tell me about The Jameson Group. What exactly is it?"

"I could tell you," he says seriously. "But then I'd have to kill you."

I roll my eyes at him. "Try again."

He chuckles and damn... the green in his eyes is mesmerizing when he laughs. His irises lighten and the tiny striations of rust turn golden.

When he stops laughing, he tells me, "I was in the Marine Corps... MARSOC, which is special forces. Did that for four years and liked the excitement and adventure of it, but didn't like the lack of control or the low pay. I decided to start a company that provides a lot of those same services and charge for it."

"What are the services?" I ask him, sliding my hands down to rest on his abs.

He gives a slight shrug. "Could be recovery of a kidnap victim or just gathering intelligence inside an enemy nation. Sometimes we're hired for protection services for dignitaries."

"And who would hire you to do that?" This is fascinating stuff.

"Sometimes private citizens," he explains. "Once we were hired by an Arab oilman whose daughter had been kidnapped for ransom. We were hired to get her back. But mostly, it's our government or one of our allies' governments that hire special-ops contractors."

"It sounds very James Bondish," I say with a laugh.

"It's not quite that exciting, particularly gathering intelligence," he quips dryly. "Try freezing your ass off for weeks while sitting in the frigid mountains of Afghanistan and doing nothing but looking through binoculars at a village and making diary entries of movement."

That doesn't sound exciting at all. "But still... you're hot like James Bond," I point out.

Jerico gives me a huge and unfettered grin. Before I know it, his hands are at my ass and he's pulling me up his chest.

"Hey," I complain as I push back. "You said I had ten minutes."

"I'm calling a time out," he says gruffly, his eyes going to the juncture of my legs. "I'm hungry."

Well, who am I to argue with that?

Jerico pulls me up his body, but I slam my hands down one more time to halt my progress. He looks at me with a mixture of amusement and irritation, but he waits for me to say whatever it is I want to say.

"You're not as scary as I thought you'd be," I murmur, tracing my finger down the middle of his chest. "Jayce told me to be careful with you."

Jerico's eyes harden slightly and his mouth parts as if he wants to prove he's scary or ask why Jayce would be wary of him, but instead he whispers, "Touch yourself."

"What?"

His eyes fall to where my finger sits in the middle of his chest. Since he's pulled me up his body a bit, it's resting not very far from the opening of my pussy. Warmth flushes my body and a sensual ache forms low in my belly before making my sex start to convulse. I slowly drag my finger across his skin, until it touches my warm, wet folds. I push just the fingertip inside and then bring it out to circle the wetness around my clit. A tiny moan pops out of me as my eyes flutter closed.

"Fuck, that's sexy," Jerico says in a gravelly voice filled with lust. "Let me taste."

My eyes open slowly and a lazy smile spreads over my face. I pull my finger away and reach out, lightly rubbing it over his bottom lip. His tongue comes out and swipes at it, and that right there... that's fucking sexy.

"Playtime's over," Jerico growls. His hands on my ass pull me all the way up until I'm straddling his face. I hear him mumble, "It's dinnertime," before his mouth is on me and he's rocking my world once again.

CHAPTER 19

Jerico

F OR THE THIRD time this evening, I leave my office and take a walk around The Wicked Horse. I hit up every room as well as The Deck. The only place I don't go is The Social Room because Trista's in there working the hostess podium. While I'd once told her I liked her working the condiment tray because she was almost naked and it was a treat for my eyes, I didn't like how it was a treat for others.

It's weird. I didn't mind fucking her last night in The Silo and people watching us, but when she's out there working, she's too stunning by half and she gets hit on a lot.

I don't like it.

I'm avoiding The Social Room and Trista because I want to make a point to myself. I'm too wrapped up in this girl and it freaks me out. Since Michelle, I knew I'd never trust another again with my heart. So owning a sex club and fucking different women each night has maintained my position on that matter. I'm on the prowl tonight as I want to prove Trista's not the only game in town and that there are a lot of other women in this club who would interest me.

I hit The Silo first and note all the rooms are taken. There's a beautiful girl in the stocks and a line of men waiting to fuck her. That has potential for sure, but nothing else in here is even making my dick stir. The Orgy Room has several potentials, but I only peek my head in for a moment. It's the same thing each night. Naked bodies tangled and writhing, the sounds of moans and slapping skin and the occasional cry of pleasure when someone climaxes. Lastly, I check out The Waterfall Room, but it's my least favorite by far. I like fucking in a lot of places but water isn't one of them, and forget about laying under the waterfall, even though it seems very popular. I don't want to be busy wiping water out of my eyes when I'm trying to keep my attention on the beautiful woman underneath me. Walking quickly through The Waterfall Room, I step out onto The Deck, which is my second favorite place to fuck.

The Deck is so much more than just an outdoor deck. It's a place where you can get a drink or a snack at one of the two large cabanas stands outside, but what really sets your teeth on edge when you step out is that the entire deck is made of a thick, clear, acrylic-like flooring that lets you see forty-six stories down. There are also clear acrylic chaises to fuck on. There's nothing like fucking a woman on her back while seemingly floating in the air. It's also not for the faint of heart or those with a fear of heights.

The perimeter of the deck has a ten-foot plexiglass wall that is one-way. The people on the Deck can see out, but those in Vegas can't see in. While The Onyx isn't the tallest casino in Vegas, the way it's situated on the strip, no building stands over it so privacy is pretty much guaranteed unless a chopper flies over. All the glass is one-way, which provides the necessary cover so we don't violate public nudity laws. The bottom side of the clear deck is covered with reflective material, which also has a one-way effect, so someone on the ground with binoculars can't get a free peep show by looking up. A lot of thought went into this deck before we had it built.

I love the adrenaline rush of being so high in the air and looking down at the Vegas lights below. Makes my cock extra hard.

There's a gorgeous woman standing at the outdoor bar, her eyes pinned on me. She's vaguely familiar, and I'm pretty sure we've got carnal knowledge of each other. She raises her glass of wine and tilts her head toward the bar... an invitation to come join her.

I think about it for a split second, but dismiss the idea completely. Giving her an apologetic shake of my head, I move back into The Waterfall Room, through it, and out into the hallway. I have an immediate need to see Trista... to see if I have a sexual reaction to the sight of her, because nothing I've seen so far has interested me. Either I've got it bad for just one girl, or my dick is broken. Neither choice is all that great to me.

I head to The Social Room and make myself look everywhere but the hostess stand to judge the clientele. The bar isn't overly crowded as it's late, meaning most have moved back into the other rooms. A couple of people are mingling with drinks, but they'll soon move to a back room where the clothes can come off and orgasms can be made.

Finally, I slide my gaze over to the podium where Trista is standing, wearing another sexy black dress I'd provided for her and that glorious hair hanging in layered waves over her shoulders and down her back.

And I definitely get a reaction.

Not only does my dick start to thicken, anger suffuses through me. It flashes so hot sweat breaks out on my forehead.

Because Kynan is standing with Trista, and it looks like they're engaged in an intimate talk that they're both enjoying. Kynan's got an elbow on the top of the podium, one leg crossed over the other. Trista's bent over slightly, resting her forearms on the desk portion of the stand, which reveals an obscene amount of cleavage. They're standing very close to each other, but what enrages me is the looks on their faces. Trista's laughing at something Kynan says, and then she reaches out and gives a playful punch to his chest. Kynan's grinning at her with a bit of a predatory sparkle in his eye, and he catches her hand before she pulls it away. He says something to her, and she gives a bashful smile and a shake of her head before pulling her hand free. But then he says something else, and she's laughing again.

She's fucking completely comfortable with him. No embarrassment over the fact he fucked her yesterday with me along for the ride. If I had to take a guess at what Kynan's doing right now, he's hitting on her strongly. No doubt wanting to fuck her tonight.

Yes, Trista and I agreed this was an open relationship and each of us could do whatever we wanted, but apparently, my sense of outrage and the caveman-like possessiveness that's welled up inside of me doesn't give a shit about what we said. She's been in my bed for two nights, and I liked it a lot. While what we did last night with Kynan was hot as all get out, I don't want her fucking him without me there.

Possibly never fucking him again.

Fuck, I'm screwed up in the head.

I stalk over to the podium, my long legs eating up the distance quickly. Trista sees me first, her eyes dancing with humor and her smile wide at whatever Kynan just said. I'm not sure what my face looks like but her smile slides right off when she sees me. Kynan sees it, turns toward me, and merely gives a chin lift. "What's up, man?"

"I need a word with you," I grit out at Kynan, the

fury evident in my voice. I feel strangely in the right here to be angry, even though I know my display of temper makes me look foolish.

This is confirmed when Kynan smirks at me before turning to Trista. "Talk to you later, darlin'."

"Bye, Kynan," she says softly... with affection... and is that desire?

I turn on my heel and walk out of The Social Room, down the private hall and into my office. Kynan follows behind. The minute I hear him close the door, I turn on him. "What the fuck do you think you're doing?"

"What do you mean?" he says innocently, but he's still wearing that smirk.

"You know what I mean," I growl at him. "Trista's off limits to you."

"She wasn't last night," he points out. "And besides, since when do you care about monogamy? I guarantee you don't have any exclusive agreement with her."

"That's beside the point—" I start to say, but Kynan cuts me off.

"It's exactly the point," Kynan says and the smirk is now gone. His expression turns serious as he takes a step toward me. "Trista is a nice girl. She's gorgeous and a dynamite fuck. But she is not your girlfriend, and I'm pretty damn sure she's nothing more than a dynamite fuck to you as well. So why shouldn't I take a shot at her?"

"What?" I sneer at him. "Are you offering her monogamy?"

"Fuck no," Kynan says, horrified. "I love the single life. I'm just saying unless you tell me your relationship is exclusive with her, you've got no right to be proprietary."

"Christ," I mutter as I turn away from Kynan and rake my fingers through my hair in frustration before whipping back on him. "I'm asking you to stand down and stay away from her unless it's by my invite to join us."

Kynan cocks a skeptical eye at me. "You going to tell every guy who's sniffing around her that?"

"Who's sniffing around her?" I ask, another flare of anger rushing through me.

"The question is who isn't?" Kynan says with a knowing look. "People have taken notice of your interest in her, and the men think her pussy must be magical or something."

My shoulders sag as my gaze drops to the floor in consternation because I realize I have no right to ask any man to stay away from Trista. We agreed this was casual and we could see—well, fuck—other people.

"Jerico," Kynan says softly, and I look back to him. "You asked me to back down and I'm your best friend, so I will. But if you want others to stay away, that's Trista's call, so you better talk to her about this. If you want to be exclusive, just lay it out there to her."

"I don't want to be exclusive with anyone," I snap at him, because I've trained myself over the years to not believe in love, trust, and loyalty between a man and a woman. The losses that could result from love are too painful to tolerate.

Kynan nods in understanding, his eyes sad for me and my unwillingness to open up. While he indeed enjoys the single life, he believes in love. In fact, he had a great love he let get away, so I think it makes him even more empathetic to what I've been through and how it's made me.

Turning toward the door, Kynan grabs the knob but before opening it, he turns back to me. "She's not Michelle. Maybe you should give her a chance."

I don't say anything in response. Kynan gives a sigh of frustration and walks out of my office.

At least I can be assured he won't go after her, but not sure what to do about her sudden popularity among the men in the club. I have no standing to say anything to them, not to mention it would be bad for business.

I stare at the door Kynan just walked through for a long time, and then it hits me.

I may not be able to say anything to them, but I'm her employer and she works exclusively for me. I can sure as hell say something to her.

Walking to my desk, I pick up the phone and buzz the podium. Trista answers, knowing it's me because it will show her from what extension the call is coming from. She cuts right to the point. "Are you done beating your chest?"

Ignoring her remark, I say, "Come to my office. We need to talk."

"Right away, sir," she says and from her tone, there's no doubt she's not happy about me pulling Kynan away from her.

Well, tough shit.

I take a seat behind my desk after taking off my suit coat and loosening the knot to my tie. It only takes moments before there's a soft knock on my door. Trista walks in confidently, her expression frozen into a mask of impassiveness so I have no clue what she's thinking. But it doesn't matter since I'm the boss.

"It's come to my attention that you have a few men interested in you here at the club," I say lightly.

Trista just shrugs. "I guess."

"You're not to have sex with any of them while you're in my employment and fulfilling the terms of our deal," I say in the most businesslike tone I can muster.

Her whiskey eyes go dark, and she glares at me. "I notice you didn't offer the reciprocal to me. That you won't sleep with any of the other women here."

"That's because I'm the boss and they're my rules," I say, and even as the words come out, I know they are way fucking wrong.

They feel wrong to me, and yet I don't take them back.

Trista pushes out of her chair, leans over, and slaps her hands on my desk. "You are the boss as it pertains to any work I do here at The Wicked Horse, but you don't have any say over what I do with my body on my own time. I can fuck who I want, when I want."

"And who do you want to fuck?" I growl at her as I stand up, placing my hands on my desk and leaning in toward her.

The fight drains out of her eyes immediately over my question, her eyes dropping to stare at the desk. She takes in a deep breath. Without looking at me, she admits almost shamefully, "I don't want to fuck anyone but you."

A wave of relief hits me followed by almost a giddiness that she only wants me. I put my hand under her chin and lift her face so she looks at me. "So then why are you so angry about me asking you to stay away from other men?"

Her eyes fire up again, and she jerks back from me. "Because, you ass, you didn't ask. You told. And without offering me the same, it screams of ownership, and I don't like that at all. It sucks I only want you, and I hate myself for it, but there you have it."

Something that feels like a wrecking ball punches into my chest, robbing me of my breath for a moment. While I was mired in these stupid fucking feelings of jealousy, it never hit me once that perhaps Trista wanted to only be with me. I mean… she did take Kynan's dick last night and she was flirting with him today, but…

Coming around the desk, I walk up to her as she

watches me warily. I take her hands in mine, give them a squeeze, and say, "How about for the duration of our deal... you and I agree to sleep with each other exclusively unless we both agree on inviting someone into our bed?"

Trista's eyes soften. The smile she gives me is one of relief. "That is something I can agree to, I believe."

Leaning in, I give her a soft kiss before pulling back. With total transparency, I tell her, "I'm sorry I was a jackass. I handled it badly."

"Forgiven," she says with a smile. "But just out of curiosity, will you be inviting anyone else into our bed?"

My hands release hers and take hold of the hem of her dress. Leaning in, I press a kiss to her neck before pulling back and telling her, "We've got three weeks left in our arrangement. I think you and I can come up with plenty of ways to entertain ourselves without involving others, but if we get bored, we can talk about it."

She smiles, draping her arms over my shoulders. With a glance down at my lips, she whispers, "Then let's seal the deal."

I'm all for that. She's inferring it will be done with a kiss, but I have something a little more wicked in mind.

In one swift move, I pull her dress over her hips and swing her around so her back is to my desk. She gasps when I pick her up and deposit her there before dropping to my knees.

"What are you doing?" she rasps out as I roughly

shove her legs apart and pull the crotch of her panties aside.

"Sealing the deal," I tell her without even looking up.

Then I put my mouth on her, giving her that kiss she wanted, just in a different place.

CHAPTER 20

Trista

I COME SLOWLY awake, taking in the soft sheets of Jerico's bed and the pillowy mattress that's like sleeping on a heavenly cloud. I roll over, open my eyes, and see Jerico's side of the bed is empty. I can't help the smile that comes to my face as I remember everything about the last several hours.

How Jerico showed a definite jealousy that he'd never admit out loud, leading to us promising exclusivity until my time is up here. I'm not sure what will happen then, but I know it's going to be difficult to part ways. As long as Jerico left things casual, I could keep my heart protected. But he's moved us out of that space and put us straight into a situation where I could get hurt. I don't think Jerico is relationship material, but I can't lie and say I'm not hoping something will change. I mean… this beautiful, successful man who is a sex god in every way wants only me right now when he's normally the whore of the club. I hate for it to mean that much to me, but

I'm such a girl… it does.

"You're awake." I roll over to see Jerico walking into the bedroom, fully dressed with damp hair. He's holding a cup of coffee that he sets on the nightstand by me, then sits down on the edge of the bed near my hip.

"How do you feel this morning?" he asks with a self-satisfied, cocky grin.

Bastard should feel cocky. I don't know how many times he made me come last night. The first time while he had me sit on his desk, then again when he fucked me while I bent over it. After that, he buzzed up Amanda, who was working the podium with me, and told her I wouldn't be returning.

Caveman Jerico picked me up and brought me to his apartment, where we had sex—I kid you not—three more times. I didn't know men could do that. It wasn't successive, one right after the other. But we'd have sex, then talk, doze off and sleep a little. Then he'd wake up, put his hands on me, and it was on again. We repeated that pattern three freaking times, the last time occurring about seven AM. A quick glance at the clock tells me it's half past one PM now.

I give him a smile. "I feel great."

"Not sore?" he asks.

"Nope," I lie.

"So if I stripped down now, climbed between your legs, and shoved my cock in you, would you scream in pain or pleasure?" he asks, and geez… I know he has no intention of doing that because he's dressed to the nines for business, but damn if the throb between my legs doesn't want him to.

"I'd scream in pleasure," I assure him.

He lifts an eyebrow at me as if I've wounded his dick's pride. "Well, to be on the safe side, I'll manage to wait until tonight to have you again."

"You're so kind," I say dryly, then my brow furrows. "You want me to stay over again?"

By his confused expression, I can tell the question caught him off guard. I think Jerico only knows he's going to fuck me sometime tonight, but he hadn't given much thought as to when and where or if he'd invite me to stay.

Before he can answer, I sit up in the bed a little more and stop any potential discomfort he's in from putting him on the spot. "I can't stay tonight. I promised Corinne we'd do something special all day tomorrow, so I need to get home right after my shift."

Jerico's eyes go soft, but I can see a level of disappointment in them. "Of course. Totally understand. Guess I'll just have to sneak some time in with you while you're on duty."

"Sounds good," I say with a smile as I start to sit up in the bed.

Jerico turns and grabs the coffee, handing it to me. "Cream and one sugar, right?"

I smile brilliantly at him. "Very good."

"I'm observant," he says by way of explanation. "That's how you made your coffee yesterday."

True enough. We drank coffee together in his kitchen before I headed home to get showered and spend some time with Corinne and Mom before I had to come back to work.

Jerico looks at his watch, and then says, "I've got to get going. Got a meeting across town in an hour, and I've got some paperwork to finish first."

He leans over and kisses me. When he pulls back, he doesn't pull back very far, our noses just inches from each other. "I enjoyed last night."

Four simple words, and they make me feel all warm and squishy.

"Me too," I murmur back.

"Okay," he says with one last quick kiss. "I'm out of here. Take your time leaving. The door will lock behind you."

"'Kay," I mutter as I sip at my coffee and watch his gorgeous backside in tailored navy-blue pants paired with a crisp white dress shirt as he walks out of the room.

When I hear him leave the apartment, I settle into the pillows propped up on the headboard and drink my coffee, contemplating how very strange my life has become. At best, my life could have been called satisfying. I had a respectable job with good benefits working as a receptionist in a dentist's office, I owned my own home and had a network of causal friends I could hang out with and do fun things. My best friend, Claudia, lives in Germany now as her husband is in the Army and got transferred there, but we text daily, talk on the phone at least once a week, and Skype as well, I mean… life was good.

Of course, there were stressors but aren't there always? I wasn't even surprised by Danielle abandoning Corinne. While suddenly becoming a surrogate mom was a little overwhelming, I wouldn't trade my time with Corinne for anything. In fact, I think she was supposed to be with us at the time Danielle chose to abandon her, because of her illness. My mom and I took far better care of her than Danielle ever could have. I'm ashamed to say that about my sister, but I'm not sure Corinne would have survived if she hadn't left her behind with us.

With a sigh, I take a sip of coffee and think about Jerico. He took my ordinary life and turned it upside down. Within a week's time, I went from my most exciting night involving club hopping and maybe having a one-night stand I always regretted the next morning, to a woman who has shamelessly let a man control her entire sexuality.

I let Jerico have sex with me in front of other people.

I let Jerico and Kynan have sex with me in front of other people.

While my face heats up thinking about it, I can't disregard the fact that the things that have happened to me this week have been the most exhilarating, liberating moments of my life. I'm sad that there's going to be an end to this. I think I have more awakening left within me. Being in this atmosphere where kink and debauchery are the norm without any judgment makes me want to take advantage of everything Jerico will teach me. And I want that knowing I can leave in a few weeks' time and never see anyone in this club ever again. It will be like a grand adventure, but one I can easily close the door on when I'm done.

Well, at least I think I could if it weren't for a gorgeous, orgasmic, charming alpha man who seems to want me.

Ugh.

I don't want to linger on it anymore. Last night was amazing and tomorrow night will be amazing. But now it's time for me to go back to my ordinary life. My mom is cool and won't give me the stink eye for not coming home the last few nights because I'm an adult and she treats me as such. I've always made sure she was fine with Corinne, and while I've not told her any details about Jerico, I think she's got some romantic notion I might have found "the one" since I've spent three nights with him. But I was telling him the truth about needing to go home tonight as tomorrow is going to be a Corinne day and I want to devote myself to her.

Setting my almost-empty cup down on the table, I reluctantly put on my black dress and underwear Jerico had taken off. The club opens at two PM, which one might think is odd and wasted because who wants to go have kinky sex in the middle of the day? But surprisingly, there's a decent-sized crowd during daylight hours. Mostly people who are seriously into their sexual fantasies and make liberal use of their memberships. I'm sure many are for adulterous liaisons too. The night crowd swells with mainly tourists looking to check off a bucket list item or something. Still, I need to stop in the locker room and get my bag of street clothes I had worn in yesterday before shift as I'd had to come straight here from running errands. Hopefully I can minimize my walk of shame by sneaking in, changing clothes, and hightailing it out of here. It's no secret Jerico and I are sexually involved, but I still don't want it flaunted.

I take my cup to the kitchen, rinse it out, and put it in Jerico's dishwasher. Grabbing my purse, I sling it over my shoulder and head out of his apartment, making sure the door locks behind me. I quickly walk past Jerico's office and then pop into the locker room to change clothes.

Unfortunately, the room isn't empty. It's occupied by three ladies, all who work condiment trays. I don't know them at all. In fact, I only know two of the women's names, Wendy and Calista. The work here is fast paced and solitary, so it's not conducive to forging friendships among employees. After shifts, people rush out, or they may take advantage of the club membership. Either way, I've barely said a handful of words to any of these girls, but I give them a friendly smile when I walk in. They're in the process of getting undressed and had clearly been talking and joking about something, but they went deadly silent when I walked in. They don't smile back at me.

I ignore them, open my locker, and grab my bag out, heading to one of the dressing rooms. This is a unisex locker room, which is the reason for privacy stalls, but many of the staff don't take advantage of it and just dress out in the main area. I guess the whole being uninhibited sexually thing applies to nudity as well.

Making quick work of changing into my jeans and a black t-shirt with "Joie de Vivre" printed on it, I put on flat sandals studded with coral and turquoise beads. It's my go-to casual wear. After putting my dress and heels away, I zip up my bag and make my way out of the dressing room.

Only to come to a complete halt as all three of the women, Wendy, Calista, and I-Have-No-Clue-Who, are standing there and glaring at me. Because I've never interacted with these girls much, and because I know I've done nothing to piss them off personally, I can only assume this is about Jerico.

I let out a sigh of frustration before straightening my spine and crossing my arms. "What's up?"

"We're just wondering how you've managed to get Jerico's attention for so long," the girl whose name I don't know asks snottily.

"I'm sorry… but what's your name?" I ask without answering her question.

"Leigh," she snaps at me.

"Well, Leigh," I say in a calm voice, then turn to look at Wendy and Calista, "I'm just going to have to tell you ladies it's none of your business what's going on between Jerico and me."

"Well, you've done something because Rico's not one to do repeats," Wendy says as she puts a hand on her hip and cocks it out. This is a bit disconcerting to me as she's standing in her bra and panties, and besides that… Rico? I'm fairly confident he does not go by that ridiculous nickname.

"Perhaps you shouldn't call him something so stupid," I reply. "It's probably a turn-off."

"You fucking bitch," Wendy practically screeches and takes a threatening step toward me. Now I'm very uncomfortable with the situation, so I take a step back.

"What do you expect?" Calista adds. She's at least still fully clothed, so it's not awkward to look to her. "Jerico probably lost a bet. Or she's into some super kinky shit none of us has seen before and he's fascinated with it. But honestly…"

And here she pauses to rake a scathing look up and down me with a curl to her lip before she continues, "She's not much to look at. I think that's why we can't figure it out."

"Good point," Wendy sneers, also looking at me as if

I'm covered in fleas or something. "But just like any woman in here who has a taste of that man, she's nothing but a live sex doll to him. So honey, just be ready... he'll kick you to the curb as soon as he gets tired of your worn-out pussy."

My shoulders slump a little because these jabs cut. Compared to these women, I'm not sure why Jerico is with me. Wendy's tall and buxom with boobs that are in the DD range. Her hair is the perfect color of blond, her facial features superb, and I've seen her give a blow job to a guy in the club. She's good. Calista has gorgeous red hair that falls almost to her ass in fiery curls, emerald green eyes that would give Jerico's a run for his money, and I've seen her in action a time or two. These girls are dirty, kinky, and adventurous. Leigh is also stunning, a blond as well but her hair is so pale it's white. She looks almost elfin, the kind of beauty that looks almost fantastical, made more so by the fact she actual has violet-colored eyes. I've never seen that before, and I'm kind of fascinated and equally jealous.

I don't have a response to their last barb, so I hitch my bag and purse over my shoulder and start to push past them. Thankfully, they step aside and when I look up, I come to a screeching halt.

Jerico is standing there, his eyes blazing with fury and I'm not sure how it's possible, but he looks even bigger. Even though he glares over my shoulder at the women I'd just walked past, I'm still intimidated as shit by the fury that radiates from him.

"Wendy, Calista, Leigh." He says each of their names, and I'm stunned at how calm he sounds despite the expression on his face. "You're all fired. Effectively immediately."

"What?" Leigh gasps in shock. "You can't do that."

"I can and I did," Jerico says brusquely. "Now get dressed and vacate the premises. Your final paycheck will be mailed to you."

Wendy and Calista's heads drop, their faces crestfallen as they walk past Jerico. But Leigh is a little spitfire. She growls at Jerico as she struts past him, "You're a dick."

Jerico laughs at her, and it sounds cruel and amused. To add insult to the injury he just handed out as the ladies go to their lockers, he says, "And for the record... I think rather than finding out what Trista has to keep me coming back, you should be asking yourselves what you didn't have that made you just a one-time fuck."

I wince, because that was crude. Calista and Wendy's shoulders sag, and they don't waste time getting their things. Leigh mumbles under her breath but loud enough to be heard. "Such a fucking dick."

Jerico turns his gaze to mine, his eyes now soft and possibly empathetic. I don't want any part of it, especially not in front of these women. I jet past him and run out of the locker room, intent on getting the hell out of there before any more attacks come my way.

"Oh, no you don't," Jerico says as he grabs me by the elbow just as I enter the hallway. He turns me around and starts to march me toward his office. I feel like a kid being taken to the principal's office again, and I wonder if I'll get paddled.

Now why the fuck did I just think that?

Once we're inside, he releases his hold on me and asks, "Are you okay?"

My eyes narrow as I hiss at him. "I'm completely humiliated. Otherwise, I'm okay. I can't believe you fired them for that."

"Why not?' he asks as he pushes his hands casually into the pockets of pants. "I'm the boss. They were being bitches to you. I kind of thought you might be happy about it."

"You do realize I'm going to be the club's pariah now?" I snap at him. "It's clear people don't like me because I have your attention, but now they're really going to hate me when they find out you fired those girls because they were a little catty with your current flavor of the month."

"That's not what you are." He looks pained and troubled, but I'm not sure why. He's the one with relationship boundaries.

"That's exactly what I am," I say softly, but the force of my reminder hits him hard. This deal is only for a month.

He looks at me warily, but he inclines his head in

acknowledgment. "What would you have me do?"

Without thought, I jerk my head toward the door. "Go back and rescind their termination."

Jerico's eyes go wide with surprise, and I can see instant denial in them. I bet he's a man who never goes back on a decision once it's made. We enter a stare-off, and I cross my arms for stubborn effect.

Finally, he blows out a huff of resignation and drawls, "Fine. I'll go tell them now."

"Good," I say with a snippy attitude. I'm not sure why since he just gave me what I asked for, but that's how it comes out.

This causes his eyes to darken and his lips to curl. "I expect gratitude for this tonight, not attitude."

I roll my eyes at him, but I don't have a problem showing him some gratitude. In fact, I'm looking forward to it.

CHAPTER 21

Jerico

I CAN'T REMEMBER the last time I've fucked the same woman monogamously. Obviously, I was monogamous with Michelle, but since her it has been nothing but one-night stands. Since the club opened, it's just impersonal, kinky fucks. Prior to Michelle, I never had overly serious relationships because I was young and didn't want one.

It's been almost a week since I fired those three bitches and Trista made me rehire them. We've been carnal with each other every single night since so I know she's not too mad at me. I was a little pissed at her though, making me take those girls back on. I never change my mind once a decision has been made like that because inconsistency smacks of weakness. Right now, those three women not only think I'm pussy whipped, but they also think I'm soft on my employees and business dealings. And fuck if I can figure out why I gave in to Trista on that. She was clearly distressed to be harassed by those girls, but even more so that I fired them. My original intent was to protect her, but I apparently made things worse. The thing that sucks about it is I normally wouldn't give a shit about something like that. I wouldn't have cared Trista was cornered, and I certainly wouldn't have come in to her rescue. I most definitely am not the type of guy who would fire someone and then go to them moments later and take it back.

These thoughts plague my mind as I stare with mild erotic interest, as well as an undercurrent of distaste, at my computer screen. It's video of Trista and me on The Deck last night. I don't need the replay to remind me of the vivid details.

Of how I stalked toward her in The Social Room and pulled her from the hostess stand without a word. She didn't resist, but I noticed her worrying at her lower lip nervously. I damn well know it's because she was wondering what everyone was thinking of her. I made one concession when I hit the hallway lobby and asked her, "Do you want this?"

She didn't hesitate in her response, but it was tentative. A light nod of her head, although I could still see the worry in her eyes about backlash.

"Are you sure?" I repeated. Even though my dick was already hard with anticipation of what I was going to do, I gave her another chance to say "no".

Her words were clear and convincing so I accepted

them, even though they made me feel weird at the same time. She'd said, "Yes, I want this. Besides, we have ten days left on our deal, then I won't have to show my face in here again."

"Are you that embarrassed?" I asked her, my gut churning that perhaps I was fucking her up in the head by doing things with her publicly.

She immediately shook her head. "Only to the extent of dealing with those looks from coworkers. It would be different if I didn't work here."

It had relieved me I wasn't corrupting her, but it also reminded me... our time together was limited.

I certainly wanted to make the best of it, so I brought her out to The Deck. We hadn't fucked out there before, and as I watch the video of what we did last night, I think it might have been the most intimately erotic thing we've done together. More so than me eating her out in The Orgy room while men held her legs, or fucking her with Kynan.

I simply pulled her out there, her sexy heels clacking on the clear, acrylic see-through flooring. Everyone's eyes were on us and I didn't need to look around to know that.

I felt it.

Everyone wondering why Jerico Jameson was interested in this girl.

What was so special about her?

I was trying to figure that out myself, almost the

entire time I was on The Deck with her.

When I pulled her right up to the acrylic wall that let us see the glitter of Vegas but didn't let the rest of Vegas look in, I turned her so the front of her body was pushed up against the glass.

I wondered about the special hold she seems to have on me as I pulled her dress up around her hips, pressed my body against hers so she was sandwiched between me and the wall, and then slipped my fingers into her underwear and got her off quickly.

You'd never know by the video that such deep thoughts were running through my head. Especially not when she came beautifully on my fingers, then I quickly opened my pants, freed my cock, and put a condom on. Granted… my mind went blissfully blank when I drove into her from behind while she stood pressed against the wall. Her palms were spread on the acrylic, fingertips trying to dig in. Her head was turned, cheek resting against the coolness, and she groaned as I moved slowly in and out of her. My legs were slightly bent to give me better upward momentum, and while I fucked her slowly, I did it deep. Every drive into her pussy, my hips rocked under and my ass muscles clenched violently.

I'm amazed as I watch that my hips have that much flexibility, but when I think about how good she felt around me, I know my body was reacting on its own instinct to maximize every single feeling between us.

Yes, it was the most intimate sex we'd had and we

were fully clothed. But it revealed a few truths. One, Trista definitely has some type of hold on me. Funnily enough, she doesn't even know it and I'll not admit it. Two, not once last night as I slowly fucked her on The Deck did I get a rush out of doing it in front of other people. They all melted away, and I didn't think about it at all. I only cared about how wet Trista was and how she made these cute little panting sounds as she rotated her hips, trying to encourage me to go faster. Even as I slid out of her after a massive orgasm that left my knees shaking and smoothed down her dress before I zipped up, I didn't think about us being in the sex club.

There was only me and her.

"Fuck," I curse as I realize something's happening to me that is beyond my control. I tap on a key to stop the video playing and extract the DVD from my laptop. It's a compilation of the greatest moments between Trista and me. While this would certainly make Jayce's eyebrows raise, it's nothing compared to the spectacular footage of her swallowing my cock while Kynan fucked her from behind.

"Jesus fuck," I mutter a second curse and toss the DVD on top of a stack of printed pictures taken from the video, most of them impressive quality. There's no doubt it's Trista being defiled in a dozen different glorious ways.

My stomach churns at the thought of turning these over to Jayce. He'll be disgusted, think horrible thoughts about his sister. He'll be beyond furious with me, but that's what I want, right? To dig the knife in. To get my revenge. To cause him the deepest kind of pain.

With a sigh, I pick up the pile of raunchy revenge. I push out of my chair and walk over to the mahogany built-in that runs the length of my office. It has cabinets along the bottom for storage of business documents, which are locked, and open shelving on the top hutch where I have displayed various knickknacks, photos, and objet d'art the designer picked out. And in the center, there is a large open space that exposes the wall behind. A framed print of Ansel Adam's famous photograph of the Snake River in Wyoming hangs there. It was a gift from Bridger when The Wicked Horse Vegas opened.

I pull on the left edge of the frame and it swings away from the wall on hinges, exposing a safe behind. It was a stupid touch to put in when the club was built because I don't have anything that secretive or expensive to protect within this office. I've never even locked it and long forgot the combination, knowing my office was secure with the digital security system on it.

I'm going to put it to beneficial use now.

To hide dirty videos and photos of Trista and me.

I throw them inside, shut the safe door, and swing the picture shut.

Shut it all out for now.

Turning, I head to the door and pull the black tuxedo jacket off the hanger before I slide it on. My tie is already in a state of perfection. It's time for me to pick up Trista for an evening away from The Wicked Horse.

♦

TRISTA LIVES IN a neighborhood that sits in between middle and low class. When I pull my Range Rover into the short, concrete driveway, I take in the small bungalow house that can't be more than twelve-hundred square feet total. There's a "For Sale" sign out front, and it surprises me. Trista hasn't mentioned she was selling her home, and this kind of bugs me. Since I learned about her niece, I've come to know a little more about her because well… in between the fucking, there's been some talking.

I know she dropped out of college in the middle of her sophomore year because she just didn't like it, that she hates raw coconut but toasted is fine, and she worked for a douche of a dentist for years who fired her when she had to miss work because of Corinne's surgery. Trista likes goofy reality shows like *The Bachelor* and *Naked and Afraid* because she says they're so ridiculous they make her laugh, but the only movies she'll watch are science fiction or fantasy because it's worth the price of a ticket to be transported out of reality for a little bit. Fuck… I know she won a spelling bee when she was in third grade over the entire middle school, but I don't know why she's selling her house.

I make my way up to the front door. It's still light

enough outside to see, but the porchlight is on anyway. I'm not nervous in the slightest, because I keep telling myself this isn't really a date. I have a black-tie function to go to tonight. When I asked Trista to go with me, it was in lieu of working at The Wicked Horse tonight. It's part of her employment with me, so absolutely nothing to be nervous about.

Nope.

Don't care I'm meeting her mom and niece.

I barely knock on the door twice before it's swung open and I'm looking at Trista's mom. They look unbelievably alike although her mom's face is slightly aged and she's a little curvier. But past that, the resemblance is astonishing. At least Trista will know she's going to be a knockout when she's her mom's age, which I guess would have to be early fifties.

"Hello," she says warmly and motions me into a small living room with a wide smile. "You must be Jerico. I'm Trista's mom, Jolene."

"It's a pleasure to meet you," I say, calling on my suave side I've cultured over the years since going into private business. I've had to schmooze with big wigs, including everything from U.S. senators to sheiks.

I'm prepared to engage in small talk if necessary, but Trista walks out of a small hallway wearing a beautiful, sleeveless gown I bought for her and had delivered today. It's a deep sapphire blue and made of satin. It's simplistic yet very elegant with a square neckline and thin crisscross straps across her shoulders. It drops wickedly low in the back. While it's not overly tight, it perfectly silhouettes her body. She did her hair in a loose bun that sits low on the right side of her head with wisps of hair left out to frame her face and long neck.

She looks simply amazing as I drink her in, perusing her up and down. When I finally catch her eyes, she's smirking at me. I give her a wink right back and tell her, "You look stunning. I'm glad the gown fit."

Trista gives a one-time around twirl, and my throat goes slightly dry at her bare back. I sneak a peek over at her mother, who has one arm across her stomach and the other pressed over her mouth where I can tell she's hiding an extremely affectionate and proud smile if the light in her eyes is any indication.

"So beautiful," Jolene finally says. "But then, I'd say that if you were wearing a burlap sack."

Trista rolls her eyes at her mom. "You have to say that. You're my mom."

Jolene laughs and waves off her daughter's comment. Trista walks over to the couch and for the first time, I notice the little girl sitting there, reading a book.

Her niece, Corinne. She looks like any ordinary child would look, and I see the family resemblance although Corinne's hair is darker than Trista and Jolene's.

Trista bends over her, putting her hand under Corinne's chin to lift it so she gets her attention. "Can you say hello to Mr. Jameson?"

Corinne's eyes cut to me, and she gives a lackluster, "Hello."

"Hi Corinne," I say with a smile. "It's nice to meet you."

Her eyes drop to her book again, and Trista's eyes go dim with worry.

Jolene walks over to the couch and sits down beside Corinne as she says, "Now, you two get out of here and enjoy your night. Corinne and I are going to read some books for a while and maybe watch a movie."

Corinne doesn't react, but I catch the look between mom and daughter that says all at once, "We love this little girl, yet we can't make everything right in her world."

Jolene gives a confident nod to Trista—a silent statement that she's got it covered. Trista smiles and bends over to kiss Corinne's head. "Night-night, sweet girl. I'll see you tomorrow morning for pancake day, okay?"

At that, Corinne lifts her head and gives Trista a delighted smile. "Can I help you flip them?"

Trista makes a scoffing sound. "Well, duh. Of course you're going to flip them, silly."

Corinne giggles, and the lines of worry around Trista's eyes disappear.

"Okay, we're out of here," Trista says as she turns to me with a smile. I hold my hand out to her, and she takes it. Turning to her mom, I say, "It was nice to meet you, Jolene. And you too, Corinne."

Jolene gives me a sweet smile as she puts her arm around Corinne's shoulder. I even get a shy smile from the little girl.

We walk out of Trista's home and when we hit the sidewalk that cuts over to the driveway, I say, "Corinne having a bad day?"

Trista sighs in frustration. "Danielle was supposed to call her today but didn't."

Never met Trista's sister, but I can categorically say I officially can't stand either of her siblings.

When we reach the car, I open the passenger door and help her in. When she settles and starts to grab the seat belt, I ask with a jerk of my head over my shoulder at the realtor sign in the yard. "You're selling your house?"

Trista grimaces. "Trying to. Had a buyer, which would have given me the equity I needed to pay off my... um... loan, but found out there's a termite problem. So that fell through. I'm kind of at a standstill now because I don't have the money to fix the damage."

Oddly, I'm relieved that's the reason she's selling, and not because she may be moving away. I give her a nod and close the door.

When I get in on my side, I turn to her. "Do you need some money to get it fixed?"

Trista's head snaps my way. "What?"

"Money," I repeat. "A loan."

Trista snorts at me. "No thank you. My indentured servitude to you is almost up. I need to get out and find a job with real benefits."

I narrow my eyes at her. "I mean a real loan. With a long-term repayment and low interest. I'd help you out if you needed it."

Her head tilts to the side. "Why? Your favor to Jayce has essentially been repaid."

If I tell her the truth, it would be something along the lines of, *"Well, Trista… see, I care for you. I think. I'm not sure. I've got all these crazy feelings that I've never had before. Not with Michelle. Not with anyone."*

But of course, I don't tell her that because this thing will be over in ten days and we'll go our separate ways. Whether I use my relationship with Trista to hurt her brother remains to be seen, but I'm not about to give in to admitting any of these feelings that might be nothing more than a passing fancy.

So instead, I just say, "If you need help, call me. If not, that's fine too."

"Okay," she says hesitantly and before it can get anymore awkward, I change directions.

Leaning across her, I open the glove compartment and pull out a black velvet box. I open it and show her the contents.

Trista gasps as she ogles the diamond necklace in horror. "You said this wasn't a date."

I grimace, because I did tell her that in a fit of anxiety after I asked her to go to this, then hid behind my excuse that it was part of her job duties to me. "Relax, Trista. It's on loan from a friend. It turns into a pumpkin at midnight."

Trista's chest decompresses with the amount of air she expels in relief, but then I reach into my coat pocket and pull out a much smaller box. Handing it to her, I say, "But... I did buy these for you to wear with the necklace. They're yours to keep."

I busy myself with taking the necklace out of the box to undo the clasp. It's a beautiful graduated diamond tennis necklace that I think Helena told me was a total of ten carats. The diamond earrings I bought are each a carat, although I could have afforded much more and had contemplated something much bigger. But that spoke too much of things I wasn't ready to talk about, so I went smaller so there was no pressure on either side.

"They're beautiful," Trista murmurs as she looks at the earrings.

"Here," I say gruffly as I hold the necklace up. "Turn around so I can put this on you."

I easily clasp the necklace around her neck, running my fingers over her bare shoulder when I'm done. I get a blast of satisfaction over the way she shivers. She turns back in her seat, taking her gold hoops out of her ears and putting in the diamond solitaires. Pulling the visor mirror down, she looks at herself with a smile.

"Thank you," she says without looking at me. Her

voice is so warm with affection, I feel my throat constrict. Almost as if she could sense my unease, she adds, "For a non-date... you know, actually just working tonight, I'm taking home a pretty nice haul."

The tension within me releases, and I laugh at her. "Just the earrings, let me remind you."

Trista grins as she turns in her seat to face me. She puts a palm on my thigh and squeezes. "Seriously... thank you. The earrings are totally unnecessary but totally appreciated."

I smile back at her, feeling like I just won something. A prize. A medal. Something big and shiny that denotes I achieved something monumental here. I'm quite afraid the warm feelings I'm developing for Trista are the achievement, and I don't know if that makes me happy or scared.

CHAPTER 22

Trista

JERICO AND I meander along the perimeter of the ballroom, looking at the items available for silent auction bids. The charity dinner is being held at the Bellagio and is set to begin soon. But first, patrons are liquored up and then set loose on the tables, all to raise money for homeless veterans.

"Do you do this often?" I ask Jerico as he strolls along with me. Each of us have a glass of champagne in hand, but that doesn't stop him from putting his other hand on my bare lower back, which is super sensitive to his fingers.

"Charity events?" he asks to clarify and I nod as I look at a set of front-row tickets to Adele along with backstage passes. I don't even bother to look at the bids, because I couldn't even afford to touch it.

I'm surprised Jerico does fancy events like this. Not that he's not suave and sophisticated as well as rich, so he can afford to do these things. But the man I know is completely satisfied to stay tucked in his club, running his business and fucking until his heart is content, so it's just a little odd. Not the charity itself. Given his military connections, I get why this would be important to him.

The next item we come to is a pair of boxing gloves that are old and worn. As I look closer, I note they've been signed by Muhammed Ali. I gasp as I lean forward to look at them, and then my eyes glance down to the paper where people can write their bids. There are several already, but the last one makes me swallow hard.

$9,500.

Holy shit.

"You a fan?" Jerico asks, nodding at the photo of Ali hanging on the wall above the gloves.

"Of boxing," I tell him with a smile. "I love it, and well… Ali was one of the greats."

"I would have never pegged you as a fan of boxing," Jerico muses. "Hockey, maybe. Football, I can see. But not boxing."

"Hello," I reply tartly with a roll of my eyes. "This is Vegas. Boxing is huge here."

"That it is," he murmurs before taking a sip of his champagne.

"Not that I've ever been to a live event, but I'll usually go to a sports bar and watch." I turn to look back at the gloves, knowing they'll fetch a very good price. "I hope more people bid on those gloves. Totally worth more than that."

"I'm with you," Jerico says. "I paid almost twice as much for them at a non-charity auction."

My head snaps around, the champagne sloshing in my glass. "You donated those?"

"Yup," he says with a shrug. "I have all kinds of sports memorabilia, and this was definitely a worthy cause. I'm sure these gloves will go for a lot more. There are some serious spenders here tonight."

He's not kidding. The number of jewels being worn by the women is almost blinding, and some of the bids I've seen have been in the tens of thousands of dollars. It's mind boggling to me.

Jerico and I walk around a bit more, and he bids on a painting by a local artist I didn't particularly care for, but that stuff is so subjective anyway. He also steps aside for a moment and talks privately with the man in charge of the auction, but I don't suppose it was a necessary introduction to me. And then someone is at a microphone, asking everyone to take their seats at their assigned tables for the meal to be served.

We're at a table with six other people who Jerico knows. It hits me suddenly that he's not just a hermit who hides in The Wicked Horse, but a real businessman. He owns a prominent security-consulting company and is probably very involved with the community if he's attending functions like this.

I sit quietly, feeling like Julia Roberts in *Pretty Women* as the men discuss business and politics and the women talk to each other and ignore me. I only hope to God they don't bring escargot because I definitely cannot eat it, and I don't feel like being embarrassed by flinging a shell across the room.

When the salad is served, however, the chatter across the table dies down and Jerico turns slightly toward me as we eat. Leaning over, he whispers, "I hate all this polite chitchat."

I have to swallow down a giggle before I whisper back to him. "Well, suck it up and eat your salad."

Jerico responds by putting his hand on my leg, giving it a squeeze, and then using his fingers to pull at the silk of my gown. He gets it to rise right to my knees and then his hand is snaking under. I slap a hand on his wrist, look around the table to see everyone engaged in food or personal talk, and then I make a decision.

Not to stop him but to pull his hand up higher. I do this while watching Jerico's nostrils flare and his eyes darken with arousal. But he does nothing more than squeeze the inside of my thigh before taking his hand away. I grin at him in satisfaction when he leans over once more to whisper, "Would you have really let me finger you under the table?"

"Yes," I whisper back to him, my skin tingling with the prospect of what I almost let him do.

"Dirty girl," he says with appreciation in his eyes. "But even I have my limits on what I'll do in public. Besides, you're too much of a screamer. We would have never gotten away with it."

He's so right. It would have been stupid, but I still cherish that feel of his hand on my leg knowing he was thinking of me in that way.

The salads are removed efficiently after we finish. Within moments, the main course is served—Kobe beef tenderloin and lobster tails—and private talk resumes around the table. Not sure this is really the norm, but Jerico is not engaging anyone, content to talk to me as we eat.

"So… tomorrow is pancake day, huh?" he asks as he cuts into his steak.

I nod as I do the same. "I'm trying to establish routines… habits with Corinne. Things she can count on. Sunday is always pancake day."

"You think her mom is going to come back?" Jerico asks, stilling his utensils to look at me.

I stop cutting my steak. "I know this sounds awful, but at this point… I hope not. She's so inconsistent and unpredictable. I don't think Corinne can handle her coming back and going away again. My mom and I are giving her a stable home. With her illness and recovery, that's the most important thing."

"And pancakes," Jerico adds with a smile as he goes back to his meal.

"God, she loves pancakes," I say with a laugh and slice off a small piece of steak. "She'd eat them every meal, every day."

Jerico nods, chewing on a piece of steak. I take the opportunity to do the same and almost moan in pleasure over how tender it is. I can't afford steak at all, much less steak like this.

"What's the one thing you would eat every day for every meal if you could?" Jerico asks, and I'm not at all surprised by what seems like an inane question, but really… we ask each other this kind of stuff all the time.

"This steak," I say as I cut into another piece. That gets me a grin from Jerico. "But seriously… I think gummy bears. I'm addicted to them."

Jerico grimaces, and I may have ruined his delicious dinner. I eat another piece of steak and make a move on my lobster tail as I ask, "What about you? What would be your one thing?"

"Easy question," he says with the same confidence and authority by which he commands me when we're naked. "Red velvet cake.

It's odd we're eating the finest meal I've ever had and yet we're talking about pancakes and red velvet cake, both of which are like little luxuries to me since I try to watch carbs and sweets. It's why I make a stab at some asparagus and ignore the baked potato.

Our conversation continues, light and steady, not too personal but not inconsequential either like talking about the weather. As the meal winds down, an orchestra starts playing music. By the time the desserts are cleared—and okay, I tried some of the chocolate mousse—people were hitting the dance floor or roaming around the auction tables again.

Jerico jumps in on a conversation beside him, but when they start talking about golf, I tune them out. Instead, I turn slightly in my chair and watch the dancers, marveling at the gorgeous designer gowns and jewelry of the other women. No doubt, I'm not wearing as much in jewels or clothing, but as I look around at the men in the room, there's a little bit of pride within me knowing I'm here with the hottest man. I've seen several women appraising him openly, and I wonder if any of them have been with him at the club.

A warm hand squeezes my shoulder, and Jerico leans toward me. "Want to dance?"

"You dance?" I ask with slight disbelief. I mean, this guy rescues kidnap victims and blows up shit. Oh, and he has kinky sex. I didn't peg him as a ballroom dancer.

"I can get by," he says with a smirk as he stands from his chair and holds his hand out to me.

When I take it, he pulls me up and immediately into him so our bodies are touching. "Well, I haven't been to a formal dance since prom in high school, although I'm sure I could probably still pull off the Macarena."

Jerico laughs and leans down for a spontaneous and affectionate kiss that's over before it begins, and then he's tugging me toward the gleaming parquet floor. I hope I can manage to handle it in my high heels.

When he reaches the center, Jerico pulls me into his

arms with such smoothness it seems as if no effort was expended on his part. He leads and I follow. It turns out that I can apparently dance, even though I'll give the credit to him.

"Enjoying yourself?" he asks as he looks down at me. It's almost a magical moment as his hand splays across my lower back, his thumb rubbing my skin. His other hand clasps mine and he holds me intimately close. I feel like a princess.

"Very much," I admit to him. "Thank you for bringing me."

"Thank you for coming," he says back politely, but his voice is a low rumble that sounds sexy as hell and makes me want to pull him into the bathroom and take advantage of him.

I try to make sure our relationship stays where he wants it to so I can't get any expectations that would later be dashed, reminding myself I am his employee first and foremost. "It was a pleasurable part of my job to accompany you."

Jerico stares at me a moment, his expression flummoxed. But then he grumbles, "You and I both know damn well it's not part of your job. It's a fucking date."

I'm completely shocked by his renunciation, which is hilarious. I laugh playfully as I look up at him. "Well, try not to sound so put out by it."

He growls what might be a string of curses, but they're cut off as his mouth connects with mine. It's a hot kiss but not erotic. One of those where his open mouth moves slowly over mine, yet only our lips touch. It's sweet and intimate and… caring?

When he pulls back, he looks a little off-kilter as if he can't believe he just did that. I've always known Jerico is the type of man who doesn't commit for the long term, and he looks almost spooked right now.

I immediately start back up conversation. "Okay, don't you think it's about time given all the dirty, filthy things I've let you do to me that you tell me a little something about your background? Like what were you like growing up and did you have a dog? Oh, and how did you come to live in Las Vegas?"

I hold my breath, wondering if Jerico will shut down on me. Instead, he gives me a smile that's filled with fondness for his past. "You know I'm from New Hampshire already and I don't have a big family, but I was extremely close to my mom and dad. My dad was a carpenter and my mom ran a home business making and selling soaps."

I smile because of the tone of affection in his voice for his parents.

"After I got out of the military and decided to start my own private contracting company, I looked at a lot of places to put down the company's roots. I considered places like D.C. or New York City, but ultimately decided on Vegas because there's a lot of private wealth here and need for security services. And for the government stuff, we don't need to be in Washington to communicate with them. In fact, they come here to us if they have a mission they want us to bid on."

"Do you miss New Hampshire?" I ask him.

"Yeah… I miss the snow and how gorgeous it is in the fall. I go back once in a blue moon on vacation, but it's hard to take time off. And with my parents gone, it's not the same."

"I bet," I say softly as I slide my hand from his shoulder to his neck. I stroke my thumb there in commiseration.

"What about you?" he asks, and this surprises me. While I'm all kinds of nosy because I happen to just like Jerico on a personal basis, I always sort of felt he didn't need to know anything about me. "You've told me about Corinne, and your mom seems nice, but what was it like growing up here?"

"Well, Vegas is my hometown, although the Vegas I live in isn't the glitzy strip. I don't go there very often."

"What about your dad?" Jerico prods.

I give a little shrug as I turn my gaze over Jerico's shoulder. It's a bit of a sore subject. "He took off when I was about two and never came back. Left my mom for another woman."

"Jayce's mom?" Jerico asks so I have to look back to him. His eyebrows are furrowed in confusion.

I give a sardonic smile, because it is a bit confusing. "My mom was married first to a man named Eldridge.

They had Danielle, but he split before she turned one. Mom then met and married Jayce's dad, Vince, within like six months after her divorce. He had Jayce already. Jayce was about three years old when Vince married my mom. Jayce's mom was apparently on drugs and unstable. They had me three years later."

"So you and Jayce share the same father, but you and Danielle share the same mother?" he states for clarification.

"I have this whole chart with a colored graph I can show you," I quip, loving the way his eyes drop to my mouth as my lips purse up. "Even I get confused sometime."

"I expect you and Jayce aren't very close then," Jerico murmurs. "I mean… he was only around you a few years. He would have been around five when your dad left, right?"

When I shake my head, the cute smile slides from my face and Jerico notices. "When I say my dad left, I mean he left. Left Jayce behind too. He stayed with my mom because he didn't want to go back to his mom, and besides that, she couldn't be found. My mom raised him with Danielle and me, and I can tell you it was no picnic trying to house, feed, and clothe three children on what she made as a waitress."

Jerico's eyes furrow again in confusion, but unless I'm crazy, I see a bit of hardness there too. Perhaps he finds it as distasteful as I do that a man leaves his children and never looks back.

But then his gaze softens, and he pulls me in close. He drops my hand, his arms going around my waist. Mine go up to loop around his shoulders. We sort of sway back and forth with our bodies pressed tight. Jerico's green eyes focus on mine with an unusual warmth. Tilting his head down until his face is close to mine, he asks, "So how did a girl such as yourself wind up working in The Wicked Horse, letting me fuck you in front of others, and learning how to be sexually uninhibited like I bet you never thought you could ever be?"

His words slither through me, leaving tingles in their wake. If Jerico wanted to drop me to the floor right now and take me, I'd let him. But the man asked a legitimate question that needs answered.

"She ended up at The Wicked Horse because she needed help and didn't have a choice," I murmur as I thread my fingers through the back of his hair. His eyes flutter closed briefly and his head pushes against my hands like a cat demanding more. "But she ended up underneath *you* learning all kinds of wicked things because she wanted to. It's as simple as that."

Jerico's eyes open. They're dark and glittery at the same time.

His lips curve up and just before he kisses me, he says, "Good answer, Trista. Very good answer."

CHAPTER 23

Jerico

"**I** DON'T CARE if you're having employee problems, Seth," I growl into the phone. "My business is based on two things. First, that people like to explore their sexuality in a safe environment, and second, that if they're a little anxious about doing so, they can have a couple of drinks to loosen up first. That can't fucking happen when the liquor I ordered from you doesn't show up."

"I know, I know," Seth hastily says in a soothing tone. "I've pinpointed the problems to the loaders. They're not double checking. But I'm getting it fixed, I swear."

"You better get it fixed and fast," I warn him. "This is Vegas, Seth. You're not the only distributor in town, you know?"

"I got it," he says with relief in his voice that he hasn't been fired. "I'm sending over the missing boxes that weren't in the delivery and only charging you fifty percent for them."

"I appreciate that," I say as my frustration starts to seep away. It's all these petty little problems of running a business that cause stress, and they can add up.

While it's true Seth isn't the only game in town, I don't want to lose him as my distributor because he has a special service that the others don't do. He carries drink condiments so I don't have to order those from a separate distributor. Salt for margaritas, cherries for Manhattans, or limes for your vodka tonic, Seth carries all that shit, which cuts down on one extra thing I have to do.

"I'll have my truck there midafternoon, will that work?" he asks.

"Sounds good. Thanks, Seth."

I disconnect the call and look down at my written to-do list. It's my habit every morning. I have a digital list on my computer which I look at but then I take the five most important things and write them down on paper. I have to accomplish the tasks before I can go to bed at night.

It's a Sunday, but that doesn't mean I don't work. I run two businesses at this point, and while I have good help to manage both, I still have the lion's share of the work. Which means I work pretty much every day.

Looking down at my list, I take my pen and cross through "Call Seth and chew his ass out."

That was number six on the list—an add-on item

after my head bartender called me freaked out after realizing half the delivery of liquor was missing. To put his mind at rest, I pick up the phone and buzz his station, giving him the good news that more alcohol was on its way. When that's done, I look at my watch and realize that it's only eleven and I have finished six of my top priorities.

I do work hard, but I also have some days where I knock off early and can do something I enjoy. That could be a rip-roaring, raunchy fuck in the club, a round of golf, or even just sitting in my apartment watching ESPN. Only the last two of those things are viable today since Trista's spending her day with Corinne.

There's only baseball or NASCAR on right now, neither of which I'm a huge fan of, so it appears I'm going golfing, which is something I really love to do. I pick up the phone to call the country club I belong to so I can find out available tee times, but I don't even get to dial when there's a soft knock on my door and it immediately opens. Only two people walk in here without waiting for my invitation—Kynan and Trista. It used to be only Kynan, but Trista's now on my allowed list. I happen to know Kynan's in D.C. this weekend so I know it's Trista before I even see her. A zinging jolt of electrical excitement courses through me.

Now that is a weird fucking feeling.

She pops her head in first and gives me a tentative smile. "You busy?"

"Not at all," I tell her as I wave her in.

She disappears for a moment, and then opens the door wider. I see she's carrying a large, plastic container that's dome shaped and has a handle on top. My eyes only flick to it briefly before coming back to her. She's much better to look at.

Shutting the door behind her, she walks up to my desk with a goofy grin on her face and sets the plastic container in front of me. I look down at it, and then up to her. "What's that?"

"Something I made for you this morning," she says, unlocking the tabs at the bottom. She lifts the dome top off, and I'm staring at a cake in front of me.

Slowly, I look back up to her. "You made me a cake?"

"Not just any cake," she says while wagging a finger at me. "A four-layer, homemade red velvet cake with whipped mascarpone icing."

"Jesus," I mutter as I look at the cake, wondering what this weird squeezing sensation is in my chest. When I look back up to her, I have to ask her again, "You made that just for me?"

"Just for you," she says with satisfaction all over her face. "You said it was your favorite, and I had some time this morning after pancakes."

I push out of my chair and wave a hand at the cake. "You just happened to have all these ingredients, huh? You routinely use something as odd as mascarpone?"

Her grin turns mischievous as she shrugs. "Well, I may have had to go to the grocery store for a few things."

Jesus fuck. I can't believe she did that for me.

My mind races over the years, and I can't remember anyone doing something so randomly nice for me. So spontaneous and with the sole intention of doing it to please me.

Picking up the cake, I round the desk and head for the side door that connects to my kitchen. "Let's take this next door."

I don't miss the disgruntled expression on Trista's face as she clearly expected me to act differently. I'm sure she was thinking I'd be a bit more effusive in my praise, and I intend to be.

Just… in my apartment.

She follows me through the door as I balance the cake on my hand. I immediately lay it down on my kitchen counter and spin around just as she's walking through the door, taking her face in my hands and walking right into her. My mouth hits hers. She gives a huff of surprise as I turn slightly and back her into the refrigerator. Angling my head, I kiss her deeply. It's possible because she angles hers the other way, opening her mouth to give me entrance.

Yes, it's a deep kiss, but it's not sexual. It's a show of unbridled happiness that makes me feel like a kid, or perhaps it's gratitude that Trista perhaps thinks this is something other than "just sex".

When I pull away, Trista's cheeks are pink and she's slightly panting. She whispers breathlessly to me, "I should make you cake more often."

The grin that breaks wide is my answer, followed by another swift kiss. Then I'm turning away from her and grabbing a fork out of my drawer. Without any pomp, and certainly no circumstance to wait for a plate, I punch my fork down into the top of the cake and pull a huge chunk out.

"Oh, my God." Trista giggles as she comes to stand beside me at the counter. I angle toward her as I bring the fork to my lips, open my mouth wide, and shove the cake in. Cheeks bulging and the taste of rich cake and lightly sweet, tangy frosting coating my tongue, I groan in satisfaction. Our eyes stay locked as I chew and chew and chew, and finally swallow the heaven in my mouth. Trista's eyes are sparkling with humor and a bit of pride.

"Good?" she asks.

I give a swipe of my tongue over my bottom lip to catch some stray frosting there. "It's amazing. Thank you."

She beams a brilliant smile as she sets the cake carrier on the counter and turns toward the door that leads back into my office. "You're welcome. Now... I've got to get going."

"Wait," I say as I snag her arm and turn her back to me. "You just got here."

"And my work is done," she says impishly, going to

her tiptoes to give me a quick kiss. "I'm meeting Mom and Corinne for lunch, and I've got to get going."

Well, there goes all thought of spending my afternoon with Trista in bed rather than golfing.

But I'd never begrudge her time with Jolene and Corinne. Their unity right now is extremely important. I do pull her into me and wrap my arms around her waist after throwing the fork into the sink. Trista's hands come to my chest as she looks up at me curiously.

"Take the night off," I tell her softly and I have to admit, the way her eyes go warm makes me feel fucking really good. "Make it an entire day and night thing with Corinne, okay?"

"Really?" she asks with sweetest type of surprise in her eyes.

"Yeah," I murmur as I tighten my arms around her. "I'll keep myself occupied with the cake tonight."

Her lips quirking, she gets a playful look in her eyes. "We could… um… FaceTime each other later."

My eyebrows rise with interest, but I play a little stupid. "FaceTime?"

"Naked. FaceTime." She annunciates each word slowly, and my dick perks up at this suggestion.

And for a man who has done about every dirty thing imaginable, it hits me hard that this is something new. Something I've never done with another woman and now, I'm glad she's not coming so I can have something new and unique just with Trista.

"What time might you be calling me?" I ask in a husky voice.

"Be ready around eleven," she says, pressing into me. "Clothing is optional."

"Wrong," I tell her with a shake of my head. "Naked is mandatory."

Trista giggles. It's a great sound. It's not girlish or immature. It's sweet and melodic, and while I like making her scream and cry out, I like making her giggle too.

"Okay, I've really got to get going," she says with a smile, then gives me another quick kiss.

With a hand behind her head, I ensure it's not quick, but one that's deep and meaningful. When I finally pull back, I rub my nose against hers. "Thank you again for the cake. It was the nicest thing anyone's done for me for as long as I can remember."

Trista sort of jerks in my arms and leans her back to look at me. "Now that's just sad, Jerico."

"Pitiful really," I agree with a pathetic downward turn of my lips.

Patting me on the chest, Trista smirks. "I'll make you another cake."

Yes, I'd like that a lot.

I don't get to tell her that because she's pulling out of my arms. "I really have to go. When you're touching me, it makes it hard to remember that."

Snickering, I make a playful grab at her, but she

sidesteps me, blows me a quick kiss, and then disappears through the door back into my office. I follow, enjoying my view of her ass as she sashays out without a backward glance. Smiling, I walk to the door and lock it, intent on spending the afternoon in my apartment now, eating cake and watching TV. Not the most exciting of days, but I figure I'll spend part of my time thinking of interesting things I can show her while we FaceTime tonight.

But first…

I head to the built-ins, swing the Ansel Adams print away from the wall, and pull down on the lever that opens the safe. After I snatch the manila envelope out, I walk to my desk. Pulling my rolling chair back, I sit down and lean forward with my elbows on my knees, staring at the packet of lewd fuckery I hold in my hands. I'd even addressed it to Jayce, having easily found out where he lives due to my contacts through The Jameson Group.

My revenge used to be very important to me, but I realize that the moment Trista showed me that cake, it's simply not anymore.

I can't risk hurting Trista just to hurt her brother.

Can't do it.

She's more important than revenge.

She makes me feel better than any retribution toward Jayce could ever do.

I look at the gray box under my desk. It's my shred

bin and it gets picked up once a month as I don't have a lot of paper documents that are confidential. Normally, there's a top on the box that locks but the slot to slide the papers in is really narrow which makes it hard to put a thick stack in there, so I took it off and God only knows where it is now. I'm not worried for the same reason I don't lock my safe. I've got a good security alarm and a lock on the door that's sufficient.

I toss the envelope into the deep rectangular box without a single worry about the contents sitting there for a few days. No different than sitting in an unlocked safe, and I'm afraid I might forget and miss the shred pickup, which is at the end of the week. Then it will be destroyed forever.

But starting this moment... I'm not thinking about it anymore. Not about the photos, or the fucking hot-as-hell video, or the fact I hate Jayce more than anything in this world except perhaps Michelle. I'm not thinking about any of that. I'm letting it go.

I'm letting everything go.

Except Trista.

I'm not giving her up.

CHAPTER 24

Trista

MY PHONE CHIMES, alerting me to a text while I'm in the elevator on the way up to The Wicked Horse. I reach into my bag, pull it out, and smile when I see Jerico's text.

You're relieved of hostess duty tonight. Your job is to keep me company. Meet me in The Social Room.

Shaking my head in amusement, I slip my phone back in my purse just as the elevator doors open. My eyes go to Tamara, who's on hostess duty, and I give her a smile. She doesn't return it, so I lump her into the category of women who have had Jerico once before. I know I should be disgusted by the number of employees he's apparently fucked, but I can't really be. He was single and had no commitments to anyone but himself. He owns a freaking sex club where inhibitions are not allowed and sexual gratification is the name of the game. Why wouldn't he fuck these women?

But he's not now and that makes me feel good.

Doesn't mean he won't start doing that again soon because I've only got nine days left on my work contract with him. Of course, the thought of breaking ties with him doesn't set well with me. I know this started as just casual, impersonal sex, but neither of us can deny it has gradually turned into something more. We've opened up and shared with each other. Committed to monogamy, which wasn't hard for me, but was a first for Jerico in a long time. At least that's what he told me, but when I'd asked him to clarify what a long time meant, he redirected me with a hand between my legs. I forgot all about my question. In hindsight though, because he didn't want to talk about it, I'm guessing whatever it was wasn't pleasant at all.

My eyes scan The Social Room. Jerico stands at the end of the bar, almost in the exact place he was the night I met him almost three weeks ago. His eyes are pinned on me and even from across the room, I can see the hunger in them. Hunger for only me, and that causes my entire being to ache for him.

I walk his way, putting a little roll in my hips. I'm wearing another sexy black dress with high heels, the standard uniform for the hostess podium, but this one is strapless and hugs every inch of my body.

But Jerico doesn't even bother giving me a critical scan. No, his eyes bore into mine and the closer I get to him, the more I'm sure I want him to just take me right to the floor and fuck me hard.

Shaking my head to try to clear the lustful thoughts—nothing I can do about the wet panties—I put a smile on my face when I reach him. "Hey, gorgeous."

"That's my line," he murmurs as he slides a hand behind my neck and pulls me into him for a kiss. It's nothing but a whisper... a soft sliding of his lips over mine before he pulls back. "Want a drink?"

I cock an eyebrow at him. "That's two nights in a row you've given me off. How am I supposed to fulfill my contract if you won't let me work?"

Jerico doesn't answer at first, but turns to the bartender and orders me a Manhattan, straight up. When he angles his body back my way, he says, "Last night and tonight count toward your contract."

I sidle in closer to him, giving a tug on his silk tie of pale blue with gray diagonal stripes. "Why are you being so nice?"

"You made me a cake," he says simply.

With a husky laugh, I lean in closer to whisper, "I've also swallowed for you many times, and I'd think that would make you a lot nicer than cake."

Jerico laughs, his eyes twinkling for a moment before turning dark.

Potent.

Intense.

Sizzling.

His hand comes up to cup my jaw, and his thumb

runs over my bottom lip. "You going to let me fuck that mouth tonight?"

"If you want," I respond hoarsely. Now my clit is pulsing.

The bartender returns with my drink. Jerico takes it and hands it over. "What do you want to do tonight?"

I take a sip—a large one to steady my nerves—and my hand drops from his tie down to his leather belt where I lay my fingertips lightly on the edge of it. "I want to try the stocks."

Jerico's eyebrows fly upward in surprise. I've not initiated any type of sex in public. It's always been him pulling me off to do something dirty in front of others. He knows part of what gets me off is the wrongness of it all, and I know in a million years he never thought I'd suggest it.

"Are you sure?" he asks, eyes filled with slight worry.

I nod. "I'm feeling adventurous. As our time winds down… well, I think I want to give it my all here. Don't want to walk away with regrets."

Jerico picks up his vodka tonic, takes a sip, and sets it down on the bar. When he turns to look at me, he asks, "What would you say if I offered you a permanent job here?"

Now my eyebrows are the ones to shoot up. "Doing what?"

"Hostess duty," he says.

I take another healthy sip of my Manhattan, all

thoughts of the stocks on temporary hold. After I set my glass down next to his, I say, "I'm not sure how I'd explain this job to my mother."

Jerico's brows furrow. "What does she think you're doing?"

My face flushes with slight embarrassment when I give guilty smirk. "She thinks I'm working as a secretary for The Jameson Group. I've told her as a security firm you're open 24/7, so she thinks I'm working the night shift."

"Huh," Jerico says, not put out by this lie. "You're in the front where no sex occurs and you're just welcoming patrons. That's respectable."

"I suppose I could float that by her," I respond pensively, wondering how to even start a conversation like that with my mom.

Hey Mom... um, I'm working at a sex club, but it's okay... I'm just a hostess who greets people coming in.

"I'm going to have to think about it," I say softly.

"That's fine," Jerico concedes, but his expression is serious and somber. It makes my stomach tighten as he opens his mouth to say something else, and I brace. "But I'd also like to keep seeing you after the contract period is up."

A physical jolt of shock causes me to jerk backward a bit. My eyes have to be as large as saucers. "You would?"

Jerico gives a nonchalant shrug and looks out over the crowd. "Well, you know... you make a fucking phenomenal cake."

I slap him on the chest, and his head turns back to me with a sinful grin.

"Let me amend that," he says with a hand to the back of my neck to pull me close to him. "You're fucking phenomenal in a million different ways, and I'm not ready to stop what we have."

My heart is thundering in my chest because I'm excited at the prospect of more with Jerico, but I'm leery at the same time. I didn't let my heart get too involved so I wouldn't be crushed when I walked away in nine days, and here he is making me open myself up again.

"When you say you don't want to stop what we have," I say carefully, so I understand exactly what he's offering, "are you talking about the club sex?"

Jerico gives me an eyeroll. It looks weird coming from him because he's always so professional and put together. "I'm talking about dating you, Trista. That would include fucking here in the club and a million different other places. Going out to dinner, movies, and whatever other shit people who date do."

"Monogamous, right?" I ask, again not daring to hope.

"You're usually not this dense," he mutters, but then smiles at me. "Yes, monogamous. And if you say you have to think about it, I'm going to redden your ass when I get you in the stocks."

My entire being is flooded with warmth over the fact

Jerico wants to be with me. He wants the emotional connection and not just an impersonal fuck. Still, I play coy, lifting a finger to tap at the corner of my chin as I look upward in contemplation. "Hmmm... let me think—"

Suddenly, Jerico lifts me and throws my body over his shoulder. I shriek in surprise and offense, slapping at his back. "Put me down, you big ape."

I get rewarded with a hard crack of his palm against my ass, crying out from the pain even as my panties get wetter from the pleasure of it.

I yell all kinds of vile curses as Jerico takes me right to The Silo and the stocks room, which is surprisingly empty, but then again, it's early. That usually doesn't get busy until very late when some girl—or even a guy— works up the courage to get locked in and then fucked by multiple people.

When he bends over to set me on wobbly feet, I make the mistake of looking out the glass wall where a few people are walking closer to watch. My nerves go into overdrive and practically explode when I see two of the condiment tray girls glaring at me. My gaze slides to the wooden device that will hold me captive, and I look longingly at it. It's a symbol to me right in this moment that I've got a naughty side that can be celebrated openly, and I have a man I can trust to lock me in there and do whatever he wants to me.

"Second thoughts?" Jerico says as his hands come to

my shoulders. He angles down to kiss my neck.

I shake my head as I stare right back out the window to those watching and shore up my resolve to do this. Right now, it's what I want and what I can accept about this relationship with Jerico. After we're done though, I'm not sure he's going to like my decision.

Jerico makes swift work of locking me up in the stocks. He doesn't even bother undressing me, only telling me to spread my legs apart, which I do. The position isn't comfortable at all. While I can rest my wrists down on the wood, I have to hold my head up. Otherwise, I'd have too much pressure on my windpipe. But what really makes this a huge turn on and well worth the tiny discomforts is that I can't see what Jerico is doing behind me. I can't turn my head and even if I could, the wooden boards would block my view.

I suck in a deep breath when I feel his hands on my hips, pressing his crotch into my backside. He's already hard and the knowledge he's ready just from putting me in this contraption makes me hotter for him. Jerico pulls the bottom of my dress up. It's stretchy and stays banded around my waist, so now my backside, which is covered by a pair of sheer deep green panties made of satin, is exposed for all to see. I feel his bare palms on my ass cheeks and he rubs lightly, sometimes squeezing the twin globes. It's not enough, but it makes me squirm. I push my backside up a little higher, giving him a silent invitation to touch me somewhere else.

Instead, one palm disappears only to return swiftly with a hard crack to my ass. I shriek from the surprise and pain and my hips tilt inward trying to pull my ass out of his reach. Another crack and I cry out again.

"Told you I was going to redden that ass," Jerico growls behind me, and I receive another sharp slap, which was just as forceful, but now I'm not noticing the stinging pain as much. Instead, my sex clenches and releases with need, and I can't help but moan when he strikes me again. Jerico alternates slaps with a soft stroking of his palm across my skin. I need him inside of me so bad I start squirming, moving my legs inward so I can press them together and perhaps ease the ache there.

"Uh-uh-uh, Trista," Jerico says in a soft, patronizing voice as he sweeps his leg left and right to get mine to spread my further. "Bad girl. It's gonna cost you."

I tense, waiting for another blow to my reddened ass, but he slaps me between the legs instead, right against the swollen lips of my pussy and I swear I almost orgasm from that.

Bracing for another blow, I'm stunned when Jerico snakes his fingers under my panties at the back and sinks two fingers into me. I'm so wet it makes a squelching noise, and I wince with embarrassment even as my hips rotate involuntarily to try to draw him in deeper.

"I didn't know spanking you would make you this wet," Jerico murmurs as he withdraws his fingers. Hell, I didn't know it either but apparently, I've got a kinky thing for spanking.

While I can't see what's happening, I know what's coming. Jerico's zipper and the tear of the foil pack to release the condom seem loud. Jerico groans when he rolls it on, and I spread my legs out a little further, my entire body quivering in anticipation.

And then he's rubbing the tip of his cock through my wet folds, having done nothing more than pull the material of my panties aside to give him access. Something about us not taking off a stitch of clothing makes this even naughtier. Jerico pushes the head inside me, pauses just a second, and then simultaneously delivers another slap to my ass as he drives in deep.

So deep my shoulders hit the wooden stocks and the breath is knocked out of me slightly. Doesn't matter though because the feeling of that hard, swollen length inside of me... pushing against the edge of my womb, feels so good I want him to do it again and again.

"Harder," I moan as he starts to slide out, and he rewards me by slamming back in.

"Yes," I hiss in gratitude, and then it's on.

Jerico sets up a brutal pace, thrusting hard and fast. He slaps my ass a few more times, but then his hand reaches around, slips down my panties, and plays with my clit. My blood is already racing and the feelings of him fucking me hard, rolling my clit, and sometimes slapping me is almost too much to bear. My climax starts barreling toward me even though I try to hold it off.

He's barely been fucking me a few minutes, but my entire body tightens as it prepares to break apart.

With a sexy grunt of pleasure, Jerico drives in so deep that my climax is released in an amazingly violent burst that makes me call out his name. As my body trembles and shudders, Jerico practically heaves himself into me, cursing and grunting with pleasure.

"I'm close," he says through gritted teeth, fucking me furiously so his words come out in short bursts.

I wait for that moment I've come to know well—when he'll bury balls' deep and grind against me as he unloads. His pace tells me he's almost there, but then he suddenly stops.

Pulls out of me quickly, so I cry out from the loss of this thickness.

But then he's in front of me, whipping off the condom and staring down at me with eyes so darkened with lust I'm not sure I even see the real Jerico residing in there. One of his hands grabs my jaw as he says, "Open up."

I immediately comply because I told him he could fuck my mouth tonight. Frankly, I love giving him head. It's one of the few times I have power over him. While I can't touch him like I normally would to roll his balls or press my fingers against his anus, I merely double up on my sucking efforts to draw him in as I stare up at him.

His hands come to gently frame my face, and he doesn't move in me the way he did from the back. He's gentle so he doesn't choke me, but he gives it to me as deep as possible.

"God, I love watching my cock slide in and out of that beautiful mouth of yours," Jerico murmurs, stroking a thumb across my cheek. "Not as much as I just enjoyed watching it ram into your cunt, but fuck, baby… this is really good."

I'd smile if my mouth wasn't so full of cock.

Jerico picks up the pace, going a little faster but not as deep. I hollow my cheeks as hard as I can, getting swipes of my tongue on the underside of the head where he's especially sensitive.

I keep my eyes on Jerico and he watches me, both of us so focused on each other the entire world outside of here seems to have melted away. I no longer even think about being in stocks or people and coworkers watching me. All I think about is making Jerico feel good, giving a little hum of need that he gives it up to me.

Jerico sucks in breath between his teeth, baring them with an almost tortured expression on his face. Then he stops, throws his head back, and groans as he starts to come on my tongue. I swallow, my throat working for every spurt in my mouth. He's salty and tangy, and I just love the taste of him.

Huffing out a breath of relief and exhaustion, Jerico pulls his cock from my lips and I flex my jaw. After tucking himself into his pants, he squats down so we're eye level and gives me a soft kiss. "That was incredible," he says huskily when he pulls back.

"Very," I tell him.

He smiles and moves to stand. "Let me get you out of there."

"Wait," I say quickly, and he bends again. His head is tilted in curiosity. "Don't you want my answer?"

"You know I do," he says with a smile.

"Yes, to your job offer," I tell him. "And yes to us continuing to see each other—"

His mouth slams into mine, but I mumble against it. "Wait."

Jerico pulls back. "But... if I'm working here, I don't want to use The Wicked Horse anymore for our... um... intimate moments."

"Excuse me?" he says, his brows furrowing inward, then he immediately stands up. "Wait... don't answer that now. Let me get you out of there so we can go to my apartment."

Before I can say another word, Jerico is behind me, pulling my panties back in place, smoothing my dress down, and unlocking the stocks. I stand up, my back stiff but the ache between my legs very welcomed.

Jerico takes me by the elbow and leads me out the door that goes into the perimeter hallway. As soon as the door closes and we are out of sight and hearing, he turns on me. "Why don't you want to use The Wicked Horse? I mean... what was that we just did?"

So much for waiting to talk until we get to his

apartment.

I jerk my thumb over my shoulder toward the stocks. "That right there was amazing. One of the best sexual experiments of my life. But I can't handle the animosity from the other staff when you like to publicly flaunt me. So, as long as I'm working here, I want our relationship to stay private and away from my coworkers' eyes."

Brows drawing in even closer together, he asks, "So as long as you work for me, no sex in the club. But if you don't work for me, we can fuck in here."

"That about sums it up," I tell him simply.

"And this is all to keep harmony between you and the staff?" he asks for additional clarification.

"Yup."

"Then the job offer to work at the club is revoked," Jerico says as he crowds in close to me. I take a step back, pressing into the wall. His voice goes low... hypnotic. "I'll hire you to work for Jameson Group. You'll work at the office over on Clark Avenue. Then some nights you can join me here, other nights my apartment. Sound fair?"

"You're selling The Jameson Group," I remind him. "That doesn't sound like good job security to me."

Jerico snickers and presses his lips to my head. "It won't be any time soon, and I'll make your employment there a condition of the sale with Kynan."

This is such an easy option that I feel terrible even considering it. Jerico's doing too much for me, and I don't like how it's making me feel. I've never been one to depend on others for help, outside of asking my brother for a loan… and I'll not be making that mistake again.

Resting my hand on Jerico's chest, I say, "Let me think about the job offer."

It's obvious he wants to argue and force me into accepting, but he holds his tongue and gives me an accepting nod. My heart almost doubles in on itself when he asks hesitantly, "But you still want to see me? Regardless of whether I have you in the club or not?"

Smiling wide, I give him a resounding, "Yes. That part's a done deal."

"Then we'll figure out everything else later," Jerico says as he drags me out of The Silo and to his apartment.

CHAPTER 25

Jerico

AFTER PULLING THE seven-iron from my bag, I reach into my pocket and curl my fingers around the golf ball and tee I'd shoved in there after the last hole. I keep my eyes on the flag of this par-three. There's barely any wind so this should be an easy shot to the green.

One foot planted, the other one rises slightly as I bend down to push the tee into the ground with the golf ball already on top of it. I step behind the tee and take a few practice swings.

"Fifty bucks says you don't hit the green," Kynan says as I move in closer.

"You're on," I say without looking at him. I've been on fire today, my confidence in my game at an all-time high. Maybe it's because Trista let me tie her to my bed last night or maybe it's just because I'm currently kicking Kynan's ass, but I know I'll hit the green.

Easiest money ever.

I position myself, rocking left and right a few times

to get stabilized. My head turns to look at the green once more, down to the ball, back to the green, and finally back to the ball. I swing. When I make contact, I know it's a good shot. My eyes lock on the ball as it sails down the fairway but only for a moment. I'm so confident I don't watch it land but rather reach down to pick up my tee. When I stand back up, Kynan's muttering a curse and pulling his wallet out to hand me fifty bucks.

Grinning, I gladly take his money, loving this day. It started with Trista's warm body beside me, and I'd forgotten how nice it was to snuggle with someone and wake up all tangled up in each other. She made breakfast—French toast—and then we took a long, leisurely, and orgasmic shower together. She headed home to get some personal things done, and I met Kynan out here at the golf course an hour ago.

Kynan follows the same routine I just did to get ready for his shot. Normally, we're evenly matched, but I'm riding high today and he won't be able to come close to the groove I've got going. After he tees off, we deposit our clubs back in our bags, which are sitting on hand carts, and we start walking along the fairway to the green.

"I want out by the end of the year," I tell Kynan, but he doesn't show any response. Not a jerk, a head snap my way, or even a "what the fuck?"

"Do you have an official buyout proposal?" he asks, getting right down to business.

It's no secret I want to sell The Jameson Group.

Military special ops have been a big part of my life for the past eleven years, but with almost fifteen months of owning The Wicked Horse under my belt, I know this is all I want to do. It's the next phase of my life. I'm leaving one career and starting another. And who knows, maybe in ten or fifteen years, I'll start another.

But Kynan is the only one I'd trust to take over the business and keep it within the exacting standards I've set. He knows I want out and I've slated him to be the one, but he had no clue my timeline would be this fast. I'm sure he felt I'd stay in another five years or so, which is why I'm surprised he's taking this so casually.

"I've worked up an official proposal and my attorney is reviewing it now," I tell Kynan.

"Without even knowing what you're going to need," Kynan says as we continue walking side by side while pulling our hand carts. "I can tell you right now I don't have the type of money I'm suspecting you're going to want to buy you out."

Here's the thing about private security.

It's expensive.

Whether we're protecting a rock star on tour, rescuing a kidnap victim, gathering intelligence, or doing something so top secret we could land in jail and the government would disavow us, the money is a big reason why I created the company rather than stay in the military for my kicks. The Jameson Group has over fifty special operatives around the world and another hundred security professionals. While the professional security services for the wealthy and elite provide the bread and butter from which we survive, it's the top-secret government contracts where we really earn the big bucks. I personally haven't netted less than three million a year in my pocket after making sure everyone else is paid very, very well and all expenses covered.

While I haven't lived frugally, I've saved most of it, and I really don't have to work another day in my life if I don't want to. But I'm not one to sit around and just play golf all the time, so I'll always be in business one way or the other.

"I've had the business appraised," I tell Kynan as we approach the green. "It came in around twenty-two million."

"I definitely cannot afford that," Kynan says gruffly.

"Relax," I tell him as I set my cart and pull out a club. "That's the value over your lifetime. But I want out now and you're the only one I trust, so I'm prepared to take seven million. Put down whatever you can and I'll finance the rest by you keeping me on the payroll as a consultant."

Kynan's eyebrows shoot upward. "That's actually a little unfair to you. And why the rush?"

I look back to the tee we just left, not seeing the next group there yet, so we have a few minutes to chat. Kynan walks to his ball, which also hit the green but is further from the hole than mine.

"I want out sooner rather than later," I give him the answer to his question. "And to let me get out, I'm willing to accept less than the value. I figure six months is enough time to transition you out of field ops and into the office to run the damn thing."

"What if I don't want out of field ops?" he asks.

"Then do them," I say with a shrug. "It will be your business to run however you want."

"You still didn't answer my question," he says with a smirk.

I blink at him. I thought I had.

So he reminds me. "But why now?"

I give another shrug, trying to act casual. I really hadn't planned on moving this fast, but I want to free up my time. Work has kept me so busy over the years that I haven't had time for things like relationships, but that's going to change. Trista has changed me. Changed what I want in life. "I just want to cut back on work. Start enjoying life, you know. I've worked my ass off doing dangerous stuff and now I want to take it easy. Is that so hard to understand?"

"Not in general," Kynan says with another smirk. "But if you want to take it easy with a particular person, then I'm very intrigued that Mr. Screw A Different Pussy Each Night is going to give that up."

"I already gave it up," I grumble, taking another look at the last tee. It's still empty so we aren't in a rush finish this hole.

"For thirty days was the deal I seem to remember," Kynan says slyly. "I'm guessing you're extending that time."

"Fine, you nosy fuck," I snarl at him. "Yes... I'm seeing Trista and I want to keep seeing her. I don't want anyone else, and I want more time to spend with her. Are you happy?"

"Deliriously so," Kynan says dryly as he lines up to make his putt. I keep my mouth shut, giving him quiet, but I grind my teeth because I know I'm going to take a ton of ribbing from him over this.

To my surprise, from a good twenty feet away, Kynan sinks his putt easily. Content to finish this out, Kynan doesn't say a word but waits for me to go. I'm only about three feet from the hole and can do this with my eyes closed.

I line up, take a few short putting swings, and then step forward. I look from hole to ball and back, then give it a tiny tap. The ball veers slightly to the right, catching the rim of the cup. I watch as it shoots around and then out again.

"Fuck," I growl, and Kynan snickers. He's totally thrown me off my game.

My ball is only about three inches from the hole so I do nothing but reach down and pick it up. It's a "gimme".

It's not until we put our clubs in our bags and start walking along the path to the next tee when Kynan starts in on me. "So… this is real with Trista, huh?"

"Seems so," I say casually, although what I'm doing feels anything but casual.

"Isn't she still under your contract period?" he quizzes.

"Four days left, but we're past that shit," I tell him. "I'll give her the money now if she wants it to pay off that loan shark. And by the way, I've offered her a full-time job at The Jameson Group so part of the buyout will demand you keep her on board."

"Seriously, Jerico," Kynan drawls. "Do you even know if she has the job skills for this?"

"She'd make the perfect receptionist," I tell him as we reach the tee. "She's got plenty of experience."

"But you already have a receptionist," Kynan points out.

I grimace at the reminder. "Yeah… but I'm going to fire her. She's always trying to get in everyone's pants."

"You're fucking right she does," Kynan says, and then points out for his benefit alone, "and she's gotten into mine several times."

And mine… but only once, and I don't do repeats except in select situations with someone like Helena with her husband involved. But still, I don't really care for her and her work is mediocre. Since I fucked her one time over my desk, she seems to think it gave her the right to be perpetually late to work.

When Kynan realizes I'm not going to give in on

this, he switches tactics, and I know this is really what he's been gunning for. "I can assume then that you've given up on that ludicrous idea to show those photos and tapes to Jayce, right?"

"Yeah," I tell him, realizing how much weight came off my shoulders when I made that decision earlier this week. "Tossed it in my shred bin."

"I'm glad," Kynan says softly. "I know you wanted to strike out at Jayce, but that wasn't the way, man."

I finally turn to lock eyes with him. "I didn't know that at first. Trista was nothing to me and I didn't really care. But that's changed now."

"Got yourself a winner there, I think," Kynan says.

I think of Trista and her great qualities. Her sass and stubbornness, her quick wit and intelligence, but most of all, her humanity. The things she's done for her niece blow me away, and she'll make an amazing mother one day.

God, that fucking appeals to me. I'd all but given up on having children after what Michelle and Jayce did, and I know that's thinking way too far into the future with Trista, but I can see it. I believe we could have something that strong. I think we already do.

"Yeah, I got a winner," I agree.

His hand comes down on my shoulder, and he gives a squeeze. "I'm glad you're letting that shit go. Not just the revenge on Jayce, but on letting the betrayal go so you can open yourself up again. I'm glad you're willing to trust again."

And that's really what it boils down to. It's been almost a month since I've met Trista, but I know without a doubt I can trust her. She is just genuinely a good human being. I'm lucky to have found her.

The funny thing is… I'm glad I didn't open myself up before because I think I was waiting for Trista to come along. After Michelle cheated on me and then aborted our baby, I quite unfairly set her as the standard by which I measured other women, when really… Trista is the standard. She's what all women should aspire to be, and what all men should hope to have one day.

I get that now.

And I'm ready.

CHAPTER 26

Trista

I LEAN BACK in my chair, shaking my head as I look at Jerico. "I still can't believe you can cook like that."

He smiles and takes a sip of his wine.

And by that, I mean he made beef wellington with steamed asparagus and a homemade hollandaise sauce, all finished with a crème brûlée that was the best I've ever tasted.

"Seriously, how did you learn to cook like that?" I ask, still in amazement.

Jerico leans toward the table, crossing his forearms on top of it. With a little shrug, he says, "I don't know. I guess you can say it's how I exercise my creative side."

"Well, you should feel free to exercise it at any time with me," I tell him with a smile and then a brief glance at my watch. "And I've got to get going."

Jerico stands up from the table with me, and I make a motion to grab my plate to take it to the kitchen. I was almost giddy when he'd sent me a text today asking if I'd come early and have dinner with him in his apartment. It was what I would consider our first real date, and to find he actually made dinner for me left me feeling warm and gooey. Things with Jerico have changed quickly and drastically, and yet tonight… sitting at his table and having enjoyable conversation as we ate seemed perfectly natural as well.

But I do still have a job to do for at least the next three days, and while Jerico told me he'd relieve me of that obligation, I insisted on fulfilling it. I always pay my debts.

He's amused by this, of course, but he's playing along.

"Leave the plates," he says and when I don't immediately drop it, he rounds the table to take it from my hand. "I'll clean up."

"But you cooked," I point out.

Jerico sets the plate on the table and his arms go around my waist to pull me into him. I wobble for a moment on the stiletto heels I'm wearing along with my standard hostess uniform of a sexy black dress. I'm steadied though when my hands come to his shoulders as I look up at him. His smile is mischievous… his eyes sparkling.

"You could always let me come and play with you in one of the rooms tonight," he says in a husky voice. "I'm thinking The Orgy Room. Maybe I'll even open you up and invite some others to eat your pussy."

My sex clenches so tight I almost whimper, even as I'm stunned by his suggestions. Having other people participate, and having Kynan fuck me... that was all well and good when it was just casual sex. Even though the idea of him opening me up for others to feast on is clearly turning me way the fuck on, I'm confused by it as well.

"You'd let other people be with me now?" I ask him curiously.

He gets my meaning right away, his eyes softening. "If you wanted it and were up for it, yes... as long as I was there, I'd do anything to give you pleasure."

"But... but... I don't think I could reciprocate that," I tell him softly. "I couldn't let another woman touch you."

Jerico's eyes get even softer. "You'd be jealous."

"Absolutely," I say without hesitation. "Wouldn't you? If other men touched me?"

"Not as long as I knew I was the one you came home to at night," he says.

"That doesn't make sense to me," I say in frustration as I pull away from him. "If you want to be only with me, then you should be jealous of other men."

"Trista... baby," he cajoles as he pulls me back to him. "I own a sex club. Swinging here is a way of life, and I really don't think twice about it anymore. This is new to you though, so I'm sure it's all confusing. So why don't we just agree that for the time being, it will be just the two of us, okay? And if you feel more comfortable down the line, we can talk about it."

"You make it sound so simple," I grumble as I look away.

His hand comes to my face and guides it so I have to look directly in his eyes. "While I might not get jealous of someone else touching you, or giving you pleasure… I'd be jealous as fuck and out of my mind if you ever looked at another man the way you look at me when I'm fucking you. That's for me and me alone."

And, oh wow… that was hot as hell and so damn sweet my teeth hurt. I immediately relax into his embrace, because he just validated his feelings for me. And he's right… this is a lot for me to get used to. I have to remember that sharing bodies in this environment does not mean sharing hearts. That's exactly what Jerico just said to me, I think.

Going to tiptoe, I give him a brief, soft kiss. Smiling at him, I say, "Okay. We'll work through this, but I'm going to head out and get down to the hostess podium. Don't want anyone thinking I'm up here doing hanky-panky with the boss."

Jerico laughs… rich, deep, and with gusto. He releases me and picks up our plates. "Go on… get to work, woman."

"What are you going to do?" I think to ask him as I grab my purse from the kitchen island.

He looks up and pins me with a brilliant smile. "I

actually think I'm going to read a book and relax until you get off work. I'll be waiting for you, and I plan to fuck your brains out when you walk through that door."

"Mmm," I say with a wink as I turn toward his apartment door. "I like it."

"Oh, wait," Jerico says and I turn back to him. "Will you do me a favor? Go through my office and in my top right drawer, I have a folder Kynan's going to swing by and pick up. It's my formal offer to sell Jameson Group to him."

"So you're moving forward with it?" I ask as I follow him into the kitchen where the walk-through door to his office is located.

Jerico sets the plates in the sink and rolls up his shirt sleeves before he starts cleaning. "By the end of the year, if he agrees. We'll need that time to transition him into the boss's chair."

"You sound completely peaceful with this decision," I say, and my heart is happy for him.

"I am," he tells me, those green eyes filled with satisfaction of a good life.

"I'm glad," I say and then blow him a kiss. "See you later tonight."

"Bye," he murmurs as I push through the door to his office. It's dim with only a small desk lamp turned on and some accent lights in his built-ins so I turn on the overhead lights by flipping the switch at the door.

Walking to his massive carved desk, I inhale deeply

and realize it smells like Jerico in here. I didn't realize Jerico had a smell until now, but it's divine and I breathe in again.

When I reach his desk, I open the drawer on the left but see nothing but pens, paperclips, and some chewing gum in there.

He said left drawer, right?

Maybe not.

I sit down in his massive leather chair and propel it to the right, reaching out for the right-hand drawer. Laying on top is a navy-blue folder with "The Jameson Group" stamped in gold foil, and I know this is what I need to bring to the front podium for Kynan to pick up. I start to push the chair back so I can stand up, but something catches my eye under his desk.

I see a plastic bin, not even half full of documents thrown in, but it's the brown envelope on top that made me pause.

Because I saw the word "Jayce" and that's not an overly common name.

I bend over and grab the edge of the bin, pulling it out so I can see a little bit better once it's out of the shadow of the desk.

And there, laying right on top, is a thick manila envelope addressed to Jayce Barnes with his address as well as The Wicked Horse's return address on it. There's no postage though, but it's clear at some point, this was going to be mailed.

Whatever "this" is, I take very keen note that my gut twists as if something doesn't seem right. Jerico never talks about Jayce, so I gathered they weren't close friends anymore. I don't talk about him either because he's a prick. So for the life of me, I can't figure out why Jerico would be mailing anything to him.

Before I can talk myself out of it, I pull the silver prongs up and peel the flap back. Without any hesitation, I reach in and pull out what I immediately recognize as photos and a few DVDs. But then my eyes hone in on the first photograph, and my stomach drops so quickly I get nauseated.

On the top, there's a black-and-white photograph of me in The Silo.

Sucking Jerico's dick while Kynan fucks me from behind.

The next one is of Jerico fucking me on the deck with just my skirt hiked up.

The photo behind it is of me sucking Jerico's dick in his office. While he sat in this chair.

I fly up out of the chair, and it rolls back so hard it hits the wall. Bile surges up into my mouth, and I swallow it back down as I flip through the stack of photos. They're all Jerico and me having sex in the club. None in his apartment, but of the handful of times we had sex in the club, there are several photos of each event.

Because I almost can't believe it, I flip the manila

envelope back over and just to make sure... yes, it's addressed to Jayce.

But why in the fuck would Jerico ever be sending this to Jayce?

Tears well up in my eyes as I realize there's something nefarious going on between Jerico and my brother, and I've apparently been a pawn in it all. I pick up a DVD, but I don't know what to do with it. I have to assume it's either more photos or Jesus—my stomach clenches—video of me having sex in the club.

I stand there... just blankly staring now at the top photograph, feeling my entire body start to turn inward from the humiliation. I wasn't humiliated when I did those things. I had loved doing them, because I was in a safe environment.

And all along... I was never safe at all.

"Trista." I hear Jerico's voice and look up to see him walking toward me. His eyes flick down to the stack of photos and the envelope in my hand, and then back up to me. They're filled with wariness and unease.

"You son of a bitch," I whisper, my throat too constricted with a million different emotions to get out much more than that.

"It's not what it seems," he says hastily as he puts his hands out in a motion to calm me down. He's looking at me like I'm a wild animal getting ready to bolt.

My voice is still low, barely audible but now it quakes with fury. "It looks like you were going to mail sex photos to my brother."

"I was, but I changed my mind," Jerico says, still holding his hands out. "If you'll just let me explain—"

"I don't want to hear a fucking thing you've got to say," I yell at him and suddenly I've found my voice. "There is nothing you could say that would justify this."

"I know," he yells back at me, then in a softer voice as he runs a frustrated hand through his hair, he says, "I know. But at least give me the chance."

"You don't deserve it," I say as I spin from the desk and run to the office door, clutching the stack of vile photos in my arms.

"I hate your brother," Jerico calls after me, and I falter. Then I come to a stop when he says, "So much that I thought this would be a way to hurt him. It was for revenge. That's not a justification, it's just the reason I was going to do it. It had nothing to do with you, and I never wanted you to get hurt. But I changed my mind and couldn't go through with it. Hurting Jayce wasn't worth hurting you."

I snort, and then give a hysterical laugh as I turn to look at him. "Well, joke is on you, Jerico, because this wouldn't have hurt Jayce. He wouldn't give two shits about this stuff."

"What?" Jerico asks in disbelief.

My voice is sharp with malice as I tell him, "Who do you think made the original loan to me, Jerico? Who do you think beat me up when I couldn't come up with the money?"

I don't miss the way Jerico's eyes flame with fury and his jaw goes rock hard.

"I'll kill him," he grits out, with his fists opening and closing tightly as his body seems to vibrate with rage.

I give a mocking laugh at Jerico even as the tears break free of my eyes and fall down my cheeks. "I don't give a shit what you do to Jayce. I don't give a shit what you do at all, Jerico. I just never want to see you again."

"Trista," Jerico calls to me as I grab the door and tear it open. I can hear him coming after me, so before I can take three steps down the hallway, I spin on him. He comes to a halt just a foot away.

I suck in a breath. In a voice laced with so much hurt and pain it hurts my own ears to hear it, I tell him, "If you have any care for me at all… don't come after me. Respect my decision to leave and let me go on with my life."

Jerico's entire body deflates as his expression turns haunted. He rubs his hands over his face and when he drops them, he looks resigned. Nodding, he says, "If that's what you want."

And oh, God… my heart feels like it's collapsing, the pain is so intense. If that's what I want, how come his capitulation is making me hurt like this?

Before I start sobbing, I turn around and quickly walk down the private hall to the lobby.

I keep my head down, although I know people are

watching me.

Then I'm out of The Wicked Horse, and I don't look back once.

CHAPTER 27

Jerico

"T HIS IS A bad idea, brother," Kynan says to me as I pull up in front of the trailer where Jayce lives.

I had him thoroughly investigated after Trista found the photos in my shred bin two days ago and shared with me her brother was the one who loaned her the money. I have to say, a few things surprised me about the Jayce of today, the first being that he lived in this dump. Jayce had been a fairly clean-cut, responsible guy when I knew him pre-fucking-my-fiancée. I wouldn't have employed him at The Jameson Group if he wasn't.

But in the last five years, he's deteriorated. My sources indicate he's not been employed in three years and makes his money from selling drugs, which is enough to pay rent on this dump and his other living expenses. I had twenty-four-hour surveillance on him for the last two days and learned he's gained at least forty pounds since I last saw him, is probably an alcoholic based on the amount of discarded beer cans in a box outside his door, and he seems to have no friends other than people who come by his house for drugs. He's low level though, basically selling pot and some prescription pills he has prescribed for him by a doctor for sciatica.

I couldn't figure it out at first.

How someone this destitute and without any ambition came up with thirteen grand to loan his sister. To say I was shocked when Trista let that little secret out of the bag is an understatement. While I wanted to just hunt him down and kill him for putting his hands on Trista, I let some maturity and wisdom prevail, deciding I needed more information before I could determine how to handle him. I had called Kynan immediately so he could start investigating the fucker.

Within a day, I had my answer. Jayce isn't a loan shark, but he did take out a loan from one himself to give the money to Trista. He charged her double the interest he was being charged, and figured he could make a little money on the deal when she gave him twenty-five thousand back. Greasing a few palms, I even found out who Jayce got the money from, the true payoff, and confirmed the ten grand I advanced to Trista to give to her "loan shark" was never received by the real shark. I'm assuming Jayce has probably spent it, but I'm going to find out for sure.

Right now.

I pull on the handle to open my door, but Kynan's hand on my shoulder stops me. When I turn to look at him, I know he can tell by the look on my face I don't have any patience right now. My original plan had just been to kill Jayce. Clean and simple. When Kynan showed up to my office that morning after Trista left, he, of course, asked what I was going to do after I filled him in on everything that had happened.

I don't lie to Kynan, so I told him. "I'm going to kill Jayce Barnes and need to figure out where to dump his remains."

Kynan's eyebrows merely lifted as he took a casual seat in one of my guest chairs. "You're going to kill Jayce?"

"That fucker is going to pay," I had growled at him, still reeling from Trista leaving me and what I learned.

Leaning forward in his chair, Kynan pinned me with a sober look. "Jerico... man... it's time to let that stuff with Jayce and Michelle go. With the baby, too. You've got to move on, buddy."

My head had snapped up in surprise, and I waved an impatient hand at him. "What are you talking about? I let that go."

"Then why do you want to kill him?" Kynan asked.

I huffed with agitation. "Because of what he did to Trista. That fucker wouldn't help his niece out. Instead, he forced Trista to borrow money from him, and then he hit her when she couldn't repay it."

Rather than chastising me or telling me what an idiot I was for even thinking I could get away with cold-blooded murder, Kynan had just grinned at me like he figured out something huge.

"What?" I'd snapped at him.

"Dude, you really have moved past all that shit with Jayce and Michelle," he'd said with awe and an even bigger smile. "You're in love with Trista, aren't you?"

I looked away, not because he was right, but because he was uncomfortably close to being right. I didn't know what I felt for Trista, but it was powerful and consuming and because of it, I wanted to make Jayce pay. It was the only control I had left, because Trista certainly wasn't going to have anything to do with me.

But now at least I've calmed down and don't intend to kill him.

I am going to make him sorry, though.

Kynan's hand squeezes my shoulder, bringing me out of my thoughts. "You cool?"

"I'm cool. Not going to kill him."

"Okay," he says, dropping his hand. "Want me to come in?"

"Nope," I respond as I open the door and get out of my Range Rover. I look at Kynan across the console and assure him, "This shouldn't take long."

Kynan nods and I shut the door, not worrying about the way my lips want to quirk upward in anticipation. After I'd received all the intelligence I needed about Jayce, I decided to pay him a visit. I think Kynan knows I won't kill him, but he insisted on coming with me.

Kynan has my back though, and he didn't come to stop me from doing something I would regret. Despite his warning me against doing so, he really came to help me hide the body in case I lose my cool.

That's a good bud right there.

I walk up to the trailer, scanning the windows, but they're all covered with lowered blinds from the inside. Up three rickety wooden steps and then I knock on the door.

Either Jayce has no worries or he's just plain stupid— the latter, I'm thinking—but the door swings open wide without any hesitation. The first thing I notice is that his eyes flare wide with shock. I take him in quickly, gathering just the barest details to assess the situation. He's gotten fat for sure. And sloppy. He's wearing a white t-shirt stretched over his belly with food stains on it. It's like he tried to dress up the look by putting on a blue-and-white checked shirt over it that he's left unbuttoned, but the shirt is wrinkled and has a rip at the shoulder. He's wearing khaki pants that are a size too small, but you can tell he's not bothered to buy anything different because he doesn't care how he looks.

Fine capillaries spread out over his reddened nose. The smell of beer on him is strong even though I'm still on the steps and he's inside. It confirms his drinking problem.

This is not the man who betrayed me with Michelle. I can't even see any of the man who used to be in peak physical shape while he was in the military and then working at Jameson Group.

"Jesus," I mutter as my gaze comes back up to him. "You look fucking terrible."

I didn't mean for that to be my first words to the asshole, but they just sort of popped out. I can tell they don't sit well with him because as he starts to shut the door in my face even as he says, "Asshole."

My hand shoots out. I push the door so hard he loses his grip on it, and it crashes inward. With two steps, I'm in the trailer.

Jayce's eyes now widen with fear. He may have changed, but I haven't. I still tower over him by a good four inches, and I've taken excellent care of my body. I'm probably in better shape now than I was in my twenties when I first kicked his ass and we were more evenly matched.

"You need to get the fuck out—"

His words cut off as my hand slams into his throat and my fingers grip hard. I push him back across his dingy living room, turning him slightly so he doesn't run into his nasty-looking couch covered in patches of duct tape to hide the rips, and slam him into the far wall. He doesn't even bother to bring his hands up to defend himself or remove my hand, but then again, I'm not gripping him hard enough to cut off his air supply.

Just hard enough that he gets my message. "Where's the money Trista brought you?"

Again, not sure if he's stupid or what, but Jayce smirks at me and says, "It's gone. Spent it all."

This does not satisfy me so I tighten my grip, pull him away from the wall, and then slam him viciously back into it. His head hits the paneled wall, the smirk disappearing.

"Where's the money?" I calmly ask again. "And you know better than most what I'm capable of, so think carefully before you give me that bullshit."

"Why?" he asks with a sneer. "You going to take it back? Renege on the favor you owed me?"

I respond by landing two swift upper-cut punches to his stomach, just below his breastbone. I was aiming for three but he was doubling over, gasping and dry heaving by the second punch. I haul him straight again by my hold on his throat and pin him to the wall. His face is tinged green, and I'm not surprised. Punching someone there with enough force can cause vomiting.

Jayce's eyes cut sharply left, and he gives a slight tilt of his head toward the hallway.

"In my bedroom," he wheezes.

Pulling Jayce away from the wall, I spin him toward the hallway and give him a hard push. He stumbles and rights himself before turning to look at me.

"Go get it," I tell him.

"It's mine," he says as he tries to straighten all the way, but he can't because he's probably got major spasms running through his stomach. "You agreed to twenty-five grand as part of the favor you owed me."

"No," I say slowly as I walk toward him. He starts backing down the hallway. "I promised Trista twenty-five in exchange for working for me for thirty days, but only when I thought she owed that amount to a loan shark. Now I find out it was her brother who loaned her thirteen grand from money he got from a loan shark, and he's gouging her so he can repay it and make a little money too."

Jayce's eyes go round with surprise that I know this information. His mouth opens and closes like a gasping fish out of water, but no words come out.

"Go get the money," I tell him again, and I'm prepared to kick his ass all the way down the hall if he doesn't move. Fortunately for him, he turns around and ambles that way.

Because I don't trust the man as far as I can throw his fat ass, I follow. He'd be the type to pull a weapon on me if he's got the figurative balls to do it, but I'm thinking not. This guy is pathetic.

I watch as he enters his bedroom, which has dirty clothes all over the floor and just a battered old blanket on the bed with no sheets or pillow. He goes to the closet and reaches up to a shoebox on the shelf.

"Stop," I command, and he goes still. "Give me the box."

"What?" he says as he turns slowly and hands it over. "You think I got a gun in there or something?"

"I sincerely hope not," I tell him candidly. "Because if you do, that means you were going to pull it on me and I'm going to beat the living fuck out of you if so."

"The money's in there," he grumbles.

When I flip the top off, there's an envelope with a small stack of cash in it. I take it and toss the box on the floor. "How much is left of it?"

Jayce glares at me. "All of it."

"I don't believe you," I say as I throw the envelope on the bed. "Count it out. And if you are one penny short of ten thousand, it's going to hurt."

"Fine," he snaps at me. "I spent about a thousand of it."

Nodding, I pick the envelope up and jerk my head toward the door. "Back in the living room."

Jayce doesn't argue with me, but I can feel the rage vibrating off him. I follow him through the hallway, and then give him a hard push toward the couch. "Sit."

Jayce glares at me over his shoulder, but he turns and sets his bulky frame on the couch.

"Trista is no longer working for me," I tell him as I take a position near the door. "She didn't fulfill her contract."

"That fucking bitch," Jayce growls.

My voice is low and filled with menace when I say, "Talk about her like that again, and I'll cut your balls off and make you eat them."

Jayce's mouth snaps shut.

"Now I want you to listen, and listen well, because this is the only warning you will ever get from me." I take a few steps toward him, and his head tilts up to look at me. "I'm paying off the loan in full, and then you and I are square."

Jayce's eyes sparkle with opportunity. "That will work. You give me the money and I'll go pay it off today."

I react so fast Jayce doesn't know what hit him, but it's the back of my hand as I smack him hard across his face. It's not enough to knock him silly, but it stuns him.

"Do you think I'm fucking stupid, Jayce?" I ask him calmly. He just stares at me with wide eyes as his hand covers the spot on his cheek. "I know you were charging Trista more than what you owed to the shark, so I'm going to hand the correct amount over to him. And then, as I said, you and I are square. Agreed?"

He doesn't answer me at first. I can practically hear the wheels grinding in his head as he tries to figure a way to make something out of this. The way it's turning out for him, he's not getting anything from the favor I owe him.

Finally, he gives me a short nod. "Agreed. Now get the fuck out of my house."

I look around with disgust. "Not much of a house."

"Hasn't been since Michelle left," he mutters with a slight whine to his tone. I had no intention of bringing her up because there's nothing to say, and I don't even experience an emotion at all over her name. I have no clue why they broke up. Don't care why they broke up. It's pathetic if her leaving is what caused him to turn out this way. But I have more important things I care about so I'm moving on from that.

"Just leave," Jayce says as he flings his hand toward the door and leans his head back on the couch. I get it... he's having a shitty day.

Going to get shittier.

"Stand up," I command.

His eyebrows draw together. "What for?"

"You hit Trista," I tell him as I set the envelope on a tiny table near the door. "You're going to pay for it. Now stand up."

Jayce just blinks at me as if I'm crazy.

"I'm in a generous mood, Jayce. I'm even going to let you defend yourself. Now get the fuck up."

He may be a slovenly pig nowadays, but he apparently still has some grit left inside as he stands up to face my wrath. "Let's do this."

Five minutes later, I walk out of the trailer, money held tight by bleeding knuckles. Jayce got three good hits on me, but I left him on the floor with a broken nose, some missing teeth, and bruised kidneys. He's going to be pissing blood for a while.

I left him conscious because I wanted his assurances he'd never hurt Trista again. I wanted to demand he stay away from her, but I can't do that. He's her brother and despite how despicable he is, I can't impede on a relationship if she wants one with him.

But he'll be on good behavior because I was very careful and exact in explaining what I'd do to him if I found out he so much as looked at her wrong.

When I climb into the Range Rover, I hand the envelope to Kynan. "I've got to get some more cash, but I want you to pay off the loan shark Jayce got the money from."

Kynan blows out a breath of disbelief that I'd do that. "By that, I take it he's still alive in there?"

I nod as I start the engine, looking at the trailer for a moment. "My debt to him has been repaid. He's nothing to me now."

"And Trista?" Kynan asks as I put the car in reverse.

Throwing my hand over his headrest so I can turn in my seat to look behind me, I give Kynan a brief glance. "What about Trista?"

"You have to fix that shit with her," Kynan says as I back out of the dirty driveway.

I shift into drive, hit the gas, and head back into the city. "There's nothing to fix. I've tried calling her and texting her. She won't respond, and frankly, Kynan… after what I did to her, I can't expect her to want to talk to me."

"But you weren't going through with it," he points out. "She needs to understand that."

"She knows," I tell him. "Didn't make a difference to

her."

"So you're just going to give up?" he asks me incredulously.

I turn to look at him for a moment, then back to the road. "Fuck no, I'm not giving up. But I am going to give her a bit of space first. She was pissed and hurt, and there's no reasoning with pissed and hurt."

"I can see that," Kynan says with amusement in his voice. "Give her a few weeks."

"That's what I'm thinking," I tell him. "And to keep myself occupied, I'm going out with Renegade Three."

From my peripheral, I see Kynan's head snap my way. "You what?"

"You heard me," I say with a chuckle.

Renegade is the name for our special-ops groups. There are four of them, and number three is leaving for a mission in the Congo. This will keep my mind occupied while Trista gets her space, hopefully loses some of her anger, and be ready to listen to me when I return. I'm prepared to beg and hound her until she gives me a chance, but I know what anger, hurt, and betrayal can do to a person. I know exactly how Trista feels right now because I've been there. This is the best course of action to take right now.

CHAPTER 28

Trista

I OPEN THE single steel door to the three-story building on E. Bridger Avenue. It's a unique building and I've seen it before but never knew what it was until now.

The Jameson Group.

To the brief glance and why it looks weird is that it appears to have no windows. White stucco square columns rise from the street to the roof on the third floor. In between, it looks like where windows could be placed, there is nothing but stucco walls. But as I approached, I saw they're glass windows that are somehow frosted so it's impossible to see inside. I wonder if they can see out from inside.

The steel door is a little intimidating. It has a classy, welcoming silver sign on the front proclaiming—*The Jameson Group – International Security Services*. The fact it's steel and the outside of the building looks like pure concrete, it gives the overall message of *stay the hell out*.

Still, I don't have time to be intimidated, so I step

inside. I'm immediately stunned by the elegant lobby I find myself in. Cream marble flooring, dark paneled walls, and richly upholstered guest seating in a mocha-colored leather. I also note it's possible to see outside from the inside through the frosted-looking glass but it is hazy. There's no one in the lobby except a receptionist behind a curved desk who is looking at me with a light smile on her face. Not exactly welcoming but not exactly not.

"Can I help you?" she asks politely.

She's quite beautiful, and that doesn't surprise me. Jerico's staff at The Wicked Horse are phenomenally gorgeous, so why not here? She's wears her blonde hair in an asymmetrical bob that hangs just above her shoulders with bangs cut straight over her eyebrows. It's a severe cut, but her face is practically perfect so it can handle it.

"I'd like to see Jerico," I say as I walk up to the desk. I'm glad to note my voice sounds strong and confident, despite the fact I feel completely out of place. I should have dressed up or something because my white jeans and pink button-up blouse seem way too casual for this place.

"I'm sorry, but he's not available," she says with a mixture of apology and aloofness, but without her facial expression changing at all.

Botox! I knew it.

I'm not put off by her tone even though it clearly says, "You can't just walk in here and demand to see the owner of this company."

"I insist," I say firmly. "It's an emergency."

Her expression doesn't change at all. She just blinks those baby blues at me slowly. "As I said he's not available."

Leaning over, I place my hands on the edge of her desk. "Listen… I was just at The Wicked Horse and he's not there, so I'm pretty damn sure he's here. Just call him and tell him Trista is here to see him."

She just smirks at me without even having the decency to say a word.

I come dangerously close to losing my cool. It has not been a good day.

Hell, it has not been a good weekend. I spent Saturday alone in my room, feigning sick to my mom and Corinne, but really, I was so angry and hurt I could barely speak without vile curses flying from my mouth… or hysterical sobbing. I was a mess. A complete and utter mess to find out that Jerico was using me for some sick and twisted plot to strike out at my brother.

I hate your brother, he'd said.

I'll admit that had given me slight pause at first, because his voice was saturated with pain, not anger. For someone who hated Jayce enough to do what he did to me, it gave me more than slight pause. I knew there was something huge underlying that pain in his voice, and for a second, I even thought about staying to find out.

But then my pain roared to life as I realized all the

intimacy we'd shared wasn't real. This slow burn we had that flamed hot in such a quick time, along with feelings that developed in such a natural way between us… it wasn't real at all, and that almost killed me.

Sunday morning, I woke with gritty eyes from crying and a hole in my heart that was felt more keenly since I'd expended some of my anger.

I hate your brother.

Gah… his voice. The pain. It made my ears almost bleed despite how destroyed I felt. How could I be so angry with someone, yet at the same time feel immensely for him?

I needed to know what happened, but I wasn't sure I really wanted to know. All day while making pancakes with Corinne and doing some outdoor gardening, it was on my mind. Finally, by midafternoon, I couldn't take it anymore and drove to see Jayce.

I was stunned when he opened the trailer door and glared at me with one eye swollen and a huge cut on his bottom lip. His jaw was twice its normal size on the left, and he was holding his hand over his rib cage.

"What happened to you?" I asked, but I knew without him needing to answer.

Jayce's voice was defeated. "Jerico is what happened. Now you need to get out of here. I'm under strict orders not to even look at you wrong."

"He did this to you?" I asked. Not because it made me angry or I felt sorry for Jayce, I just wanted to make sure it was Jerico and not someone else.

"Of course he did," Jayce snapped. "Now go."

He started to shut the door, but I called out, "I can't repay you the money."

"You don't need to," he muttered, still shutting the door.

My hand slapped out on it to stop the momentum. "What?"

"Jerico handled it," he said angrily. Why he was angry, I have no idea. He got his money.

But that was something I really didn't care about. I honestly was not put out at all by the fact I was losing the extra fifteen I owed to Jayce had I just stayed on a few more days and completed my contract. I had decided that Jayce could go fuck himself on that money. He was an asshole, and I wasn't afraid of him.

Something else interested me. "Why does Jerico hate you? You sent me into a lion's den to a man who had a vendetta against you, and I want to know what it was."

Jayce's eyes glittered with malice. He sort of leered at me as he hung onto the door for support. "Go ask him yourself. I'm sure he'd tell you all about it. You're his girl, right? I've got busted ribs and I'm pissing blood because you're his girl."

"I'm not his girl," I muttered.

I never was.

Jayce didn't care though. He slammed the door in my face, and I heard the lock snick.

And that, I'm sure, was the last time I'd ever see my brother.

Sunday night, I fretted. I couldn't sleep. A dozen times, I almost called Jerico to ask him to tell me the truth about everything. I needed someone to tell me the reason I was hurting so badly, yet I never dialed because I wasn't sure I could handle it.

Instead, I woke up Monday morning, my eyes still gritty from intermittent crying and my inability to sleep, and decided I had to have the answers.

Unfortunately, Jerico wasn't at The Wicked Horse. The few staff members I ran into were aloof when I walked in, but it didn't stop me from asking if Jerico was in. No one knew, so I went to his office and knocked.

No answer.

No answer from his apartment either.

That's when I decided to try The Jameson Group. It was the only other place I figured Jerico would be on a Monday morning.

"He's not here," the receptionist says smugly, and I blink my eyes to clear the haze of this weekend's memories.

My lungs deflate with disappointment that I'm not getting my answers or the opportunity to try to mend my broken heart with the true story behind why Jerico did this.

"Trista?"

I turn to see Kynan standing just inside the entrance,

having clearly just walked in. "Kynan," I say distractedly, still immersed in the discontent welling within me. "Hey."

He looks good, but Kynan McGrath can't look bad in my opinion. And his eyes, which are always light with amusement and a free-spirited attitude, appraise me with a sympathetic warmth.

That means he knows what happened on Friday and probably has some answers.

"What are you doing here?" he asks casually as he walks toward me. From the corner of my eye, I see the receptionist lean forward to place her forearms on the desk, which I'm betting makes her deep cleavage deepen even further. Kynan doesn't spare her a glance.

I can't tell him in front of this woman why I'm here, so I go with what pops into my mind. "Jerico said I could have the receptionist job here, and I came to find out when I start."

"What?" the receptionist screeches as she sits up straight in the chair. I don't turn to look at her, keeping my eyes directed at Kynan. He smirks at me, knowing I did that on purpose, and then takes my elbow.

"Let's go discuss this in my office. You can tell me why you're really here," he says with amusement, and then he turns to the receptionist. "Hold all my calls."

"Kynan," she snaps at him, and I'm shocked by the temerity of her tone. "Is my job in jeopardy?"

He gives a nonchalant shrug. "That's Jerico's call, not

mine."

"But… but…" she stammers.

"You can ask Jerico when he gets back," Kynan assures her as he starts leading me to another steel door that has a security keypad on it.

"But he's not going to be back for a few weeks," she calls out.

"A few weeks?" I come to a halt and turn to look at Kynan. "Where is he?"

"On a plane to the Congo," Kynan says smoothly as he punches in a code at the door.

After he opens it, he sweeps his arm toward the opening to indicate I should precede him, but I'm stunned and rooted to the floor. "The Congo?"

Kynan's hand goes to my lower back and he gives me a soft push forward. My legs move even though my head is spinning, and I let him direct me down a maze of halls that I really don't pay attention to until we come to a conference room that has a long table that probably seats around twenty. On the far end of the wall, there are six large monitors and I wonder what they're used for in this line of work.

Kynan closes the door before turning to me. Without any pretense or polite consideration, he says, "Now why don't you tell me why you're really here?"

"I'm here about the job," I say stubbornly.

"You're here about Jerico," he counters.

"Fine," I snap, the stress and pain causing me to be a

bit cranky. "I want to know why he did what he did."

"And what exactly did he do?" Kynan asks as he crosses his arms over his chest and leans against the door.

"You know what he did," I tell him. "I saw the look on your face when you spotted me out in the lobby. You know."

Kynan shrugs. "You're hurt. I get it. But explain to me exactly what he did to cause that."

"He… he…" I stumble over my words, because Kynan is now making me doubt Jerico did anything nefarious at all by his laid-back attitude. But then I get my bearings and hiss at him. "He recorded us having sex. To show my brother."

"But he changed his mind," Kynan says smoothly.

I roll my eyes. "Just stop it. Don't try to defend him. You know the intent was wrong and deceitful—"

"And you're very hurt and pissed off," Kynan interjects. "You want answers."

The air in my lungs whooshes out, and I deflate. My eyes drop to the floor—gleaming maple hardwoods—and I whisper, "I want answers."

Next thing I know, Kynan has pushed off the door and pulls a rolling chair out from the table. "Sit. I'll tell you why he did it."

"You will?" I ask as my eyes snap to his.

He nods as I sit down, taking the seat beside me and turning so we face each other. "I'm telling you only because I know Jerico wanted you to know the entire story before he left, but he wanted to give you some space so you could calm down a bit."

"So he went to the Congo?" I ask, suddenly remembering that info. "And what's in the Congo?"

"Famine, war, and disease," Kynan says. "Raping and pillaging. Africa is a mess."

I cock an eyebrow at him. "And Jerico's going to bring peace to the country?"

Kynan grins at me. "He's taking a team to help reclaim a natural gas plant that's been taken over by rebels."

My breath gushes out again, this time with fear. "Is he safe?"

"Of course he's not safe," Kynan chastises, as if I should know better. "But he's good at what he does. I'm sure he'll be fine."

I nod, swallowing hard, but the thought of Jerico dying has distracted me now.

Thankfully, Kynan gets me back on course. He doesn't pull any punches, either. "He's in love with you. That's why he couldn't go through with his plan."

My entire body jolts. It's the last thing I ever thought I'd hear Kynan say. My heart squeezes painfully because I doubt what he said, so I ignore it. "I want to know why he was going to do it in the first place. He said it was for revenge against Jayce. What did Jayce do to him?"

"Are you sure you want to know?" Kynan asks me bluntly. "Because this could change everything in your life. It could make you hate your brother, or it could make you get past your anger to give Jerico another chance."

I snort at both suggestions because I don't give a shit about Jayce, and I can't imagine what could ever make Jerico want to do something so vicious to me just to get revenge. "I'm sure."

"Jerico was engaged years ago," Kynan says, and this startles me. I thought the man was relationship averse. "Her name was Michelle. They were weeks away from getting married when Jerico came off a mission to find your brother and Michelle in bed together."

I wince, because that just sucks for Jerico, but then I flush with renewed anger at this revelation. My voice quakes with anger. "He was going to show pornographic images of me to my brother just because Jayce was bumping uglies with his fiancée?"

That asshole!

Kynan rolls his eyes at me. "Please. Jerico would never stoop so low."

"Then what?" I ask frustrated as I lean toward him. "What in the hell happened to cause him to do this?"

"Michelle was pregnant at the time," Kynan says softly, and my stomach turns over. I swallow the bile down and tightly clutch the armrests of the chair. "Jerico was over the moon about it. And when he and Michelle split up because of the affair, Jerico was still over the moon about it. It's really what gave him the ability to not sink too low over losing Michelle."

"What happened?" I ask, my voice coming out raspy.

"Jayce talked Michelle into getting an abortion," Kynan says.

I sink back, my energy seeming to dissipate. My head hits the back of the chair, and I look up to the ceiling as tears fill my eyes.

"Jayce hated kids, and I think Michelle actually loved him. He talked her into the abortion and paid for it. When Jerico found out, he instantly became a different person. It destroyed him. When he built himself back up, he shut himself off from anything that could remotely get his heart crushed again."

Oh, God. Poor Jerico.

"Until you," Kynan adds, causing my head to lift. The tears overflow and spill down my cheeks. "You became way more important to him than his revenge. And whether you believe he was justified in wanting his revenge or not, he decided he couldn't put you at risk of getting hurt to assuage his own pain. He changed his mind. That's when I knew he was in love with you."

I wipe the tears from my cheeks and blink my eyes to push the rest out. Staring out the frosted window and seeing the hazy bodies that walk past on the sidewalk, I ask, "Did Jerico pay Jayce off?"

Because he doesn't answer right away, I turn to see Kynan scratching his head, his expression filled with humor and guilt at the same time.

"What?" I demand. "What aren't you telling me?"

With a sigh, he says, "Jayce didn't give you money he had. He got that thirteen from a loan shark. He only owed twenty-thousand back, and he was charging you the extra five to make a profit."

"That son of a bitch," I snarl as my eyes narrow at Kynan, and I try to figure out how to plot Jayce's death.

He holds up a hand for me to calm down. "Jerico handled it. He got the money you gave to Jayce and paid the lender off. That was his favor owed, so he and Jayce are square now."

I nod and turn to look back at the window. "This is a lot to take in.

"What are you thinking?" Kynan asks hesitantly, and I can hear the love he has for his friend in his voice. He desperately wants this to work out for Jerico.

I look back at him with a watery smile. "I think it sucks I had to hear that Jerico is in love with me from you."

Kynan's eyes turn bright with relief, and he chuckles. "I'm sure you'll hear it when he gets back."

"When will that be?"

"No clue," Kynan says. "Could be days, could be a few weeks. But I'll keep you updated."

I nod as I stand, focusing my gaze on him. "Thank you. For telling me the story… and for being his friend."

"Want me to give a message to him when he checks in?"

I shake my head at first, because our words need to be said to each other in person, but then I change my mind. "Wait, yes. Tell him I said to please be safe. It's um… important to me that he stays safe."

Kynan smiles. "You got it."

"And I'll be in to work on Thursday," I tell him. "Jerico promised me a job."

His smile gets bigger as his eyes sparkle. "Then I guess I'll see you here Thursday."

CHAPTER 29

Jerico

I'D NORMALLY HEAD straight home after landing in Vegas so I could get showered and rinse the stink of secret military operations off me. Ten days in the Congo, much of it just waiting as we gathered intelligence before we could act, with very limited use of showers, and I was not looking or smelling my best. I had almost two weeks of beard on my face—I was distressed to see a few gray hairs mixed among the dark—and the last shower I had was two days ago. I'm wearing a pair of black BDUs that are at least clean, and I brushed my teeth at the airport bathroom. It would have to do as I couldn't wait another minute to see Trista.

She'd told me to be safe. That it was important to her.

At least that's what Kynan had said on an encrypted satellite call. He'd said, "I've talked to Trista and she knows everything. She said it was important that you stay safe for her."

Since then, time has stood still. I was about going out of my mind waiting for this mission to be completed. Outside of the boredom of gathering intelligence, it was actually quite dangerous when we went in to overtake the energy plant. Renegade Team Three had five members, and we were joined by three Navy seals as well as a United Nations liaison. It was more than enough power to overtake the scraggly band of rebels who had wanted nothing more than to protest human rights violations by trying to stop the flow of natural gas to Europe, thereby hamstringing the unpopular government. There wasn't a single shot fired, and the rebels were turned over to the U.N. to deal with. After debriefing, my team hopped an outbound French military flight from Kinshasa where we flew commercially back to New York and then into Vegas.

I'm exhausted, hungry, and haven't looked this bad in a long time. The last year and a half of wearing silk suits and fucking beautiful women with abandon didn't make me soft. I still have what takes to operate at a high special-forces level, but it did fucking make me appreciate being clean.

It also made me miss Trista so badly I would get distracted, and that wasn't good.

I have no clue what is in store for Trista and me, but if it works out, I know that was absolutely my last mission with The Jameson Group. Hell, I'm ready to hand the reins to Kynan now so I can concentrate and enjoy building something with the woman I'm meant to be with.

My Range Rover swings into Trista's small driveway and I note the sale sign has been removed. I smile to myself. Kynan does excellent work. I had him make a decent offer under a shell company, and Trista took it. According to Kynan, she, her mom, and Corinne are going to move into an apartment in a nicer area of town.

Or so they think.

Going to be different if this works out for me.

Putting my car in park, I see the front door open and Corinne comes running out the door. For a split second, I think she's coming out to say hello to me, but she cuts left and runs over to a large tree that's providing some ample shade from the hot sun. She has a blanket laid out with some stuffed animals perched around in a circle, and she takes a seat in between two of them as I get out of my vehicle.

My glance goes to the front door, but it's shut. I know Trista is in there because her car is in the driveway right in front of mine, and Kynan's been keeping close tabs on her. Been easy since she apparently muscled her way into the receptionist job I promised her. No clue how Kynan handled terminating our current receptionist, but I'm sure he did just fine.

Corinne's head comes up when she hears my car door shut, and she turns to look at me as I walk around the back. "Hey, Corinne. I'm Jerico. I met you a few weeks ago when I picked up your aunt."

She smiles shyly at me. "I remember."

I look down at the blanket and see she has little teacups and saucers in front of each stuffed animal. There's a purple dinosaur, a brown bear, a Mickey Mouse, and a gray rabbit. "You having a tea party?"

Corinne's eyes brighten as she nods. "You want to join me?"

My eyes flick to the front door, but it remains closed. While I'm anxious to see Trista, there's no reason why I have to do it right this second. In fact, perhaps a moment or two before I'm face to face with her to collect myself would be good. So without any further hesitation, I say, "Sure. Where do you want me to sit?"

"By Barney," she says as she nods to the purple dinosaur. Reaching over, she moves the bear and rabbit to make room for me. I sit down on the blanket, groaning slightly because my back is a little sore from the extended plane travel, and manage to get into a cross-legged position without too much effort. I sit quietly while Corinne takes a teacup and saucer from the rabbit and pretends to pour tea it in. She hands it to me, and I take it with a smile. "Thank you. It smells delicious."

I pretend to take a sip, and then I dramatically roll my eyes upward. "Wow. This is the best tea I've ever had. What's your secret?"

Corinne giggles and takes a sip before she says, "Lots of sugar."

"But of course," I say with a smile. As Corinne giggles, I hear the front door open. My eyes slide over to Trista standing on the stoop with a guarded expression, but thankfully, there's a small smile on her face.

Holding my cup up, I say, "We're having tea."

Her lips twitch. The amusement in her voice is evident when she says, "So I see."

"Want to join us?" I ask.

Corinne adds, "Yeah… come on, Aunt Trista. Come have tea."

Trista's smile automatically beams at Corinne, but she shakes her head. "Not now, sweet pea. I've got some packing to finish."

"Okay," Corinne says in a chirpy voice, so I take it she's not too disappointed.

Trista's eyes come back to mine. "When you're done, come on in… we'll talk."

"Be there soon," I reply softly.

Her smile turns wistful, and she nods before opening the door and disappearing inside. I have no clue what to expect from her. She certainly didn't run and jump in my arms, but she didn't scream at me to leave her property either. I'm only slightly disturbed to hear she was packing, and I'm not sure exactly what that means.

I turn to Corinne and decide to pump her for intelligence. After I take another sip of tea, I ask carefully, "Why is your Aunt Trista packing?"

Corinne takes a sip with her little pinky out, and I

immediately snap mine out to mimic her. When she lowers her cup, she says, "She sold her house, and we're moving soon."

I swallow hard, as I did not intend for Trista to move so quickly when I made the offer on her house and it was accepted. "Where are you moving to?"

"An apartment," she says with dancing eyes filled with excitement. "It has a playground and a pool, and I get to stay in my same school where my friends are."

My heart rate decelerates as I realize she's not going far. Not leaving Vegas.

"That sounds nice," I tell her. "I bet Trista's excited."

Corinne shrugs and her eyes turn sad before they drop down to her cup. "I guess."

Reaching over with my free hand, I give her a little tap on her knee to get her attention. "Hey... what's wrong?"

When she looks back up at me, my chest contracts so hard I almost wince. She's got a light sheen of tears in her eyes, and I want to slay whatever monster put them there. "It's my fault she has to sell the house."

"No, sweetheart, it's not," I hastily reassure her, but she's already denying my words by nodding her head vigorously.

"It is," she insists. "I heard her talking to Grandma. She had to pay for my surgery, so she had to sell her house. Now she's sad she has to leave, and it's all my fault."

A single heart-wrenching tear slides down her cheek, and I'm at a loss as what to do. I love kids. Always wanted them, but I'm woefully unprepared and ill equipped to handle a bereft six-year-old with guilt issues.

"Hey, Corinne," I say in a soothing tone as I reach a hand out and wipe her tear away. I'm absolutely not in a position to guess how Trista is feeling, but I'm going to take one for the team. "Trista isn't sad about this house, I promise you. She's sad about something I did to upset her. It's got nothing to do with you."

I didn't realize a six-year-old could cock their eyebrow so effectively, but that's exactly what Corinne does. I can also tell she's intrigued. "She's sad because of you?"

I nod quickly. "I was an idiot and did something stupid to hurt Trista's feelings. I didn't mean to do it and I'm really sorry, but that's why I'm here now. To tell her how sorry I am. Hopefully, she'll be happy again."

"Do you love her?" Corinne asks solemnly.

My eyes cut over to the front door, and I mutter to myself, "Shit... this is awkward."

But no sense in doing anything half-assed. I'm already committed to getting Trista back, which means I've got to open myself up to everything that's been pushed away for so long, which will be a little uncomfortable.

Sliding my gaze back to Corinne, I nod with a smile. "Yes. I love her."

Corinne nods again and gives me a look of such sage

wisdom, I doubt she's six for a moment. "When you love someone, and they do something bad to you, it hurts worse than if you don't love them."

Fucking hell. She's talking about her mom, but her logic is spot on. "Yeah… that's why I really need to make sure she knows I'm sorry."

♦

I FOLLOW CORINNE into the house. We finished our tea first. She also invited me back for another tea party, and I'm hoping I get that opportunity. I hope I get a lot of opportunities, and I swear to myself I won't waste them. Not like I have been doing.

Jolene meets us as soon as we enter the house with a purse over her shoulder. She smiles at us, and then holds her hand out to Corinne. "Come on, honey. Grandma needs to go grocery shopping, and you're coming with me."

"But I want to stay here and see Jerico apologize to Aunt Trista and tell her he loves her," Corinne says in a slightly whiny tone that would be absolutely fucking adorable if that didn't just embarrass the shit out of me.

Jolene's eyes cut to me and they're twinkling, but she's insistent with Corinne as she wags her hand at her to take. "We're going to give them some privacy. I'm sure Trista will tell you all about it when we get back."

Corinne grumbles but takes her grandma's hand. Jolene glances at me. I try to wipe the sheepish look off my face, but she sees it. Her eyes twinkle harder. Nodding her head to the hallway, she says, "Trista's in her room packing. The room on the right."

I nod in acknowledgment. "Thanks."

I wait until Jolene and Corinne leave the house. When I turn around, I notice the living room has been completely packed except for the furniture. I walk by the little kitchen, seeing the cupboards are all opened and half the contents gone, with boxes on the floor that have already been sealed up. Apparently, their move is imminent and that means Trista's been making big decisions. I wonder if I'm included in them.

The door is open and as I near her room, I take a deep breath and let it out slowly.

This is it.

I square my shoulders and enter, my eyes immediately seeking and finding Trista as she stands on tiptoe in her closet, pulling a box off the shelf above where the clothes hang. I rake my gaze quickly down her, my body tightening as I take her in long, tanned legs in cutoff shorts, as well as a thin t-shirt that's raggedy and seen better days. Her hair is in a high ponytail, and she grunts as she manages to grip the edge of the box and pull it down.

When Trista turns, she's not surprised to see me standing there. I'm assuming she heard her mom and Corinne leaving, but I can imagine her continuing with her packing to keep herself busy. I'm assuming she's as nervous as I am.

"Welcome back," she says softly.

"Am I?" I say in challenge, preferring to cut to the heart of the matter. "Am I welcome?"

She sets the box on the dresser near the closet, and then tucks her hands in her pockets. She's standing on one side of the bed and I'm on the other, but it feels like miles apart.

"Kynan told me everything about you, Michelle, and Jayce," she says, also apparently preferring to get to it. "It explained a lot to me."

I nod. Kynan had told me he spilled the beans, and I don't begrudge him that. I was thrilled Trista had sought me out so quickly after our fight wanting to know the truth of everything. I hate I wasn't here to give it to her, but I'm thankful Kynan was and could put her mind hopefully at ease a bit until I returned.

"Trista," I say as I start to round the bed to move closer to her. I stop just a few feet away and disclose my heart to her. "I swear to fucking God I changed my mind. I wasn't going to send that stuff to Jayce."

"I believe you," she says, and I hear the truth in her words. She's not blowing smoke up my ass. But she's also not just accepting it either. "When did you change your mind?"

It's probably not going to set well with her, but I tell her the truth. "Not until you brought me the cake. I put the stuff in the shred bin that day."

"So for almost three weeks that we were together, you were planning to give that stuff to Jayce?" she presses as she crosses her arms over her chest, and I wince internally. This is not going well.

I nod my head, refusing to let my gaze waver from hers. "Yes."

Her eyes turn so sad, and my stomach twists over the pain I've caused her. I know all about how that pain feels. It kills me I was no better than Michelle and Jayce in causing it to someone else.

Trista's gaze falls away, and she stares at the bed blankly.

"But—" I say to catch her attention.

Her head lifts. Those beautiful eyes come back to me with a wariness I have to wipe away and I need to do it quickly.

"From the very day you and I first met, I knew what I was doing was wrong. I warred with my own con-science, and I'm ashamed to say the good part of me lost those battles time and time again. But Trista... I just didn't know you well enough at that point to open myself to the potential for more. It started out as casual sex, and we were both trying to stay closed off from each other. But every day I was with you, it became more and more difficult for me to keep my eye on my revenge. Until one day... I realized the way you made me happy couldn't compare to whatever fulfilling that vendetta was going to do for me. And I wanted more from you. I still want more from you. I am so ready to build something with you. I never thought I'd have that again. Never dared to think I'd dream so big as to fall in love again and consider a future with a family. I just need you to—"

"You're in love with me?" she butts in, and I go still as she takes a step toward me.

I swallow past the lump in my throat, but I nod. "I'm pretty fucking sure I am. I mean… I've not actually felt this before, but it's so damn powerful I can't ignore it. I think I've actually been waiting for you."

Trista lets out a quavering breath and takes one more step toward me. "Jerico—"

"Trista—" I say at the same time as I take a step to her. We are only inches apart now. "I am so goddamned sorry I hurt you, and I'm begging for another chance. We can start over or go full steam ahead, or whatever… but please don't cut me out. Let me make this right."

And that's when her smile changes. It's no longer slightly aloof, bordering on polite. And the sad quality is gone. Her eyes light up as her lips form into a generous, beautiful smile directed just at me. My heart lightens, and I finally feel like I can breathe.

"I forgive you," she says as she steps all the way into me, placing her hands on my chest. I want to grab her and pull her tight to me—squeeze the hell out of her in relief—but I keep my hands at my side. "I can't even imagine what you went through, and it sickens me that my brother did it to you."

"Not your fault," I mutter, because I can tell she's pained by her relationship with Jayce.

She nods and gives a slight tap to my chest with her right hand. "I know, but I do understand your motivation. I get that you didn't know me from Adam, and based on the terms of our relationship, you didn't owe me any loyalty. I appreciate that you're sorry for it, but I agree… things changed between us. I wasn't expecting it to happen, but it did. And that's why I was so hurt when I saw that package to Jayce. Because I'd started to fall in—"

I don't even let her get the words out. I'm pretty fucking sure she was about to say she had fallen in love with me, but I jump the gun by grabbing her face and crushing my mouth against hers. She gives a tiny yip of surprise that I swallow up as I wrap my arms around her to hold her to me. She lets out a sigh of pleasure onto my tongue, and I kiss her harder and deeper. I want to go on kissing her forever, and then I want to fuck her, and then I pretty much want to move to a desert island with her so I have her all to myself.

But that's not feasible, nor can I possibly hog Trista for my own selfish purposes. She's got a niece to take care of, and I'm going to do whatever I can to help in that respect.

I pull away. As I tuck a lock of hair behind her ear, I study her eyes. So warm and peaceful and slightly sizzling, meaning she wants me to fuck her, but I tell her something that's more important. "I've asked my attorney to help you get guardianship of Corinne if you would like to pursue that."

"You didn't have—"

I put my finger over her lips. "Don't even refuse. It's there if you want it, and if you don't, that's fine too."

"You do too much," she grumbles.

"I don't—"

"You bought my house, Jerico," she chastises me.

I flush and give her a guilty smirk. "Sorry."

"Also forgiven," she says with a giggle. "But really… you don't have to do these things for me."

"I'll do these things," I tell her, then give her a soft kiss. "And so much more. You're not going to believe all the things I do for you, Trista. Because I have a hard time believing all the fucking amazing things you do for me and to me."

She sighs and presses into me, laying her cheek against my chest. My hands stroke her back, and I go weak kneed when she murmurs, "I'm glad I fell in love with you."

"Me too," I murmur back. "Me too."

EPILOGUE

Trista

THE ELEVATOR DOORS open, and I step into The Wicked Horse. My eyes search for Jerico, but The Social Room is packed and I'm having trouble locating him, despite the fact he stands taller than most men.

"Hey, Trista," I hear from my left and I turn to see Larissa manning the podium as she eyes me up and down. "You look phenomenal."

She's very sweet and very new so she hasn't, nor will she ever, have the pleasure of Jerico's company. She only knows me as Jerico's very significant other and that has afforded me a lot of respect now I'm not working here anymore. Some of the original staff still ignore me, but they wouldn't blatantly attack.

Not as protective as Jerico is of me.

While I can't prove he did it on my behalf, certain employees who were bitchy to me in the past… well, let's just say they no longer work here. When I noticed and asked Jerico, he would never confirm nor deny he'd fired them, but simply told me it was none of my business. That doesn't offend me at all, and actually... it's kind of cute how he's all caveman on my behalf.

I give Larissa a grateful smile, tucking a lock of hair behind my ear. "How am I supposed to find Jerico in this crowd?"

"It's crazy, isn't it?" Larissa says as she looks out over the crowd with excited eyes. "I truly didn't think many people would show up."

I smile as I look at the people packed shoulder to shoulder and standing three deep at the bar waiting for a drink. This makes me happy because tonight is about celebrating the second year anniversary of The Wicked Horse. I don't find it strange how much pride I have in Jerico and this business he's built up to epic levels. I've realized since knowing him that there is no shame in expressing sexuality, and I look forward to the rare nights we will spend in here. We don't do it often, mainly because I'm working fifty-plus hours a week at The Jameson Group, having quickly ascended from recep- tionist to office manager. And Jerico... well, he doesn't like to really hang out at The Wicked Horse unless I'm there hanging out with him. So once or twice a month, we'll do a "date" night there, and we freely show our love by getting it on in one of the public rooms. I find it as invigorating and as liberating as the first time that Jerico took me in The Orgy Room all those months ago.

"There he is." Larissa points with excitement, and I

see his head weaving in and out of people as he locks eyes on me from across the room.

"Thanks, Larissa," I say and start moving toward him.

We come to meet in about the middle of the room, and he looks at me with worry. "Is Corinne okay?"

"She's fine," I assure him because he didn't expect me here tonight. I totally wanted to be, but Corinne has the flu. While my mom was happy to watch her, she was also tremendously nervous as this is the sickest Corinne has been since her surgery. I give him further reassurance, "Her fever broke, and well... I just wanted to be here with you."

Jerico smiles in relief and pulls me into his arms. When Corinne got sick two days ago, I knew it could interfere with my plans to attend the celebration tonight. But Jerico insisted I stay home tonight when he saw how freaked my mom was. I personally felt she was going to be fine on her own, but I love how much Jerico cares about my mom and Corinne. He felt it was more important I stay back.

"I was just getting ready to leave," he says before pulling back to look down at me. "Everything is in hand here, I've done my duty giving a toast, and I'm ready to get home and relax."

"Oh, my God," I say as I laugh, bringing a hand up to his face to touch his jaw. "You've turned into an old fuddy-duddy."

His eyes narrow at me. "An old fuddy-duddy?"

I snicker and press in closer. "I thought we'd go have a drink on The Deck. Maybe fool around a little. Celebrate your success."

Jerico cocks an eyebrow, his gorgeous green eyes sparkling with interest. "This has potential."

Going to my tiptoes, I put my lips as close to his ear as I can get. "I'm not wearing any panties under this dress."

"Jesus," he grumbles before bending down and shoving his face in my neck. "I work really hard to maintain a cool reputation here, and you come and give me a hard-on in about ten seconds. You're ruining my rep, babe."

I laugh again, feeling his chuckle against my skin. But then he pulls back and asks, "Are you sure she's okay?"

God, I love this man. I love him, I love him, I love him.

And let me tell you why...

Sure, he had nefarious intentions when we first met, but what I've come to realize is that he has a heart of gold. I know deep down, even had we not developed feelings for each other, he wouldn't have sent that stuff to Jayce. Jerico doesn't have it in him to hurt an innocent. That's old history, and I rarely think of it.

But since then, he's shown me just how generous his heart is. After purchasing my termite-infested home, he had the damage repaired as well as put in new flooring and appliances. He handed the keys over to my mom once it was painted and had new furniture. This stunned me because he did this without even telling me what his plans were.

In fact, it was sort of highhanded of him, but after he turned the keys over to my mom, he took Corinne and me for a ride. He picked us up at the apartment I'd moved into with Corinne and Mom, and we got ice cream. Then we drove into a gated subdivision where he pulled into a Mediterranean-style home that was massively big and made my eyes bug out.

"What do you think?" he asked us when we got out of the car.

"It's like a castle," Corinne said in awe. "Like Aladdin would live there or something."

"It's gorgeous," I said hesitantly, then turned to look at him with suspicion. "Why are you asking us?"

"We'll go inside and take a look around," he said as he took Corinne by the hand. She latched onto him tightly, a strong indication that her feelings were growing deep.

Just like mine.

"Whose house is this?" I asked as I followed them up to the door.

"Ours," he said casually as we walked up the steps of the porch. "If you like it, that is."

"Ours?" I asked hoarsely, my throat having gone dry.

Jerico turned around, Corinne with him. She stared

up at me as he brought his hands to her shoulders, and he said, "Trista… you're it for me. And Corinne is yours, so I want us all to be together."

It's true. Corinne is mine. It's another thing Jerico facilitated quite easily once I was able to reach Danielle and have a heart to heart with her. It took about five conversations, but Danielle eventually asked me to take custody of Corinne and I agreed. Jerico got the paperwork done within a month, and she was officially mine.

Well… she's ours, like Jerico said.

It's my hope that one day Danielle will realize what she's lost and hopefully try to have some type of relationship with her daughter, but only time will tell.

Corinne, Jerico, and I moved into that massive home four months ago, and I couldn't be happier. My mom lives just twenty minutes from us, Corinne is healthy, moderately happy, and doing well in school, and I have a job I love. And to put the perfect icing on the perfect cake, I have Jerico and he loves me.

"Corinne is fine," I tell him firmly. "Mom has everything in hand. This is your big night and you should celebrate. And because it's your night, we're going to do whatever you want to do. If you want to take me to The Deck and fuck me, I'm yours. If you want to go home, get in our pajamas, and watch TV in between hovering over Corinne, I'm yours as well. Just tell me how you want me."

Jerico's eyes go soft as he looks at me. "I love you. I

want you any way I can get you."

"You can get me any way you want me," I tell him with a smirk. "And I love you too."

"Let's go home," he says as he turns me toward the elevator door. "It's too crowded here tonight. Home sounds nicer."

Jerico's arm slips around my waist, and we walk slowly through the crowd. I think about cuddling on the couch with him, munching popcorn and watching an old black-and-white movie. I like that idea better too.

"However," he says as he leans to the side and murmurs, "I intend to take advantage of you not wearing panties before we get those pajamas on."

Yes, home sounds like a better idea, indeed.

Thank you for visiting The Wicked Horse! If you enjoyed reading *Wicked Favor* as much as I enjoyed writing it, please consider leaving a review.

The seduction continues at The Wicked Horse Vegas with ***Wicked Wish (Wicked Horse Vegas, Book #2),*** coming August 15, 2017!
Pre-order Wicked Wish now

Jorinda Pearce thought she did everything right – graduated from college, married her college sweetheart, established a career. But what does she have to show for it now? A degree she doesn't use, a job she hates, and an ex-husband that spent more nights bending his secretary over his desk than he did sitting at the dinner table with her. Now that the dust has settled, Jorie is needing a drastic change in her life and Vegas is just the place.

Looking for a long overdue adventure, Jorie takes a walk on the wild side and attends the annual masquerade ball at The Wicked Horse Vegas. It's exactly the escape she's looking for, and even better, she can explore anonymously. Drawn to the man masked in black leather with the body of a god, Jorie finds the greatest pleasures of her life at the hands of a stranger.

Cason Brooks is the most sought after man in The Wicked Horse and sex is nothing but a game to him. He appreciates the anonymity the club offers and he loves that he can leave at the end of the night without looking back. But there's no way he can walk away from the mysterious green eyed beauty behind the mask of sapphire feathers, because he knows exactly who she is.

Jorie is his best friend's little sister and there's not another woman in the world that's more off limits than her.

What happens when Jorie discovers that the only man able to fulfill her wicked desires is the one man she never dared to wish she could have? And will she survive falling for a man like Cason, that doesn't know how to love at all?

Connect with Sawyer online:

Website: sawyerbennett.com

Twitter: www.twitter.com/bennettbooks

Facebook: www.facebook.com/bennettbooks

To see Other Works by Sawyer Bennett, please visit her Book Page on her website.

About the Author

Since the release of her debut contemporary romance novel, Off Sides, in January 2013, Sawyer Bennett has released more than 30 books and has been featured on both the USA Today and New York Times bestseller lists on multiple occasions.

A reformed trial lawyer from North Carolina, Sawyer uses real life experience to create relatable, sexy stories that appeal to a wide array of readers. From new adult to erotic contemporary romance, Sawyer writes something for just about everyone.

Sawyer likes her Bloody Marys strong, her martinis dirty, and her heroes a combination of the two. When not bringing fictional romance to life, Sawyer is a chauffeur, stylist, chef, maid, and personal assistant to a very active toddler, as well as full-time servant to two adorably naughty dogs. She believes in the good of others, and that a bad day can be cured with a great work-out, cake, or a combination of the two.

72806389R00202

Made in the USA
Columbia, SC
31 August 2019